SOUL SAVIOR

Immortals of the Apocalypse: Book 2

DANIEL DE LORNE

For Dion
Because he lost his previous dedication
(and because he damn well deserves one)

❧ I ❧

THE LIGHT OF THE MOON SHONE ON EMRYS STONE, AND Emrys Stone shone back.

All the human souls he'd ingested in his five hundred years of life radiated out of his body and reflected off the helmets of the armed soldiers whose guns were pointed at his chest or head. They blocked his access to the warehouse containing the secret second entrance to the underground ark of Providence. If only he and Galen had made it inside before the moon gave these soldiers another reason to kill him.

Other soldiers knelt in the dirt and dust, their helmets off, their mouths open, their expressions ecstatic. If only he and Galen had made it inside before the moon gave these soldiers something to believe in.

And pinned on the ground was his lover, Galen, with that same look of wonder shining from his eyes. If only he had made it inside before the moon gave Galen a reason to think of him as anything but human.

If only he wasn't a soul-eater.

On numbers alone, six soldiers believed him to be

more than a man and, while they would be right, they likely came to the wrong conclusion. They probably thought him something to be revered. Ever since the night his daughter Sian died, Emrys had tried to keep his light hidden. Hell, he'd even hunted down those soul-eaters who encouraged fantasies about being angels—or worse, gods.

And yet, there he was, five hundred years old, glowing for all in a post-apocalyptic world that fumbled in the dark for salvation.

A salvation he couldn't deliver.

Emrys tucked his hands into his armpits to hide some of his glowing skin. "I am not what you think I am."

One of the armed soldiers lifted the visor on his helmet. "You're a freak. And you'll be a dead man if you don't stop that glowing."

Emrys had seen that look before. The curled lip, the twitching eye, the sheen of sweat on skin. The only difference was that his daughter wasn't screaming for him to save her. He shut down the memory. He couldn't save her, but he could save Galen.

"I can't do anything about the light, but I'm not here to cause trouble. I'm just returning Galen to you, then I'll go."

Emrys had already been exiled for admitting to the murder of Brink, one of Providence's soldiers. Factions inside the ark knew it wasn't true and demanded a fair trial, hence Galen coming to bring him back from the ruined and desolate wilderness. Emrys had agreed, but that was before the moon got involved. The best he could do now was ensure Galen returned to safety and, as much as he hated the thought, leave him behind forever.

"Emrys, no!" Galen struggled to get up, but a soldier forced him down again.

Emrys jolted as if the palm of the soldier's hand had

shoved him in the back, but he refrained from retaliating. A gun might go off. Galen might get hurt. If that happened, he wouldn't leave a soul alive.

"Galen, I can't go back with you." He wrenched his gaze away from Galen and back to the assumed leader.

Isaiah—head of Security, one of the Five, and Galen's father—had been clear. Emrys had taken the blame for Brink's murder in exchange for being exiled from Providence. Galen would be cleared of any involvement, and his life would go on. But Isaiah hadn't banked on riots inside Providence rising up against his extrajudicial dealings.

"Please, take Galen back to Providence with you." He squeezed the words out like they'd been wrung from his heart.

"What crap is this? We don't take orders from you."

One of the believers on the ground shifted to glare at the soldier. "Don't you understand what you're seeing, Thomas? Emrys is an angel."

"Don't be a fucking idiot, Trellain. He's nothing but a murderer. He killed Brink. Whatever he's doing to make that…that light or whatever it is, it's not real."

"I know what I believe." Trellain got to his feet and faced off against Thomas. "Emrys has shown himself to us for a reason."

Emrys pitched himself forward but stopped as the guns refocused. "Yes, and that reason is to return Galen to you. Then I'm leaving. As agreed."

"You can't leave us, Emrys." Trellain and the other soldiers got to their feet, letting Galen up, and protected them both.

Galen stumbled forward, hand out to touch Emrys. He backed away from Galen's adoration, a look so pure that any person alive should feel blessed to receive but to Emrys was a torment that rent his heart from his chest. He had to stop this. He had to turn Galen back towards Providence and force him through to the safety of that underground ark. Humans couldn't yet survive out in the world.

And neither could a soul-eater if they didn't harvest a human soul every thirty days.

At least Emrys knew what day he would die. That knowledge was more than most humans were granted.

Galen kept coming closer. "Emrys, please, you can't go. Not now, not after I know the truth."

"And what truth is that? I am not what you think I am." The words trickled out of his mouth like water from a strangled river.

"But I've seen it, and I can't believe I was so blind. The way you and Nimue came out of the wilderness…the way you and Nimue survived the journey from Endurance…the way Nimue helped me escape the cells and then vanished. The way you destroyed those two men and left nothing but ash. Only something—someone—divine could do that."

Emrys's heart caved. He leaned close, his light shining upon Galen. "Divine? If that's what you think me to be, then I can't live in Providence. But you have to go back." His voice was nothing but vapors.

"But the people need you."

"They should forget me." He touched Galen's cheek and stared into those soulful eyes. "And you should too."

Galen's eyes and face hardened like clay that had been fired, his beliefs molded and set. "Never." He grabbed Emrys's hand and raised it above his head so more of him glowed in moonlight. "Soldiers! You have witnessed this miracle. We must return to the city, and the citizens must be shown the truth."

"Oh, we're returning all right," Thomas said. "But only so that thing can go on trial for Brink's murder. And

Isaiah says if you give us any trouble, you're going up there with him."

Now Isaiah wanted a trial? He'd expected it of the other councilors, particularly Laurence and Kira, but for Isaiah to press for a public hearing…something must be up.

Galen stepped in front of Emrys. "Emrys didn't murder Brink, and I will proudly stand before the citizens and tell them so. Then we'll see who the people believe."

Thomas raised his weapon, and so did Emrys's defenders. A firefight was imminent.

"Everyone calm down." Emrys pulled Galen behind him. Only one of them could survive getting shot. As difficult and unpleasant as it was to abandon Galen, he forced himself to agree to the original bargain. If he didn't, he'd allow what was only a whisper of an idea, an ember of a possibility, to grow. "I don't care about your orders, Thomas. I signed the confession Isaiah gave me. I kept my part of the bargain. I left so Galen could stay."

"Isaiah ordered us to bring both of you. That's final."

"Emrys, you must lead us," Trellain said.

"Have you lost your senses?" Thomas's voice was strained, a high-pitched caustic sound. "He's no leader. He's a murderer, and Providence is in chaos because of him."

"Chaos reigns because Isaiah expelled Emrys and angered Heaven," Trellain said.

Their bickering nicked Emrys's skin and rubbed the wounds with sand and salt. He was trying to do the right thing. But what was the right thing to do?

He had two choices.

He could run and leave the humans to sort out their own mess. He could run and leave behind a story of a glowing thing—man, monster, or messiah. He could run and leave Galen and his heart behind.

Or he could stay. He could stay like he really wanted to, and not just to ensure he had souls to feed on. He could attempt to do some good. Staying meant guiding Providence to a brighter future. Staying meant keeping Galen safe.

That was all.

That was everything.

Half of the soldiers believed him to be an angel without him even trying. Could he convince half of Providence of the same with a little prompting? Or would it be better to hide his light under hundreds of feet of dirt and do everything he could to make them believe he was an ordinary man?

But ordinary men had a way of falling victim to those who exercised greater power. And who had greater power than him?

He held up his hands, caught more light, and called for silence, pleased to see that even his adversaries obeyed. They might not believe him to be an angel, but they knew he was not like them. He'd take their fear if it helped him get back inside, but he wasn't yet ready to declare he was their savior or that he could do anything special. He needed more time to make that decision.

"I will return to Providence with you, but I have no desire to lead. All I want is for the chance to make things right." They could take that however they wanted.

He turned to Galen, belief bursting within his eyes. A belief built on lies. But what was one more among many when the truth of what Emrys really was would push Galen away? Galen could love an angel, but he'd never love a soul-eater.

"I'll go with you willingly."

"You'll go in handcuffs. Both of you." Thomas ordered two of the soldiers to cuff them, but neither soldier made a move. The last time Emrys had been cuffed, he'd taken a soldier's soul and killed him. That was only two days ago. That memory must have flitted through their brains and caused them to hesitate.

"Handcuffs won't hold me, and if you try to put them on Galen, it'll be the last thing you do."

The soldiers stepped back and formed a guard to march him into the warehouse. Once inside and out of the presence of the moon, the glow from his skin shut off, plunging them into darkness. More than one sharp intake of breath followed.

"Emrys." Galen gripped his bicep, his voice like icy mist. "What happened to the light?"

The soldiers turned on torches to show their way. How he wished he could turn his light on and off at will.

He scrambled for an explanation, sensing the anger of those who'd been staunch in their disbelief at seeing the trick fail. His throat was closing, and each step towards Providence restricted the flow of oxygen to his lungs. Believing him an angel had benefits but believing him to be something less than human would come with problems.

"Told you it was nothing but a hoax," Thomas said.

Trellain rounded on the soldier. "His light is a reward for those who serve as witnesses. Those who see it are blessed, but only those who see it and believe are truly saved."

"How convenient," Thomas said.

"You're lucky you don't get struck down where you stand, Thomas."

"And you're lucky I don't knock the sense back into your head. Keep moving."

In the dim light, Emrys couldn't see how well Trellain's

explanation pacified them, but the party advanced. They reached the small squat building in the center of the warehouse. Trellain entered his access code, the doors opened, and they were bathed in generated light. They entered, Thomas dealt with the controls, the doors closed, and the elevator descended.

Four of the non-believers stepped forward, lowered their weapons, and sank to their knees in front of Emrys.

"Please, forgive me, Emrys. I didn't believe at first, but now I do."

"As do I."

"And me."

"Accept me, too."

Emrys blinked at this display before the two men and two women were joined by the believers in asking for his benediction. Galen joined them. A short, sharp, breathy laugh exploded out of Emrys's mouth. It was grotesque.

Thomas's dark lips rippled into a sneer. "You're all fools."

Their heads turned as one in Thomas's direction, hate glinting in their eyes, so directed, so pure, so ready to commit violence that a shiver raced up Emrys's spine. A shiver that brought some satisfaction. He only had to give the word and they'd tear Thomas limb from limb.

Thomas backed against the elevator door and tightened his grip on his gun.

That power...

He understood those Darisami who'd revealed their abilities, who'd played up their differences, who'd conned humans and presided over thousands. He understood what they'd been drunk on. And he understood how it could all go wrong. He would do better than them.

"Thomas, you have nothing to fear from me or these people. You do not have to believe in me."

"There is nothing to believe in." Thomas's voice turned to gravel. "You are a murderer, and your trial will prove that."

"He is an angel, and we are his Defenders!" Trellain screeched, which gave rise to the other's crying out for him.

It took far too long to settle them, and even when they did, Emrys's heartbeat stayed elevated. "It doesn't matter what I am. I am only here to make things right."

But unless he inspired unity, he would only bring about greater division. And overcoming that would be no easy feat.

Not for a human.

Not for a Darisami.

Not even for an angel.

✦   2   ✦

THE ELEVATOR SLOWED. EMRYS'S PULSE QUICKENED. THIS was it. The surveillance cameras outside the warehouse would have picked up his little light show, and soldiers would have scrambled to meet him on his return. But what kind of welcome would he get? Isaiah wanted a trial, but that was when he thought Emrys was human.

He positioned himself in front of the door to be the first thing anyone saw when they opened—and the first thing to get shot. He asked his defenders to lower their weapons and present a peaceful front, hoping that orders hadn't come through for them all to be shot on sight.

The doors slid open to the sound of guns being raised and armed. A unit of about fifty soldiers formed a solid wall of black-garbed brutality. Helmets and visors, bullet-proof vests, black cargo trousers and thick black boots heralded Emrys's return.

The sight of all that firepower sent his heart fluttering, but he kept his arms wide, his chest open, and his smile non-combative. About half the muzzles were pointed at him, the rest were on his followers, including Galen. If the soldiers started shooting, he would not be able to shield them all.

"This isn't necessary." He took one step forward. Guns readjusted. He stopped. "You don't need to be afraid of me."

An opening widened in the middle of the soldiers to allow Isaiah to come through. He was dressed in protective armor. Three soldiers knelt in front of him to form a barricade.

"These precautions are necessary to protect Providence from a violent criminal and whatever disease you're carrying. You'll go into quarantine until we know we're safe from you, and then you'll stand trial."

"Why would you want a trial? Aren't you afraid I'll tell the people what I know?"

"Our deal still stands. While you confess to the people that you murdered Brink, Galen will be in a cell under guard."

As a hostage. Would Isaiah really kill his own son? Emrys didn't want to find out.

"Soldiers, seize them," Isaiah said.

They marched forward, and so did Emrys's defenders, ensconcing him in their protection and arming their guns. The soldiers halted.

Isaiah's gaze flickered between his soldiers and Emrys's, calculating who would die if they started shooting and whether he would be one of them.

Emrys had to be the voice of peace and reason. "There is no need for force, Isaiah. I'm ready to speak to the people now."

"You'll speak to the people when I tell you to speak to the people."

"There are riots. You can't afford to delay. We are going to the Tower, and we are going now."

Isaiah growled. "Fine. But everyone is to hand in their weapons."

Isaiah could have everyone shot once the guns were handed over, but considering the fifty witnesses to such a crime, Isaiah's reputation would not survive.

And once everyone else was dead and Emrys was left standing, Isaiah's life would be finished.

Emrys instructed his followers to hand over their weapons.

"After you, Isaiah." Emrys started forward.

"Wait! He's got a knife." Thomas rushed up behind him and grabbed the hilt of the golden blade hooked through Emrys's belt.

Adrenaline surged through Emrys and swept all rational thought out of his body. He spun, clasped Thomas's wrist, and crushed it until he could feel moving bone fragments. Thomas howled and fell to his knees.

"The knife stays with me," Emrys said between clenched teeth. He pried the knife out of Thomas's limp grip. "Now, let's get this over with."

He marched forward, Isaiah's soldiers falling back, and Emrys's followers forming a V behind him. He stopped at Isaiah and the soldiers blocking his path.

"Well?"

This ridiculousness was going on far too long. He was trying to be good. He was trying to keep Galen safe. And he was trying very, very hard not to kill everyone in his way.

Isaiah's green eyes, so similar to Galen's for their color, so different to Galen's for their humanity, tried to determine the game Emrys played. He'd never understand that Emrys did this for Galen and Galen alone. That kind of love didn't exist in Isaiah's heart.

Emrys saw, too late, Isaiah's eyes flicking past Emrys's

shoulder. Emrys heard, too late, the warning cries of his followers. And Emrys felt, too late, the gun pressing into his back.

His heart braced but it did nothing to stop the bullets exploding into his body. They stung as they cut through his spinal cord and blasted open his internal organs. He crumpled to the floor while noise like a hyenas' feeding frenzy erupted behind him. Isaiah and his soldiers fell back as Emrys's defenders turned ferocious and attacked Thomas, whose shouts turned to shrieks as nine people tore him apart.

All except Galen. He pressed his hands to Emrys's wounds. "Emrys, please, don't leave me. You can't leave me." Tears clogged Galen's throat, and they were the most beautiful thing in the world.

He could never give Galen up, and if that meant he needed to be an angel, then a-fucking-men.

"I'll never leave you."

Isaiah commanded his soldiers to prepare to shoot and made no exception for Galen. Emrys's heart lurched, kicking him back into action, and he forced the healing to hurry and repair what had been broken.

His spine healed, and he forced himself to stand. The blood slowed to a dribble then stopped as the wounds closed. Beside him, Galen praised the Divine. Behind him, his defenders continued their terror. In front of him, Isaiah's soldiers backed away. Emrys tore the tunic from his body to expose the healed wounds. The guns didn't lower, but some did shake.

"You have seen my power! Your weapons do nothing!"

His shouting cut through the Defenders' screeching, and they turned in fanatical belief to him, their bloodied hands touching him to make sure he was real, that he was alive. They praised his resurrection, but he didn't take his eyes off the soldiers.

"Lower your guns. No one else needs to die for your foolishness. Every shot rips a wound in the heart of Providence. I have come to make things right, but you have a choice. You can try to stop me from my salvation, or you can accept that I will speak to the people now. Your future survival and that of the human race counts on it. Make your choice, but be warned: my patience has limits, yet my ability to heal does not."

❦   3   ❧

Emrys entered a Providence unlike the one he'd left barely more than twenty-four hours earlier and trailing a procession that contained Galen, Isaiah, Defenders, and Unbelievers. A cacophony rose up and down the ten levels, a mix of alarms sounded to no real effect other than to stir blood and raise tensions, and so much noise prevailed it was hard to determine where it all came from and what it was all leading to.

He didn't want to talk to Isaiah, but he needed information. "What's happened?"

"Aren't you the Great Almighty? Shouldn't you know?" Isaiah's smirk had returned but not the color to his face. He wasn't the only one. About fifteen soldiers had defected following Emrys's rise from the dead and joined the Defenders whose uniforms and skin were stained with Thomas's blood.

"If I knew everything, I would have been able to prevent this."

"I'm sure. We both know you're a fraud. That light, your supposed return from the dead, all fake. It won't be long before you're exposed. But in the interests of expediency, Laurence's Workers and Kira's Scientists have gone on strike and launched protests. They've shown themselves for the traitors they are and will pay the price. Once you're dealt with, I expect their trials to be swift and their executions swifter."

"You don't have the luxury of murdering thousands of people. Providence wouldn't survive."

"That's a risk I'm willing to take."

But as they crossed the corridor and made for the raceway that connected level four to the Tower, Isaiah hesitated, bolstering himself for the gauntlet ahead.

"Shields up!"

His soldiers raised their shields, blocking out the light, and the unit surged forward with Emrys in its midst. Projectiles thudded into the shields, but none were strong enough to stop them while they ran away. That wouldn't do.

Emrys fell back and turned to face the rioters above. If he were them, he would have gladly pelted Isaiah with anything he could lay his hands on, but instead he needed them to stop. He hoped they could see who he was. Thankfully, he provided enough of a distraction to halt their assault, allowing the Defenders to seek shelter in the Tower.

Galen tugged at him, arm up to protect his head. "Emrys, come on. You need to get inside." Love poured out of Galen's eyes, but it was laced with the love of the divine, a love filled with certainty, with faith, without question. He smiled, knowing that this falsehood would be their downfall in the end, but glad to have Galen look at him still with love, not horror.

After all, how many lovers came back from the dead?

"I'll be there shortly." He pushed him away.

Worry streaked across Galen's forehead, but he hurried to safety.

Emrys refocused on the rioters on the balconies above. His gaze landed on a black-haired woman two levels up. He didn't know her, but that didn't matter. She just had to see him. He spoke to her and only her, and prayed she heard him.

"I am Emrys Stone, and I have returned. Lay down your weapons, quiet your hate, and come to the council chamber. All will be made right."

She stared at him, disappeared, and returned with another woman and pointed at him. That second woman called someone else over, more and more until people lined the balconies and the noise lessened a few decibels. He again implored them to come to the chamber, then turned to leave, a smile broadening across his face at the effect he had, but as he looked back the way he'd come, he froze.

Juliet stood at the end of the raceway, confusion rife upon her face. Her eyes were red and her skin patchy, like she'd been crying.

Crying for Brink.

A broken heart didn't stop breaking during a riot.

She narrowed her eyes at him and rushed him, her fist raised. Workers followed behind her.

"It was you. You killed Brink. You killed Jared."

He wrestled with her but could not stop her rage. He pleaded with her to stop. She didn't give way to tears, such was her strength, but she demanded answers.

"I'll tell you everything soon. Just get the riots to stop and bring everyone to the Tower."

"Why should we trust you or Isaiah's soldiers?"

"That is a risk you are going to have to take, but I'll do whatever I can to make this right."

"And Brink? What about him?"

"I didn't kill Brink. I promise you that. But yes, I killed Jared. And I'm sorry."

Her face broke, his admission stunning her and allowing him to step away. He reiterated his plea for them to come to the chamber and turned to the Tower.

Galen watched from the doorway, his brow knit together, and as he arrived, his gaze shifted from Emrys to Juliet.

"Come on." Emrys pulled him away. "Don't worry about her. She'll bring them."

But though Galen allowed himself to be led inside, something about the look on his face made Emrys uneasy.

They closed the door behind them. The Defenders were waiting. He ordered them ahead, buying some time and space for him and Galen.

"Galen, look at me." He grabbed Galen's chin and forced his gaze to lock onto his. "You have nothing to worry about over Juliet."

"I'm not—"

"I know you two have history, but she's hurting over Brink and Jared's deaths."

"And that's a good reason not to trust her. She thinks you killed them both."

"True or not, I share some responsibility in Brink's death, but she's not unreasonable, and you don't have to protect me from her. Whatever happens, she'll do what's right for Providence."

"Even if that means betraying you? She and Laurence used you just as much as Isaiah did. What if they don't believe in you like I do?"

A fist formed in the pit of his stomach. Where did Galen believe he was taking them, and would he follow until the very end? Would he follow even as Emrys ruled over an ark and took souls to keep himself alive?

"And if I told you I'm not an angel?"

"I would say you were testing me."

"And if I said I was something else?"

"It wouldn't matter." He placed his hands over Emrys's. "I believe in you and have since the moment you arrived. I know we can do great things, and I am willing to serve you to make them happen."

"Even if you think I'm not human?"

"Even then. You give me strength, Emrys. You give me surety that we are on the right path. I had a glimpse of it with Tristan and another taste of it when you arrived, but now, I know with all my heart what is the right way for us and for me. You show the way, and I will follow."

"But will you love me too?"

"Always." Galen kissed him, his soft full lips pressing against his own, a kiss of pure fire and devotion that made Emrys's heart rise into his throat and stop all the lies and all the truths from pouring forth. He would do everything he could to be the angel Galen believed him to be. He couldn't take that faith away from him, couldn't destroy his heart any more than he could destroy his own with his golden knife. And as long as Galen loved him with the heart of a man, as well as a believer, he could be anything for Galen.

Their kiss broke slowly. He wanted more, *craved* more, but that would have to wait. Their breath was heavy, the closeness of their skin, the smell of his sandalwood–and–summer scent a promise that filled him.

"Come on," he said. "Let's save Providence."

❧ 4 ☙

Bare-chested and covered in blood, Emrys stood on the dais in the center of the council chamber. The Defenders formed a circle around him and kept to their places, projecting an aura of calm in the midst of the tumult that swirled around them.

The chamber filled, releasing waves of sound that reverberated through Emrys's chest. The councilors took up on opposite sides and hurled insults at each other. Laurence and Kira defended from Emrys's left, and Isaiah, Christos, and Elaina attacked from his right. Their factions filled the seats, wary that the right had guns while the left was armed with little more than steel rods and tools. Would the bullets run out before they could kill everyone?

Isaiah made multiple attempts to gain control over the crowd, but his bellowing fell beneath the claims of dirty dealings from the other side. And when they saw Emrys, bloodied and surrounded by guards, they thought him there against his will and demanded his freedom. Very few were interested in taking note of what was before their eyes.

That he was not manacled.

That he was not injured.

That he was not concerned.

At least not outwardly.

On the inside, his stomach was as wild as the storm raging around him.

He waited and used the time to construct his speech, every so often catching Galen's eye and his concern for Emrys's protection. No one had yet leapt over the low wall that separated him from the citizens, but how long would that barrier be respected?

He raised his hands above his head and took a deep breath. "Citizens!"

A few of the people closest to him started and closed their mouths, but otherwise his call was one more bit of noise lost in the maelstrom.

"Citizens!"

The Defenders took up his cry and chanted as one. The swell of twenty-five voices speaking in unison created a ripple that swept through the babble, taking out more of the opposition.

"Citizens!"

As all eyes turned to him, the yelling died.

Isaiah seized on their compliance. "Citizens, we are here to oversee the trial of Emrys Stone for the—"

Jeers and booing drowned his words, but the Defenders called for silence. When it came, Emrys didn't allow Isaiah the chance to usurp him again.

"Citizens, the last time I spoke to you, I had come out of the wasteland in search of a new home for me and my daughter, Nimue. I told you that we had come from Endurance, seeking shelter, but I must tell you now, that was a lie."

Many on the right lobbed jibes and curses at him, but he held his hands high and waited for quiet to return.

"Nimue and I are not what we appeared to be."

"You are a murderer!" a citizen cried before being shouted down.

"We came to Providence to welcome it into a great and glorious future. And while I stand here accused of the murder of Brink Ford, I am not the one on trial." He pointed his finger towards Isaiah, Christos, and Elaina. "These councilors are the true traitors of Providence. They have conspired to stop me because they are scared of losing their power. They exiled me for a murder I did not commit in the hope of holding onto Providence for their own selfish gains. They have denied you your rightful place as my chosen people."

His words were met with confused looks. He was just a man, not glowing, not special, not one of them. Laurence and Kira's factions held their breath. He was the one they had entrusted as the figurehead of a new revolution that would lead them to the surface, but was this delusion really what they had signed on for?

Meanwhile, Elaina gradually distanced herself from Christos and Isaiah.

He turned back to the crowd. "I accepted my exile because I know that the future waiting for you is to be led by this man here, Galen Rhodes. But such was Galen's love for me and for the people of Providence that he could not let their corruption stand. He risked his life to bring me back to you, braving the surface and standing against tyranny. His faith has saved you, as has the faith of the men and women in front of me now. He implored me to return, and while Nimue has gone in search of others she considers more welcoming and more worthy, my love for Galen and for you has brought me back to

Providence. Citizens, I am an angel sent from Heaven to guide you—"

Isaiah and Christos's factions met his words with raucous and forced laughter. He wanted to smile through their taunts and of the other side's blind faith, but his confidence wavered. He was not an angel, and he was less than a man. He was a monster and a liar and had no more right to rule than anyone or anything else.

His faith slipped. Had he done this wrong? It seemed so foolish. He could have pleaded his case, laid open Isaiah and Christos's conspiracy and said they'd employed him as an assassin to kill Jared and Laurence, sown the seeds of discontent further and walked away while Providence's halls ran with blood.

Galen turned to him while the hurricane blew. Emrys was in danger of the storm passing him by, of the calm center moving on while he and Galen were torn apart in the onslaught of an evil wind.

"Show them a miracle," Galen shouted above the din. "They need to see something."

But what could he show them? He couldn't shine on command. He didn't want to get shot in the head and resurrect. And taking someone's life would lead to panic. In all of his five hundred years, he had never wished for anything that would make him stand out as different, doing everything he could to blend in and—

He had it. He hoped it would trick their common sense into believing he was what he said he was.

He took a deep breath, raised his hands, and slowly brought them down. His body changed. His skin lost its wrinkles, smoothing out and regaining its suppleness. He became young again, slipping from thirty to twenty and into his teens. His muscles changed and shrank, and he appeared as a teenager, but he never stayed at one age for long, keeping up a gradual yet swift transition through his years as his arms descended.

And once he became as young as he could appear, he reversed the effect and aged. The older and more decrepit he became, the quieter the crowd fell, struck silent with the horror of what they witnessed.

"Citizens, I have roamed the Earth for five hundred years, watching humanity's decline yet shaping it toward a time when the sins of your forebears would be swept away, and you would emerge into a new dawn." His skin wrinkled and thinned, his dark brown hair faded to white. "It has been a long journey to this point, but the time for a new future is now."

The Defenders fell to their knees in praise of this new miracle. Many in the crowd did the same or hid their faces in terror.

"I have the luxury of time, but you do not." He brought his hands together in a loud clap and immediately returned to his fixed thirty years.

Wide eyes watched it all, believing yet not.

"These men and women before you have witnessed my other miracles and recognized my divinity. They have seen my light. They have seen me return from the dead. They have seen the new path before them and wish to walk it, but we cannot do so without the rest of you. Though these councilors have attempted to thwart me and lead you further into despair, I do not wish to fight them. They are welcome in Heaven's good graces if they so choose. And I extend the same to you."

"What is this future?" Laurence called out. His skin had gone as pale as his white robes.

"Your time living beneath the surface is drawing to an end. I am here to guide your return and ensure your continued survival in the new world."

"Treason!" Christos roared. "There is no life outside Providence."

"Your fear blinds you, Christos. Humanity cannot live confined forever, and the time has come to break free."

"Into what? Have you turned the grass green and the sky blue? Will you turn the soil fertile and the Earth plentiful once more?"

If only he could.

"That is for humanity to do. I am here as guide, not savior. Anything worth having must be hard fought, as you well know, Councilor. The Divine has given you the chance to redeem yourselves and make a bright future."

"One full of burning sun and blisters. You are a fraud! You are nothing but an ordinary man trying to start a coup, a puppet of those two over there." Christos pointed his finger at Laurence and Kira.

"I am no one's puppet. I serve the people of Providence, and I will take my lead from them, as should you. Many here know that the time has come to return to the surface. Working towards that must be the ark's only goal. It won't happen quickly. The Earth is still healing, but the surface is your rightful home. The time has come. The fights between your factions are a symptom of how broken you are.

"When you should have worked together, you strove to break apart.

"When you should have treated each other with compassion and kindness, you showed duplicity and scorn.

"When you should have opened your eyes to the truth, you blinded yourself with lies.

"I am here to heal these rifts, but I will not force together those who are unwilling. And so, I give you all a choice. Allow me to stay, and I will work with you to rebuild life on the surface. Vote for me to leave, and I will willingly, accepting of my fate and of yours."

He paused. No one spoke. He had them.

"Those who wish for me to stay, raise your hands now."

Isaiah's eyes widened as he caught the importance of what Emrys had done. The room was more than half filled with Laurence and Kira's supporters. The Soldiers were the largest faction within Providence, yet most of them were not in the room, and a good portion of those who were now guarded Emrys. By speaking to the citizens directly, he had bypassed the uneven numbers of the councilors and their three-against-two imbalance was rendered obsolete.

The Defenders' hands rose first, followed by Laurence. Most of the Workers took their lead from him. Some refrained, but they were in the minority.

Kira, who'd not responded quickly but was not hesitant, raised her hand, and her Scientists followed.

Emrys's smile broadened as more and more voted in his favor. He spun to see hands raise around the circle, stopping at the line that divided them from those who refused. But from his position, those hands accounted for more than two-thirds of the vote. There was jostling as those caught on Isaiah's side pushed their way through to join the winning team.

He turned to the three councilors.

Elaina had separated herself from Isaiah and Christos. She raised her hand, though he could not be certain if that was of her own volition or because many of her medical team had done so first. Either way, there were now three councilors for and two against.

He smiled at Isaiah.

"The people have spoken."

5

THE CITIZENS DISPERSED, AND EMRYS FORCED THE FIVE into a closed-door meeting. The councilors watched as he pulled the gold knife from behind his back and laid it on the table, knife pointed between Isaiah and Christos.

"It seems you two are the only dissenters." Emrys took the cloth Galen offered him and wiped the dried blood off his body.

"Yes, we are the only ones who see sense." Christos cast hateful glares at the other three before swinging his reptilian stare back to Emrys. "I don't know how you did that trick out there, but you are no more divine than I am."

He smiled and put on a fresh tunic. "It's of no matter. The people believe, and that's what's important. I have given them hope and a direction, something you have been unable to do for many years." He took a seat and indicated Galen should do the same. "But let's talk about my divinity for a moment. Galen, Isaiah, and the Defenders have seen what I am capable of. You should know I am not going anywhere."

Christos levelled his gaze. "Neither are we. It is foolish to think that the surface can sustain life."

Emrys sat back in his chair. "I agree."

"You agree?"

"Yes. As it stands, the surface is unsuitable."

Christos blinked at him. "Then what is all this? Why tell them that you're going to lead them out if you have no intention of doing so?" He turned to the other councilors. "You see? He is a fraud."

"I agree that the surface cannot sustain us as it is *now*, but like Laurence and Kira have tried to make you understand, if Providence is to survive, a return is the only possible solution, and for that to happen, we must *start* now. And I have consensus to do that. The question is, will you two abide by the citizens' decision?"

Isaiah smirked. "I think the question is will Laurence continue to betray Providence once he knows you killed his nephew?"

Heads turned to Emrys, but he only met Laurence's eyes.

"Is this true? Did you kill Jared?"

Isaiah had no proof that he'd done it. Emrys had left no mark on him nor contaminated his system with poison. But Emrys had already confessed to Juliet his involvement, and Laurence would learn of it.

"Yes, I took his life."

Laurence frowned. "But why?"

Emrys could have told the truth, but he didn't want to be seen acting under another's orders. He was already accused of doing that for Laurence.

"Because his soul was crying out in pain. I'm sorry for what I did, but it was an act of mercy. Jared would never have made it to the surface and would not have been able to handle what awaited him there. I am sorry for lying to you and bringing you this pain, but he died peacefully, a relief that even you would have wished for him."

"I would have preferred him alive." Laurence's hard stare didn't shift, but Emrys wouldn't buckle.

"Then Providence should have taken better care of him. You all knew he was a problem but did nothing to help him nor any of the multitudes that live here and yearn to be free. Confinement cannot last forever, and yet you have avoided making any meaningful decisions to ease their suffering." He faced Isaiah. "Instead, you fight among yourselves and tried to make me the object of the people's hate. I have only been in Providence for three weeks, but already I am tired of your games." He stood from his chair. "I would do this by consensus to save precious souls, but if that cannot be done, you only have yourselves to blame. Isaiah, Christos, I will have your answers. Will you be a perennial thorn in my side, or will you accept my rule?"

Isaiah, calculating as ever, weighed and assessed the numbers in the room. He licked his bottom lip, a fat frog tongue that slipped out and retracted beneath a snarl. "I will never bow to you, but I will not get in the way of this foolishness. Instead, I'll await the day that the citizens realize you give nothing but false hope. Then I will see all of you step down from the council and defer to me. And you…I'll see you expelled for good."

Emrys pressed his palms into the table. "If I fail, then I will accept. But Isaiah, you've seen me come back from the dead. You know I'm not so easily beaten."

Isaiah's glower slipped but he regained it, like rebuilding a wall of sand that the sea had washed away.

"And you, Christos?"

"I accept nothing." He got up from his chair and walked around the table towards the exit.

Emrys let him go and sat back in his chair. "Then you

will get nothing in return."

The councilor came towards him and bent down to stare into Emrys's face. His wrinkled skin filled Emrys's vision. "I know what's best for Providence, and it's not you."

He met the councilor's eyes. "Your longevity is noble, and your experience of Providence's history is useful, but I have been on Earth for centuries, and this is what must happen."

"Ah yes." He got closer. "Centuries. And yet here we are. Humanity has not benefited from your existence. You have already admitted to Endurance's collapse." Blood vessels and wrinkles filled his focus as the councilor sought to intimidate him. "Can you handle the deaths of thousands more?" The councilor was nose-to-nose with him, the hot breath of his old mouth blowing on him.

"You know nothing of Endurance."

"And you know nothing of Providence." Christos bared his teeth and grabbed the golden knife, pulling it back to strike.

Galen called out, and the councilors shoved back from the table.

Emrys's heart thudded inside his chest as the glinting blade came towards him, but within the space between heartbeats, he grabbed Christos's wrist, braced his other hand against Christos's torso, and flipped him over and onto the table. He held Christos's arm wide and barked at everyone to stand back. The councilor lay dazed and confused, pinned with Emrys's hand around his wrist.

"I had hoped to do this without taking life, but you have failed the people of Providence. You kept them safe, but your pride kept them from returning to their rightful home. You attempted to keep them from my divinity and from my salvation. And now your time is over."

Christos cried out for aid, but none came to help either councilor or savior.

The harvest symbol flared in the front of Emrys's mind, the lines and curves interlocking and shining a vibrant blue. He placed his hand against Christos's cheek.

"Wait, I'm—"

The symbol shot down his arm and entered Christos's body like the Holy Spirit on Pentecost. His soul separated with clinical precision and speed.

Christos's soul was his.

Emrys drew it in slowly, wanting every councilor to witness the power of his touch, so there would be no doubt that he did this himself, with no weapons, no poison, no little tricks that could lead anyone to believe this was anything but the work of a higher power.

Christos's weary soul tickled his palm and trickled up his arm, into his chest, and swirled around his heart. His memories filtered into Emrys's brain, and he bathed in the secrets Christos had cultivated over his eighty-five years. He went slowly, day by day, hour by hour, so he could learn every moment of Providence's history, of Christos's life, and exploit all its secrets for his own ends.

Everybody loved miracles.

And now he had the codes to unlock them.

He hurried through the rest, seeing his life as a young man before the Fall, believing in nothing but progress and the strength of the dollar, that there really would be an eternity.

And when there wasn't, when the blood had been splattered on the wall, and the Earth dried up and the rain stopped falling, when desperation entered into the minds of his neighbors, his wife, his children, when the news gave no hope and everything told him to prepare for the worst, he found opportunity and saved himself first and no one else second.

The last drop of Christos's soul slipped into Emrys, and his body went slack.

And then there were Four…

Nobody moved.

Nobody breathed.

He picked up the gold knife from where it had fallen onto the table and slid it behind his back. He faced the ensemble and a small part of him enjoyed the quiet, god-fueled terror.

"I do not strike unless I am struck," he growled at them. "Christos was given more than enough chances to understand what must happen next. But the life he came from and the one he led would not permit anything else. Understand this: I act for the good of Providence, and I will not stand for anyone working against my will. You may disagree, and Isaiah, you may continue to dissent, but if you actively work to thwart me or my plans for Providence's future, you will share the same fate as Christos. Do you understand? Do you *all* understand?"

Execution had its drawbacks, especially those that were extrajudicial, but he knew that none of the councilors ever cared for Christos, just as he now knew Christos never cared for them. He had to bank on the fact that they saw more opportunity in working with Emrys than against him, and a bit of fear would go a long way to help ensure that.

The councilors nodded, even Isaiah.

"Good. Now Christos's death leaves an opening in the council which Galen shall fill."

"What?" Isaiah and Galen said in unison.

"Galen is Providence's newest councilor."

"But he hasn't been elected," Kira said.

"No, but he has been chosen by me and will oversee

matters in my stead when I cannot deliberate. He will also take Isaiah's position as head of Security."

"That's mine!" Isaiah bellowed.

Emrys raised an eyebrow, tickled by Isaiah's outburst. "Not anymore. You will replace Christos as the head of Service, although Food will now be under Laurence's purview." Truly, he would have preferred Isaiah had no access to any position of power, but Service was the only place left for him.

The councilors argued at the change, hitting him with questions and demands over Christos's corpse.

"Enough! That is what I have decreed. Galen is already well respected in the military, more so than you, Isaiah. Meanwhile, you can prove your loyalty by keeping Providence's bureaucratic processes going. Does the council accept?"

Silence from them all as the realization sank in that they were nothing more than figureheads. They had given away their power because they could do nothing else. One by one, they assented.

"Very well," Emrys said. "Isaiah, do whatever is required to hand over control of Security to Galen. The rest of you, go encourage your people to return to their lives. It's been a long day and night. They need their rest, and peace must prevail."

"And what of Christos?" Elaina said. "What should we tell the people?"

"Tomorrow, I will inform them that he has passed. How he died depends on what happens between now and then and what rumors abound. Either he died a legend, his heart giving out from accepting the Divine into his life, or he died a traitor for trying to hamper the Divine's plan for Providence. A punishment that could be visited on anyone. Understand?"

❄ 6 ❄

Emrys left Galen to coordinate the handover of Security from Isaiah and ensure that no one got any inspired ideas about staging a second coup. The military shifted its allegiance from the senior Rhodes to the junior with little fuss. If soldiers refused to bend the knee, they were stripped of their position and marched out. But such was Galen's nature that none could accuse him of being tyrannical and they left with as much pride as they wanted to keep. Emrys didn't know these people, but Galen did, and he knew best how to handle them. Meanwhile, Emrys toured Providence.

It was late, but not all citizens had returned to their quarters. Trellain went with him, as did broad and blond Micah, one of the first five Defenders. They journeyed through the levels of Providence repeating a path he had trod when he and Nimue first arrived in the ark.

He spoke to the people, gathering a crowd eager to hear from the Divine. Though he implored them to go to their beds, they stayed. The number of faithful grew, some eager to hear what he had to say, others eager to believe like their fellow citizens.

Hope had been scoured from this desolate time in history. What was there to look forward to but an endless stream of days in confinement, doing their best to ignore that they were living in an underground prison? He had experienced it in Endurance, where one day blended into another.

Where the sun didn't rise.

Where the moon didn't shine.

These were people who had grown up on stories of an apocalypse before their time. To hope for anything different was pain.

He gave them a future. He gave them hope because he had come from a time where hope delivered. He came from a time of plenty, a time when the Earth was bountiful, a time of phones and travel and watches and jewelry and cars and an endless stream of stuff. A time when so many—and yet not so many when you really got down to it—took food and water and shelter for granted even though more than half the planet starved.

Yet everyone had hope. Even in the worst places. Even in hospitals. Even in prisons and refugee camps. Everyone had dreams of something better.

But not in Providence.

Not until him.

While he left the running of the city to the councilors and pushed them to rebuild on the surface, he could feed the people hope on which they could grow fat. He understood the dangerous weight of their expectations, but if he did it right, he could channel their hope into something real.

He just had to believe that himself.

He proselytized in a mess hall on level six talking to the

people and building on his promises for their future. They sat enraptured, unwilling to leave him. He couldn't deny the thrill. He no longer had to hide. After five hundred years he was seen.

Trellain came up to him and begged his forgiveness for intruding, but Galen was requesting to meet with him. Emrys extricated himself from the crowd and implored them to return to their lives and serve Providence. Not everyone complied to his command, some following him out of the mess hall.

Emrys managed to leave behind the bulk of the followers when they reached the elevator, but when he and his escort emerged on level four, he created another spectacle. Not everyone was happy to see him. He was called a murderer more than once, and while Micah and Trellain itched to strike down any who besmirched Emrys's name, he forced them on. But instead of going to the military base, Trellain and Micah took him to apartments inside the Tower. Micah stayed outside the door.

The rooms were larger than the standard set aside for Providence's population. Four rooms deviated off from a central meeting area apportioned with couches, tables, and chairs. It had its own kitchen and would have easily accommodated a family of ten.

"Why have you brought me here?" he asked Trellain.

"Captain Galen has had everything moved to these quarters. He believes it will serve you better to be in the center of Providence. We have put your things in that room." Trellain pointed to the first door on the right. "I hope that's all right, Immortal One."

Emrys paused at the title. *Immortal One.* He'd been called it his whole life without hearing it in such stark terms. Emrys was Welsh for immortal. And yet, hearing it spoken that way made it seem like a pact that he had to uphold.

He was no longer Emrys Stone but The Immortal One, a responsibility he must bear.

He smiled. "It will do nicely. Thank you, Trellain." He walked over to the large glass window that looked out onto Providence. The crowd had amassed on the balcony across the way. "Can they see me?"

"No. It's tinted."

I'm here but not here. Real but not real.

"Do you believe in what I'm trying to do here?"

"Of course, Immortal One. I have seen your light and know where my future lies. Thank you for choosing me."

If only he had. If only there was some actual plan to all this. But he could do worse than Trellain whose deep brown eyes provided some comfort and reassurance. Even if those eyes now drooped.

"Trellain, thank you for saving me and bringing me back to Providence. You should get some rest."

"Captain Galen has asked me to stay until he arrives in case you need anything."

"There is nothing I need now. But if your duty forbids you from leaving, please rest in that room over there. I would like to have some time to myself before Galen arrives. When is he due?"

"He should be here soon." He stifled a yawn, failed halfway through, and succumbed as his face contorted. "Perhaps you know best. It has been a long day." He placed his hand over his heart, bowed his head, and retreated to the other room.

Emrys's gaze slipped out the window at the growing crowd that was now his responsibility. He was thankful for the distance between him and them. It gave him a moment of clarity to consider the task ahead. A moment of clarity that blurred the more he thought about what he had to do. He pinched the bridge of his nose.

He turned from the window and went into his room. He pulled the boots off his feet, freeing them of their binding, stretching his toes, and massaging his soles. He peeled off his clothes and entered the bathroom. He turned on the water and stepped beneath the spray to cleanse the dirt and dust of the outside world and of two dead Darisami out of his hair. The remains of Thomas's dried blood liquefied, dripped down his body, and gurgled down the drain.

The lingering touch of thousands of people followed.

The physical remnants of all that had happened in one day washed away, but the effects were not so easily scrubbed.

The water cut off. He would've liked to stay beneath the shower and dissolve into nothingness, but the impulse was fleeting. He was committed now. Not for himself, but for Galen.

He scraped the water out of his hair and off his body, then stepped out to find Galen holding a towel for him. His gaze drifted down the length of Emrys's body. Being watched by this man shot a charge up Emrys's spine that buzzed at the base of his skull. He took the towel from Galen but let it hang and allowed Galen's eyes to take in all of him. His cock pulsed from the attention, and the sly smile on Galen's lips made him hard.

"I'm glad you like what you see."

Galen blushed, the skin from his neck up to his ears flashing red. "Sorry. I was looking for any sign of damage."

"Oh."

"Don't get me wrong, I'm very much enjoying what I'm looking at, and the chance to finally see you like this in proper light without having to sneak around is amazing.

But after what happened to you today, I'm surprised there's no permanent injury." Galen raised his hand as if he were about to touch Emrys and confirm what his eyes told him, but he hesitated.

Before he could withdraw, Emrys took Galen's hand and pressed it to his chest. "I'm whole. I'm healed. And you can check whenever you like."

Galen beamed in return and slid his rough palm down Emrys's stomach. Their eyes remained locked as Galen's hand descended to rest over his thickening cock. He took it in the palm of his hand, a jolt shooting through Emrys at Galen's strong touch. He stroked him, slow but firm, an erotic flare in his eyes.

Emrys obliterated the small distance between them, kissing Galen's full lips and diving his tongue deep into Galen's eager mouth. He grabbed the front of his uniform and dragged him into the bedroom, breaking the kiss long enough to push him onto the bed. Emrys bore down upon him. His tongue slipped into Galen's mouth, his lips working harder, his kisses becoming more desperate.

He wanted to wipe away the past forty-eight hours when Brink's death complicated things further and take them back to a time when they were fucking in their secret room, when he didn't have the whole of Providence waiting for him to save them.

He wanted to become lost in Galen.

His fingers worked rapidly to undo Galen's uniform, pulling off boots, unclipping belts and buttons. He unwrapped Galen like a Christmas present wrapped in black paper though not so easily shredded. He inhaled the rich, manly scent that rose off Galen's body. Emrys's mouth at Galen's neck made his back arch then his pelvis thrust upwards, meeting the full weight of Emrys's body pressing down upon him.

He slipped down Galen's body, kissing along his clavicle, his chest and his nipples. He flicked one with his tongue and bit it lightly. Galen's body crunched from the small jet of pain. He did it again, sucked at it, teased with his teeth as Galen moaned. He continued lower, kissing along his abdomen to his groin where his cock strained for attention. The veins pumped hard. Emrys prepared to dive down to taste all of him when Galen sat up.

"Fuck me, Emrys. I want you to fuck me."

Emrys's cock twitched at the raw lust and desire in Galen's eyes. The fanaticism of zealots paled in comparison. Galen spat onto the palm of his hand, turned onto all fours, and wiped the saliva over his hole, spreading his cheeks, enticing enough for all conscious thought to shut down. Emrys grabbed hold of his own cock, let saliva fall out of his mouth onto the head, and rubbed it all over.

"Do you want lube?"

"I don't need it."

And Emrys didn't need any further invitation. He slowly entered Galen, meeting small resistance, but Galen's eagerness urged him on. Inch by inch as he was swallowed whole and slipped into Galen along the full length of his shaft. Galen buried his face into the pillow, and his hands turned into fists that bunched the sheets. He moaned into the mattress while Emrys held himself together, a delicious pressure that started in the tip of his cock and spread throughout his body. Galen held all of him, and he did not move, taking his time to savor this connection.

"Fuck me hard, Emrys."

Galen's order detonated the little bit of peace he tried to hold onto. Lust overtook Emrys, and the raw eroticism of knowing that Galen wanted him drove him hard, fast, and deep.

He grunted as they fucked, his fingers digging into

Galen's hips, spurred on by the loud moans and swearing that came from Galen's mouth, sometimes muffled, sometimes clear. Hearing those noises, especially after they'd had to make love in near silence before, made Emrys growl and fuck harder.

"I'm going to come. I'm going to come."

Galen's hurried declaration kicked Emrys's heart into higher gear. Sweat poured down his body, forcing him to hold on to Galen while his hands turned slick. Tension built in his balls, and he came in Galen with force, crying out as the orgasm exploded through his body, showering up and down his body. He kept going to bring Galen to climax. His hips drove back, his hand pumped his shaft, then Galen froze and swore as he came with powerful shudders.

They took a breath and another. Galen collapsed onto the bed, and Emrys lay on top of him. He didn't want to pull out. He wanted to stay this close forever.

Galen breathed beneath him, the rise and fall of his chest, and Emrys rested his head between Galen's shoulder blades. He kissed his sweaty skin and listened as Galen murmured his pleasure and gradually drifted off to sleep.

But slumber eluded Emrys, and in its place amassed worries for the days, weeks, and months ahead. He stayed curled against Galen's body, but his muscles were primed for action. It was in this mess of worry that Nimue's presence bloomed in the back of his mind thanks to the soul they'd shared in Endurance. She gave him the courtesy of announcing her presence when they both knew she could have entered without permission. She intimated that she had already done so.

So, they're calling you 'Immortal One' now?

It appears so.

He gave her an overview of what had happened, certain she already knew more than she was letting on.

Her laughter ran through his skull, so loud he was surprised it didn't wake Galen. Every moment he thought she'd stop, that her ridicule at his predicament was abating, she would start again.

It's not that funny.

It is from where I'm sitting.

Which was currently somewhere outside Providence.

Do you think I've made a mistake, Nimue?

I think it hilarious that you are doing the thing you punished so many for—and would have punished me for if not for the fact that I reminded you of Sian.

Do you hate me for it?

Through all the years of tense friendship, her regard had mattered more than he chose to admit. And he liked to think it wasn't just because she reminded him of his daughter.

I could never hate you, Emrys. You are doing what needs to be done to survive, and the people of Providence are lucky to have you.

Not all of them would agree.

Then you must convince them. Out of all the Darisami, I believe you are the best placed to make this succeed.

It was his turn to laugh, even as his stomach curdled with the idea. *Why me? I am no better than any other.*

Perhaps no better but you are different. You helped keep some sort of order among a race of beings that could easily have enslaved the human race. You are the best of us, Emrys. There is no cruelty in you, no matter the death your touch brings. I have seen that as your friend and as someone who has squatted inside your head these past few months. You are strong, and you do not shy from what needs to be done, but you are good where it counts, and so much better than I. Not as clever, I'll grant you, but better.

I worry that won't be enough.

You only have to look at that man lying in your arms to under-stand that you are more than enough. I have hardly heard you hunger for souls since this began, which tells me that you do this for him and not yourself. Never forget that. Have faith in yourself, Emrys. Real faith that you can turn this around.

Her confidence nestled inside his heart.

What will you do now?

Now that you're back inside Providence, I thought I'd go see Clara.

The Darisami still resided in Endurance as far as he knew.

Are you going to kill her?

Only if she decides to attack me first. It might be handy to leave her to take care of the remaining humans trapped inside that city while I explore. Like an insurance policy. But don't worry about me, Emrys, I will survive, as will you.

She bid him farewell, and the pressure at the back of his skull abated, leaving him with the weight of Galen against his body. The day was warming up, and they would need to attend to many things, but for now, for a few precious moments, he allowed Galen to sleep, and the warmth of his body fired his heart for the trials he would have to endure.

❧   7   ☙

A COUGH AT THE DOOR DREW EMRYS'S ATTENTION TO THE rising activity happening in the next room. Micah was standing there, eyes fixed on the wall ahead, while Galen slept in Emrys's arms. But even that small sound and the slight lift of Emrys's head roused Galen and, like all good soldiers, he was immediately awake and scrambling out of bed to don his uniform.

So much for a morning in bed together.

"Yes, Micah?" Emrys shifted himself back to rest against the headboard. No way would he feel uncomfortable, either physically or figuratively.

"Forgive my intrusion, Immortal One, but one of the supervisors from the Factory is demanding a meeting."

"Who is it?" More than half of Emrys's attention was on Galen as he pulled on his boots. The rest of the uniform was on but not yet done up. Disheveled yet sexy.

"Her name is Juliet."

Emrys's attention shifted back to Micah. "What does she want?"

"We had some trouble with groups of rioters outside

the Factory earlier this morning. Nothing that we thought you needed to worry about, Galen, but they did get rowdy, and we had to drag some of them off to the cells. She's come to demand their release. I wouldn't worry you with this, but Councilor Laurence was throwing his weight behind her and we need your guidance on what to do about them. I'm happy to have them detained."

The old prejudices between Security and Workers remained. They were going to make this job harder.

"No, let her in. I'll be out there in a minute."

Micah pressed his fist to his heart and bowed. Guess that was the Immortal One's salute from now on. The soldier left and closed the door.

"Do you think it's a good idea to let her in here? Let me handle her." Galen sat on the edge of the bed, his body secured behind his uniform.

"That won't work. We all need to pull together for this to have any chance of success. And right now, the Workers are my best allies."

The muscles in Galen's face tightened a pinch. "What about Security?"

"Apart from the Defenders, do you think the rest of Security are committed to what we're trying to do?"

"They are loyal."

"Yes, but to who?"

"To you and Providence."

"But do they think they're one and the same?"

"I'm sure they do, and if they don't yet, they will in time. I know them." Galen picked at his thumbnail. "And because I know them, I think it would be best if I don't share your bed again."

"What? No." Emrys took Galen's hand, stopped him from picking his nail to shreds, stopped him from leaving. "I can't do this without you."

"And you won't. But it doesn't look good for me to be fucking our savior. People will think it's favoritism."

"You *are* my favorite. You are the only one I am doing this for."

"But you have to be doing it for everyone else as well, and for now, at least while there's such scrutiny, it would be better if I slept in my own bed and if I was not given… preferential treatment."

"Did I do something wrong last night? I thought you wanted it."

"Very much so." Galen played with Emrys's fingers. "But I was selfish. And I hope you'll forgive me. For a moment, I wanted to be the only person that mattered." He tried to smile, but it was like his lips didn't have the strength. "I wanted to take everything. It's been harder than I expected, watching how much the people have turned to you. I was afraid of losing you, and so I gave what I thought no one else could give you."

"You give me more than anyone else possibly can."

"You might think that now, but I can't put myself above anyone else here. Then I would be no better than the other councilors. You don't need that kind of selfishness serving you. I love you, Emrys, but at least for now, you need me to focus on putting your plans into action, and you need everyone else to believe that you are here for them and them alone, not for me."

Galen kissed him, but it was a chaste kiss, like a disciple to a holy man, and it was a kiss that Emrys hated to the depths of his being.

This couldn't be happening. What was the point of being divine if you couldn't have what you wanted? Galen's words struck Emrys dumb, giving Galen time to stand and walk towards the door.

"You are the only thing that matters," Emrys said.

"It pains me to walk away from you, but I know that this is the right thing to do. Micah barely knew where to look. And now I have to go out there and listen to their reports. I won't have them thinking I have slept my way into my position."

"But they would be right." Emrys regretted his words immediately.

Galen's face went blank. "Then all the more reason to prove to them that's not the case. If your love for me is as pure as I believe it is, it should not matter that I sleep in your bed. Perhaps when things are easier, and our position is more secure, it will change. I hope it will, but I am giving myself to Providence and to your plan." Galen shook his head. "I hope you won't hate me for it. I will wait for you in the other room."

And he was gone.

Emrys stared after him and could see the movement of soldiers in the other room and hear Juliet's voice demanding to see him before the door closed. He slumped back into the bed and released a heavy breath.

Well, I made a fucking mess of that.

He wished he had some skill in foresight, but he doubted even the great Cassandra could've predicted that. One thing was for certain: he was now more motivated than ever to ensure that Providence held itself together under his firm hand, so the scrutiny on him and Galen would ease.

Beneath the lust and selfishness, he knew Galen spoke the truth, that it was sensible to proceed as angel and acolyte or ruler and minion. It may not have affected his own position much, but anything that threatened Galen's authority could not be permitted. Galen needed to be considered a leader in his own right, not just a concubine for the Immortal One's pleasure.

Emrys should have anticipated this, but he was only divine in name, not in nature.

He threw back the covers and walked over to the wardrobe. Opening it, he found white robes hanging beside his old Worker's uniform. Whether this was Galen's idea or Trellain's, he saw sense in separating himself from the rest of the populous. Only councilors wore white.

He put on the robes but kept his feet bare. He picked up the gold knife and turned it over in his hand, the light reflecting off the blade. He would have to do something about it. He could strap it to himself and use it as a symbol, say he was there to cut through closed minds and the bonds of Providence that kept them below, but the truth was that keeping it by his side made it only too easy for people to stab him with it.

But what to do…

He would give it to Galen, bestow it upon him during a ceremony that would mark him as his high priest, as his first among many. Then everyone would know absolutely that Galen walked with his authority. He slipped the knife through the belt at his waist, careful not to cut himself. As it was, even through the fabric, the proximity of the metal made his skin itch.

The door opened, and Emrys spun at the riot of voices that tumbled into the room, of Juliet's and Galen's and Micah's and Trellain's and Laurence's, the closeness of their bodies to each other, the snarls and anger and demands on their faces. That was humanity encapsulated in one depressing image. All fighting and shouting over each other to be first, to be heard, to be accepted. It made him tired.

"Shut up, all of you!"

They obeyed.

"Juliet, you wanted to see me. The rest of you, leave."

"But Emrys—" Laurence said.

"Leave!"

The soldiers bowed and muscled the councilor out of the doorway. Galen cast a disparaging look at Juliet before closing the door on the two of them.

"You're hurt," Emrys said. She had a gash on her forehead and her cheek. Her red hair was a matted mess, and her eyes had dark shadows beneath them. But nothing wavered in her demeanor, she was as upright as ever, as formidable as ever. She was not made of dying embers but an eternal flame. "Are you okay?"

"I'm fine. The blood makes it look worse than it is. Do you know how long I've been waiting out there while you've been lounging around in here? With Galen?"

"What I do in the privacy of my own quarters is no concern of yours."

"That's where you're wrong. It's *everyone's* concern. You've been missing in action."

"Security can handle any problems."

She laughed an exhausted laugh, and he regretted his defensiveness. "Do you know what's been going on out there? Because they can handle things so well? We've had Christos's old supporters fighting Workers outside the Factory. Scientists have been battling Medics in the hospital, and Defenders are storming around Providence like they own the place. You need to be more involved."

He did. He was a fool to think that his coup would be anything but bloody. "Has anyone been seriously injured?"

"Three Workers are in the hospital."

He sighed. "You're right. I'll do better. Micah also said people are being taken to the cells."

"For no reason other than that they were in the wrong place at the wrong time. I want them released."

"I'll make sure it's done. Thank you for bringing this to

my attention." He walked towards the door, but she didn't move. Her arms remained folded across her chest, her weight on her right foot, disapproval crowding her face. "Is there anything else?"

"Is there anything else?" Her voice rose an octave. "Don't you think you owe me an explanation?"

He stepped back. "About Brink?"

"Yes, about Brink."

That one was an easy one to explain. "Isaiah had him killed and used his death to blackmail me into leaving Providence."

Her face dropped. "I don't believe you. If that were true, why haven't you charged Isaiah?"

"Because I don't have the proof, and I don't want to destabilize Providence further by removing another councilor. Isaiah has some uses yet."

"Like as a scapegoat for your crime."

"You'll believe I killed Brink but not Isaiah?"

"Brink attacked you, and they said it was you. I have lived here my whole life while you have been here less than a month. It was easier to believe. And now you're parading around like you're the Messiah. I'm not sure this wasn't all part of your plan all along."

"Believe what you want, but I did not kill Brink. I would've liked to but killing him would hurt you and it would've hurt Galen."

She scoffed. "As if Galen ever gave a shit about Brink."

"I admit no love lost between the two of them, but Galen didn't want him dead. For what it's worth, I'm sorry he's gone for the pain that it brings you. I can see how much you loved him."

Her eyes watered, but she didn't give way to tears. "I don't know why I did. He didn't love me. Only Galen." She tucked an errant strand of hair behind her ears.

"Which made him vulnerable. Like it's made you vulnerable."

"Meaning?"

She rolled her glistening eyes. "Meaning Galen's not strong enough to lead Security. He's too good. He's too willing to follow another's orders. That'll be his undoing in the end."

"We'll see."

"I already have. You forget I've been here longer than you."

"And I've been alive a lot longer than you."

"Ah yes, you're supposedly five hundred years old."

"Four hundred and ninety-eight to be exact."

She gaped at him. "I don't know how you can stand there and come up with these fantasies. And you thought Jared was delusional."

"Jared was broken. I am very much whole."

"Was that why you killed him?"

He couldn't tell her the truth that he'd traded Jared's life for the right to stay in Providence, back when everyone thought him human. "Jared's death was part mercy and part necessity, but I tell you truthfully, he did not suffer. I wish I could say the same about Brink, but I had nothing to do with his murder. Isaiah killed him because he thought he could ruin Laurence's plans for returning to the surface. And considering Brink's history with Galen, Isaiah was ready to frame Galen too unless I agreed to sign a confession and leave. I did it for Galen, and I would have left Providence forever if he hadn't wanted me to stay."

"So why didn't you both leave?"

"Would you give up and walk away from your dreams, too? What does it matter what my reasons are? I have given Laurence and Kira the opportunity to rally behind something greater and use that to push their agenda, one you share. I believe—I know—that Providence cannot survive underground forever."

"Then you have a plan for getting us out of here?"

"Yes, but it involves everyone, especially you."

"What makes you think I will do anything to help you?"

"Because I do this for Providence and not myself, just as you work tirelessly in the background to ensure Laurence remains legitimate with the Workers."

"He is one of us; you are not."

"Which is why I'm allowing him to stay on council. But I want you to advise me. You know you can do more, and I am giving you that chance."

She scoffed. "You've got to be crazy. If I throw my support behind you, that's me done for."

"Don't be so sure. You are the leader they need. While Providence loses its head believing I'm an angel, you will maintain your sanity. You did it while Jared lost his mind and in the face of Brink's obsession and jealousy over Galen. That kind of level-headedness, that kind of surety, is what Providence needs. It's what I need. And I need your help in leading the mission to the surface. Will you do it?"

She studied him with a mix of disgust and disbelief on her face, but curiosity glimmered in her eyes. He wanted to press his case further, but she needed time.

"I'll think about it. In the meantime, have my Workers released. Then I'll know how committed you are." She turned and left the room, conversation halting as soldiers noticed her. With a tilt of her head at Laurence, the two of them left Emrys's apartments. She would be back.

Galen hurried over, but Emrys exited his room. It was time the Defenders saw him and time he took a firmer hand in shaping Providence into what it needed to be.

"Is everything okay?" Galen fell into step beside him.

Emrys walked over to a bank of computer screens that had been brought in to establish a remote command center. Surveillance cameras fed him visions of Providence's citizens. Most were orderly but a large congregation on one of the screens bothered him.

"What's this?"

"Level seven. Food production." Christos's people. "Things are getting heated up there. People are…upset about the rumors of Christos's death."

"Are they violent?"

"Not yet, though we found some of them picking fights outside the Factory, and they've been detained."

"Monitor them, but do not send Security in unless I order it."

"But Emrys, we need to maintain peace."

"We're sowing resentment. Release everyone who's been locked up since this morning."

"But they might start fighting again."

"Then Security will stand by unless life is threatened."

"I disagree."

The chatter of the other soldiers in the room stopped.

"Go on."

"Security must show that there is still someone in charge."

"*I* am in charge. Not Security. Not Science. Not Labor. Not Service. Me. So if there are complaints, I will address them and not put anyone else's life in danger. Understand?"

Galen's mask fell into place. Official. Offended. Off-limits. "Understood." He signaled to Trellain and gave him the orders to release the prisoners. Trellain hurried out.

"Is that all?" Galen asked.

Emrys wanted everyone out of the room, but he couldn't do that without it looking like he was going to give

Galen a dressing-down. He had to keep it authoritative but collaborative.

"I've asked Juliet to lead the missions to reclaim the surface."

Galen's mask slipped. "Is that wise?"

"I trust her more than the Five."

"Of which I am now one."

"That's not what I mean. She's different from Laurence, and I like her ideals and values. She could be useful."

"I don't trust her."

"But I do. She knows about what I've done. I told her about Jared."

Galen closed his eyes. "I wish you hadn't done that."

"It was right she knew. Now that she knows the truth, she can deal with it and help us."

Galen cast a glance at the soldiers on the other side of the room. He stepped closer and lowered his voice. "Am I not enough?"

"You are more than enough for me, but Providence needs more people working towards the same goal. I am conscious of how much pressure this is putting on you."

"I can bear any task you give me."

"But you cannot be everywhere at once."

Galen breathed out long and loud, but his shoulders stayed square like he refused to buckle. "If that's what you think is best, I will go along with it. I...I trust that you know what's best for Providence."

If only Emrys shared that faith.

"Thank you. Let's get the Five together this afternoon. Juliet can attend too. I'll then address the people in the evening about Christos. That should keep them going for a while."

"I'll arrange everything. Is there anything else I can do for you?"

"I…"

He wanted to say how much he hated this distance between them when less than an hour ago they had been so close. Back when Emrys had everything he wanted. He wanted to say he wished things were different.

All this jostled and jabbed in his chest while Galen looked at him from behind the subservient mask of a faithful disciple. But Galen had been clear. He was there to serve the Immortal One and Providence, not love him as Emrys Stone. Not yet. He just had to hold onto hope.

"No, but thank you."

Galen nodded, smiled—forgiven—and left to join the Defenders while Emrys was left alone.

8

"You must have had a plan." Emrys leaned over the table and pressed his fists into its surface. Any more force, and it would crack. But he had to channel his rage into something other than Laurence's face.

The councilor stammered, giving Kira the opportunity to intervene. "You must understand, Emrys, that discussion and investigation of a return to the surface was thoroughly suppressed, specifically by some of the members around this table." Her wide eyes with their almost-black irises shifted to Isaiah and Elaina.

"But to have no plan whatsoever. You aimed to use me as your rallying point, but for what? You should have had some alternative available, something for the people to believe in and hold onto when their questions came. You were willing to destroy Providence over nothing more than fancy words."

"We had hope," Laurence said.

"And we had you," Juliet said.

Isaiah's smile became ever thinner. "Excuse me, Emrys, oh great Immortal One—"

"Watch your tone, Isaiah," Galen warned.

Isaiah glared at his son before continuing. "If you are as powerful and all-knowing as you say you are, surely you must have a plan of your own and not have to rely on us mere mortals."

"I am here to guide. My experience of the world before the Fall will help you, but I am restrained by many of *your* limitations. And when I look at you, Isaiah, I am reminded of how many there are." He returned to Kira. "What of your experiments? I was led to believe you had made some progress."

Kira's face remained as bland and unemotional as a research paper. Any qualms at a breach of ethics were invisible. "We may have exaggerated our findings. A necessary and strategic move on our part."

Isaiah's face reddened. "I was not aware of any developments. How did you manage to keep that a secret?"

Kira swiveled towards Isaiah. "We told your son about it. You are not the only one who claims to be working for the good of Providence. We were forced to use whatever we could." She looked at Galen. "I hope you are not offended by our subterfuge."

"Only if it was for nothing," Galen said. "Your scientist was very convincing. He believed you had made real progress. As a fellow council member, I hope that was at least true."

"As do I." Emrys sat in his seat.

"Much of our work has been theoretical," she said. "The data Isaiah's units supplied us with was incomplete despite repeated requests for better samples. We have made careful use of the seed bank to try to grow seedlings, but this has been difficult to do while maintaining secrecy, even within my own teams. Not all Scientists agree with what we are doing."

"Hopefully, they will become more agreeable," Emrys said. "What of the plans for returning to the surface that were laid down by Providence's founders?"

"Limited at best," Laurence said.

Emrys knew for a fact that the architects of Endurance had provided very little detail when it came to repopulating the earth. Their focus has been on saving as much humanity as could fit inside the ark, not worrying about how to get back out again.

"They provided measures of what radiation levels should be observed," Kira said. "And we have copious amounts of information about how to grow crops and test for soil richness, et cetera. And we will, of course, go back into the records for a more thorough search, as long as they haven't been scrubbed. For that, I think you would have to look to Isaiah, or perhaps Christos…which is a little harder now that you've killed him."

He brushed aside the pointed remark but couldn't remove all the splinters. "Galen will ensure you have access to all historical information available. Meanwhile, the restrictions on the Scientists and the Workers returning to the surface will be lifted."

"We should keep some restrictions," Juliet countered. "We don't want people going up there if they don't have a purpose. It would put them and us at risk. And what happens if they don't want to come back inside?"

A few days without food and water and they'd be banging on the gates to be readmitted.

"I agree with Juliet," Kira said. "I am keen for my people to see the surface, but I would like to keep that number small to begin with. If they begin to dig around in the dirt, there's no telling what they might turn up."

Emrys traced the symbol for infinity on the table. "Very well. You do what you think is best, but I would like to see people on the surface by the start of next week. Is that enough time?"

If Kira was happy about this, she didn't let it show. "I can work with that timeline."

"Good. Laurence, what of the Workers? Will any be willing to go to the surface? We need structures. These skills need to be honed after being allowed to go lax these many years."

"I can find volunteers, but the essential work of the city needs to continue. And since giving me Food to oversee, my attention has been focused elsewhere."

More stalling. More excuses. And Laurence was meant to be the keenest.

"In that case, I'm putting Juliet in charge of the service mission."

She hadn't come back to him with an answer to his earlier request to lead the mission, but she was there at the meeting. That indicated enough willingness.

Though Juliet didn't appear to agree. She sat up straight in her chair. "Emrys, it would be better if Laurence were in charge."

"By his own admission, he has his hands full, and I would prefer him to ensure the city doesn't starve. Collaborate, as I am grateful for his support and his contribution, but I need someone who can focus on this and this alone."

Laurence gave her a silent, definite nod. At least he was big enough of a man to know his limitations and would not stand in the way of Juliet achieving what was needed.

"So, we have agreement?" He looked from Juliet to Laurence and back to Juliet. Both gave their assent.

"Excellent. Now, what else?"

"I've heard that you're planning a little presentation at tonight's…meeting." Isaiah couldn't bring himself to say the word ceremony. "May one be permitted to know what it's about?"

Emrys intended to bestow the Golden Knife upon Galen as a sign of his loyalty and his primacy in Emrys's ministry. He was surprised Isaiah didn't know all about it already. There had to be a leak if he knew this much, but he was too shrewd to reveal everything.

"You'll just have to wait for the surprise."

"You can provide them with all the circus you want, but they see you for the invader you are."

Galen surged to his feet, but Emrys placed a hand on his forearm and bid him sit. He smiled as benignly as possible, knowing it looked strained. "I don't expect everyone in the ark to love me as Galen does, or Trellain, or Micah, or the many thousands I have spoken to since my revelation. The only strife that comes is from those who refuse to accept that this is the way of things. But I am benevolent. There will be rewards for those who help Providence. Those who don't believe in me must merely contend with their conscience. A place will be provided for all."

Every life was precious, especially to a Darisami on a rationed diet.

His little speech forced them to hold their tongues. After all, the people, on the whole, were behind him. For now, he had that.

"But in the interests of cohesion, reciprocity, and respect for your positions, during tonight's ceremony, I will declare Galen my First and bestow upon him the Golden Knife of the Immortal One."

"More pageantry!" Isaiah threw up his hands and blew out a disgusted breath.

"It's more than that. He will assume the leadership of the Defenders, and the knife will serve as a symbol of his willingness to cut through the fear of the past and lead us into glory."

"You are turning us into a theocracy." A chill laced Elaina's words as she failed to suppress a shiver.

"For now. While the essential work is undertaken. Who can say if I will stay with you once it is done? For some, that will be a welcome relief."

"If we live that long."

"Something to look forward to either way," he said. "Now, that is all, and you may go." He stood from the table. "I expect to see you at your positions in the council chamber tonight."

Everyone rose. Isaiah stormed from the room as if he'd been called to battle. Juliet and Elaina followed, but Laurence remained behind. Kira stalled too.

"Excuse me, Immortal One." The honorific fell easily from Laurence's tongue like oil on water. "I know it might be impertinent of me to ask, but that gold ring I gave you…is there any chance of having it back?"

Laurence had given it to him two weeks earlier, and Emrys had melted it into the golden rod that he'd used to kill Wyatt. Nimue had taken it with her. At least he could tell Laurence part of the truth.

He put his hand on Laurence's shoulder, and the councilor stiffened. He'd seen Emrys kill with a touch. It wasn't unreasonable to think he'd do it again.

"I wish I could, Laurence, because it was a fine token of how far you were willing to go to ensure our vision would be achieved, how willing to help Providence achieve great things to give up that which was so important to you for the good of others."

Laurence did not look like he was buying the bullshit. "I am glad that it meant so much to you, but considering my continued support of your endeavors, perhaps it could be returned to me as a sign of our covenant."

Emrys licked his bottom lip. Now for the truth. "I'm afraid it's no longer here. Nimue took it with her."

The councilor frowned. "Why?"

Emrys gave a small laugh, the kind politicians gave when they were fobbing off a difficult constituent. "She liked it a little too much. But I will have another commissioned. I know it will not hold the same sentimental value with its link to your grandfather and the old world, but not everything should be remembered. The world before the Fall had many faults, and I aim to ensure they do not happen to Providence. I hope that will be satisfactory."

Laurence's eyes hardened, but the councilor swallowed down his displeasure and forced his lips to curve in a near approximation of a grateful smile. "Thank you, Emrys."

They turned to the exit—and to Kira. Her pallid face was neutral but no less inquisitive, those large dark eyes taking in everything she could. What did she see? As a human, she must have seen a threat. As a scientist, a quandary. As a leader…a rival.

"Is there anything you would like to discuss, Kira?"

"No, I was waiting for my friend."

He smiled at her, knowing full well that hers and Laurence's plans may have aligned for some time but the two of them were not close. Christos's memories—and his spies—provided that information.

The petite scientist with her dark brown eyes and young features was in her mid-thirties, but Christos had long ago singled out the brilliant woman as someone to watch. Her studies and excellence brought her to his attention, and he considered her someone to form an alliance with. He wanted a way into the Scientists' camp as the previous councilor lost support and grew weary of jockeying. That councilor still lived in Providence in quiet service—not quite a mentor, not quite a pariah. Christos had plenty of secrets on him. That's what Christos had done. Collected secrets.

Kira, however, had none he'd been able to extract, except for her reticence in forming attachments. Intelligent to the extreme, smart enough to know how Christos groomed her in more ways than one, cunning enough to use it against him and withhold her loyalty. Collaborating with Laurence put more distance between her and Christos, even though her allegiance remained to herself. Christos only learned that too late, once she'd attained her position on the council.

Like all the councilors, she was someone who would have to be watched.

"I am pleased that the bonds of friendship remain between you and, I hope, between us. As far as I am concerned, our aims are the same, no matter how we choose to get there. I also hope that you will come to me, both of you, whenever you have concerns."

"I'm surprised to hear you say that, Emrys," she said. "You have given quite the opposite impression."

"I won't listen to petty arguments, but I always have time for constructive feedback, especially considering we both want the same thing. I think we all know that Isaiah is our greatest challenge, so providing a united front will benefit us all."

"I don't presume to speak for my fellow councilor, but I continue to reserve judgment until I have gathered more evidence about whether this is the right thing for Providence."

"Isn't this what you were working towards?"

"Religious anarchy was never in my plans."

"Nor mine, so I will do everything in my power to ensure order prevails."

"Then let us pray it is enough." The corner of Kira's mouth ticked up at her small joke. She bobbed her head and left the room with Laurence limping behind her, leaning on his cane.

The older councilor seemed more weakened than ever, as if he had not the strength to see this through to its conclusion. This worried him as the leader of one of the largest factions within Providence. If Laurence wavered, so would the Workers. He had to get that ring made fast. He would make it himself, but not of the same precious metal as the one it replaced. Providence couldn't spare the gold, and Emrys couldn't risk his skin burning every time he touched the councilor's hand.

But for all his concerns over Laurence and how to bolster him, it was Kira's analysis and assessment that left him cold. His hopes of building consensus being easy had little ground on which to stand. He had to find a way to ensure they didn't lose their footing in the howling winds of revolution.

9

"WHERE DID THEY GET THE GUNS?"

Emrys stood before a screen in the military command center that showed twelve rebels on level eight holding machine guns. When the screen changed, it revealed more armed rebels. He counted a total of thirty guns and a growing swell of people blocking seven and eight from anyone who followed Emrys or merely abstained from choosing sides.

The ceremony the night before had gone well. The crowd had been pleased to see him, and the response to Galen receiving the Golden Knife of the Immortal One had brought on a frenzied rapture. Galen was now First Defender, High Priest, and Head of Security. Enough to ensure a strong hold on command.

All of this was helped by the propaganda video that Galen and his team had put together. Footage of Emrys glowing flowed into the scene of his assassination and resurrection, which was then embellished with footage of his transformation in front of the masses during the ceremony. Everyone had been enthralled.

Well…almost everyone.

Cries of forgery and fraud reached him, even if they had focused on the wrong thing. The miracles were real; it was the divinity that was fake. And while the video had convinced many more of his holiness, it had hardened a minority against him. A minority that accounted for about ten percent of the population. They had congregated on those upper floors. The one bonus being that it was easier to identify who was for him and who against.

The biggest problem now being that those who were against him also had guns.

"They smuggled the weapons out of the armory over the past few days. Some we thought were on our side have gone over to the rebels." Galen grimaced.

"Are we putting in place better procedures now?"

"We are, and we're tracking down every weapon, but the question is what do we do to retrieve the guns?"

The rebels stationed themselves facing the elevator door and at strategic points around the balcony, pointing up, down, or across, as well as covering the rarely used back access points. Being an even-numbered floor, a gangway connected the level to the Tower, but with more of their followers having taken over level seven, that presented a problem-in-waiting. A frontal assault would be costly.

"I say we attack," Trellain said. "This is treason, and a threat to Providence's safety."

"I agree with Trellain," Micah said.

He and Trellain had taken up positions as Emrys's Shadows, bodyguards and runners to answer to his every beck and call. The other seven Defenders who'd first bowed to Emrys had been promoted and put in charge of units throughout Security.

"I know you don't want Security to intervene, but this

is serious, Emrys. We can't have an armed militia in our midst while working towards a return to the surface."

"I understand but if we go in there with an armed force, we risk people dying." The last time Security got involved people had been injured. He needed to maintain the semblance of being a benevolent creature—no matter how bloodthirsty the gods were in times gone by. He also disliked the idea that hundreds of people could be killed in one offensive. As a Darisami, he would prefer that the only killing that took place was done by his own hand and at thirty-day intervals.

He rubbed his chin, the back-and-forth action getting harder and rougher, hopeful of uncovering a solution. "Have they made any demands?'

"They want your death or departure. Preferably the former."

"And in the meantime?"

"Their numbers are growing, but we're also getting migration. The Faithful have shifted to the lower levels, while the rebels occupy the top. We've also seen some on nine. The undecided are somewhere in the middle."

"Acting as a buffer."

Galen nodded. "But they'll get caught in the crossfire if they don't choose a side. There are more believers than non-believers, so we're going to get cramped if the rebels are allowed free rein at the top."

No one lived on level ten but having the rebels so close to the main entrance worried him.

"What function happens on seven and eight?"

"The school's on eight, but the important thing is food production is on seven."

"Anything else?"

"Isn't that enough? Christos used to live on seven, and most of his people were there as well."

"We should get Laurence in there."

"It won't make any difference. They've rejected him, too. Christos has been turned into a martyr for their cause, and they want you tried for his execution."

"Treasonous bastards! Immortal One, let us clear them out. We'll be swift. We cannot let this insult stand."

Trellain breathed fire into his words, but they chilled Emrys's spine until he thought it would snap. "Your devotion warms my heart, but if we raise our hands against them, then they will never have the opportunity to be welcomed into our new kingdom. Everyone, no matter how misguided, should have that chance, even if they are given many."

The soldier frowned at him. He wasn't the only one. Despite Providence's army being largely untested, the military was no different from those in previous generations. Kill first, hide the bodies later. But Trellain's commitment kept him from arguing further.

Galen could afford to speak up. "I understand your reticence to treat them harshly, but what do we do about them now?"

If he didn't send in the military, he could do only one thing.

"I'll go speak with them."

"Is that wise? They've got guns."

"I'll survive." Bullets hurt but they weren't fatal. The gold knife was strapped to Galen's belt. What did he have to worry about? "I'll try to convince them to lay down their weapons and join us, but if they refuse, I'll offer an armistice. They can separate themselves from the rest of Providence, but they have to give up the guns. If that's what they choose, can we also isolate one of the elevators so it only services their floors?"

"Yes. We'll give them elevator four."

"Good. I'll be back shortly."

Trellain and Micah turned to follow him. The newly stitched golden knives on their sleeves flashed.

Emrys stopped them. "I'm going alone. Get me an empty elevator and take me up to eight. It's safer this way."

A concerned look passed between them, but he was adamant, and they relented.

"We'll be watching," Galen said.

Emrys made his way out to the elevator and rode up alone, heart rising faster than the metal box in which he travelled. Dressed in white robes and with his feet bare, he hoped he'd provide a calming effect.

The doors opened.

He smiled at the rebels.

Five bullets pumped into his chest, a sharp pain radiating from their entry points, and thrusting him back into the wall. Shock ripped the air through the holes in his lungs as he crumpled to the ground.

He should have worn armor.

The elevator doors closed on the rebels' cheering, and he started to descend.

He forced himself up, pressed the stop button, and shouted at the camera to return him to eight. Galen would be mobilizing a squad to retaliate but that could not happen. Seconds stretched long before the elevator ascended again. He examined the holes in his bloodstained tunic and tutted. He pulled off the shirt and held it in his right fist. When would they stop trying to shoot him?

The doors opened. He didn't bother looking beatific. He was pissed. He glowered at the rebels, and their cheering stopped. The thunderous look he cast upon them sent them scurrying back.

Perhaps now they would believe he was immortal.

Two dropped their weapons and retreated, but the one

who'd shot him stayed and trembled. He was young, probably no more than twenty with barely any meat on his body. Lank and wiry, he had brown hair, brown eyes, and a cherubic face that looked like he was about to be cast out of Heaven. His eyes searched Emrys's chest for the bullet holes and widened as the last wound closed.

Emrys held out his hand. "Give me that before you hurt someone."

Nobody made a sound. Quivering, the young rebel passed the gun to Emrys. When the weight transferred to his hand, the boy's eyes flooded with tears. He sank to the floor, pressing his forehead to the ground, begging for forgiveness, sobbing for his life.

The sound cut Emrys more painfully than the bullets. He could have given him a peaceful death, freed him of this strife and end his torment. Or not. His anger was strong enough to want to make an example of him. But with all that attention, with all those people watching, with all his potential to be a cruel Darisami tyrant, he wasn't yet ready to kill.

He cracked his neck and streamed air through his nostrils. If he expected understanding and compliance from those who opposed him, he had to be willing to do the same. Better to try to mold a benevolent society than one built on kill-or-be-killed.

Emrys reached down and touched the rebel's shoulder. "Stand up."

It took a few nudges of encouragement to get him to his feet. When he did, the boy kept his eyes downcast.

"Tell me your name."

"Owen." His voice collapsed halfway through. He sniffed and his breath stuttered. "My name is Owen, Immortal One."

"I forgive you, Owen, as I forgive everyone here who accepts the truth." He took Owen's hand. He wanted to break it but simply knowing he could and didn't was enough. "You have made the hardest journey of all. You have come out of a place of darkness, trusting the lies others have told you instead of believing the truth that I have come to save you. But you believe now, don't you? You understand what I am?"

Owen understood he'd been given a second chance. And like all people, smart or dumb, he wasn't going to waste it.

"I do." He wiped his nose with the back of his wrist. "I believe." His watery eyes flicked to Emrys's chest, to his bloodied but whole skin, then down to the shirt.

Emrys held it out for him. "Show this to the people."

Owen raised it to display the holes.

"I know you have your doubts, but trust what you have seen with your own eyes." Emrys gestured to the ruined cloth. "I am here to be with you always, to see you survive the time ahead, and to bring you into greater glory. You are welcome to follow me, and together we can bring harmony to Providence."

The crowd kept back, kept quiet, and kept their mistrust.

Give them time.

"I am here to speak to your leaders, but when I leave, anyone waiting here is welcome to follow me without prejudice or reprisal. You have my word." He made eye contact with as many people as possible, some hard-faced and angry, others uncertain, and a few wide-eyed and terrified, awe gripping their minds in its claws.

He turned to Owen. "Take me to the people who would turn you into a killer."

Owen walked in front of him, a hurrying faltering step

—half shy, half eager—wanting to please but also wary of being duped.

They didn't have to go far as news of Emrys's visit spread, bringing out an armed group of five men and women. He recognized one of them from Christos's memories. Warwick was a big brash brute of a man, taller and broader than Emrys, with a thick reddish-brown beard.

"You've got a lot of guts coming up here." Warrick's deep gruff voice sounded a little strained.

"I could say the same about you. Barricading two levels of Providence is an act of war."

"Which you started when you killed Christos. We're just protecting our people."

"From what?"

"From you."

He smiled. "Guns won't do that. As Owen and many others can attest to."

"Cheap tricks, that's all."

Warwick's refusal to accept the truth hit Emrys's back teeth. His appetite for killing Owen had only been luke-warm, but wiping Warwick out made him *hungry*. Perhaps he should have let Galen storm the level and clear them out. Negotiating with this wannabe warlord was an aggra-vation he didn't need.

"Then take another shot. But I warn you, you will suffer the same fate as Christos for your crime."

Warwick tightened his grip on the gun's forestock, but he didn't aim. "What do you want?"

"A truce."

"That would imply you have legitimacy."

"It would mean you do too. I don't want a war in Prov-idence. We have too much work ahead to let squabbling derail us."

"Work that involves returning us to the surface when it is dangerous to do so. You are sentencing our people to death, and we won't stand for it."

"It will happen with or without you."

"Let's see how far you get when your people are starving."

"You don't want to do that, Warwick. Threaten us, and I will send troops in to reclaim this floor. Your people will die, and my work will continue. But I don't want war, so I'm prepared to negotiate."

Warwick licked his bottom lip. "What do you propose?"

"You and your people can have seven and eight."

"We want nine as well."

They couldn't have nine. Science operated out of there.

"There aren't enough of you to occupy those floors, and we can't sacrifice the space." He also wanted a buffer between them and the main exit out of Providence. "You can live on seven and eight, and come and go freely, but you must give up the guns."

"We're keeping the guns."

"They won't protect you from me."

"But they'll protect us from your thugs. We keep the guns."

"If you refuse to hand them over, you will be restricted to seven and eight and barred from accessing the other floors. Elevator four will be for your use alone and will service these two floors."

"You're imprisoning us."

The crowd talked over each other, demanding freedom, demanding he go.

"Hand over all your weapons, and I'll consider giving you free access."

"Not a chance."

"Then you will not be allowed to roam. This will be for your protection as well as others."

"As if we'd trust you to keep your word."

"Right now, my word is the only one in Providence you can trust. Hand over the weapons, and you're free to move. Keep them, and you'll be restricted to seven and eight. It's your choice."

"Not much of a choice."

Emrys's lips strained as he stretched a smile across them. "It's the only one you'll get. Do we have a deal?"

"What if we need medical assistance? What if we need things fixed?"

He was inclined to tell them to go fuck themselves but that didn't seem the right response for an angel. "You will have a direct line to the control center and be allowed to go to those levels as necessary, in exchange for continuing to keep the supply of food going."

Warwick sneered. "You want us to feed traitors?"

He got closer to Warwick, and while the bigger man tried to bolster his bulk, his size did nothing to weaken Emrys's resolve. "You will continue to feed the people, or I will clear you out personally, one by one."

The muscles beneath Warwick's eyes spasmed. "I want to talk this over with my people in private. You will have our answer by the end of the day." He spun and led the other leaders away.

"One more thing," Emrys said.

They stopped.

"Anyone who wants to follow me must be allowed to leave whenever they wish."

"Anyone who wants to leave can do so, but they'll be tossed over the balcony for the traitors they are," Warrick roared loud enough for the people to hear.

Emrys held his lips in a straight line, fighting the smile that wanted them to bend and bow. Better that Warrick appear the villain. The rebels walked away, and Emrys turned for the elevator with Owen following close behind. The doors were partially blocked by a group of about thirty people—women mostly, some children, a couple of men.

"Will you follow me?"

They nodded, some smiled. Others kept their distance, but they had chosen him. That was encouraging. The elevator door opened without his needing to do anything, and in he walked with a new group of Faithful and Owen by his side.

❧ 10 ☙

WHEN THE ELEVATOR STOPPED ON FOUR, THE DOORS opened to a wall of military might. The former rebels cowered behind Emrys. He stepped forward. "What is this?"

"It is for yours and Providence's protection, Immortal One. These people are to be taken to cells for interrogation before being allowed to join the rest of the population." Trellain ordered the soldiers to advance.

Emrys knew it was the right thing to do. Any among them could be a spy, but the abject terror on many faces was a lock on his throat. "I promise you they will not hurt you." He tried to sound convincing and calm.

Owen looked at him, his mouth shut but his eyes were wide and pleading.

"It will be fine, Owen. Tell them everything you know, and you'll be free soon."

Some seemed placated by him, others resigned, and a few resistant. The last would receive the most attention.

Once the prisoners were dragged away, Emrys was left with Trellain and Micah. "Who gave this order?"

"It was unanimous among us, but Galen gave his final consent," Trellain said.

Emrys had wanted Galen to be an authority in Providence. He wasn't sure he wanted it to look like this. "Make sure the Defenders understand that their interrogation is not to be invasive, brutal, or cruel in any way, because if I hear it is, then that person will answer to me. Do you understand?"

"Yes, Immortal One," they spoke in unison.

"Good, then make sure my orders are passed on. Now!"

Trellain bowed his head and beat a fast path behind the prisoners, leaving Emrys with Micah. He jerked his head for the Shadow to follow at a slower yet no less determined pace and re-entered the command center.

Emrys spoke before Galen could. "I've told Trellain and I'm telling you: those people are to be treated with respect and care."

Galen blinked rapidly. "We are doing this for your protection. If they have nothing to hide, then they will be fine. But it would be stupid of us to let traitors roam freely. They will not be harmed unless they give us cause, a tenet that is in keeping with your own doctrine."

Galen had him there. He could not expect mercy when he had not shown any to Christos. The threat of being stuck with the gold knife and his long life ended had been all the justification he'd needed to take the councilor's life. What difference did it make to the Faithful? A traitor was a traitor, and all traitors would be dealt with, in one fashion or another.

"Fine, but I expect you and the Defenders to do the right thing."

Galen sighed in happy relief. The tension in the room eased as whatever held breaths were released. Galen asked how the meeting with the rebels had gone and Emrys filled him in.

"Food production is going to be a problem, no matter how trustworthy you think they might be," Galen said.

"I agree. Have Laurence meet me in my chambers in an hour. I'll get him started on an alternative supply chain."

"Good idea." And no doubt one that Galen had already had. "Would you like me to attend the meeting as well?"

"As much as I'd appreciate you being there, I think this is something I can handle myself."

"As you wish. If it's all right with you I will have military standing by in case the rebels try something drastic while we await their response."

LAURENCE APPEARED IN EMRYS'S QUARTERS AN HOUR later. He no longer gave off the affable uncle routine, leaning on his cane as if it were a crutch and plastering his face with a non-threatening smile. Now he wielded his cane like a weapon and his face was that of a general being brought forth to answer difficult questions that he wasn't in the habit of being asked. He must have had a decent night's sleep. Though Emrys offered him a seat, the councilor chose to stand.

"I'm sure you are aware that you have lost control of Providence's food supply."

"I never had it," Laurence said. "Their allegiance to Christos was too strong, and his death hardened them against me. I don't say this as an excuse, but to point out the reality of the difficult situation in which we find ourselves."

"Either way, this must feel like a blow to you. And while I am disappointed, I'm realistic. I want you to establish an alternative food supply."

Emrys did not like the way that Providence's functions were so clearly demarcated. In Endurance, they had strived to make the systems as foolproof as possible, so that when one went down, a backup came online. It also helped that the council had been relatively large and of similar mind, or at least easily swayed by the majority of Darisami who occupied its bench. Clara and Ragnar's factions had always been at loggerheads for supremacy, but they had the common sense to see the benefit in having a devolved system. No such luck in Providence with its five councilors.

"That may take some time, Emrys. The expertise in setting up those systems and maintaining them is largely among the rebels."

"But not everyone who knows how to work them is on their side. At least thirty came over today, so talk to Galen and find out if any have knowledge we can use. I am certain that the original plans for Providence will give you some indication of what can be done."

"The only assurance I can give you is that we will try. My main concern is having enough people available."

"Let me worry about that. You worry about making sure people don't starve."

"Wouldn't it be better to arrest the rebels?"

"And lock over a thousand people into cells? I would prefer to win them over slowly than act fast and threaten the tenuous peace I am trying to negotiate. When the time comes for us to return to the surface, we will need as many people as possible. The rebels are armed. If they believe they have nothing to lose, that will lead to greater tragedy."

"I hope your approach is the right one." Laurence's

hand tensed on the top of his cane. "If that is all, I had best get to work."

Emrys stood. "Before you go, I have something to give you." He went into his bedroom and came back with a piece of white cloth fashioned into a pouch tied with black thread. He handed it to Laurence.

The councilor undid the knot, folded back the fabric, and stared at the golden ring lying in the center.

"I promised you a replacement. I'm sure your informants already told you about my late-night efforts in the Factory, but I hope it is a surprise nonetheless."

Laurence held up the ring and stared at it, his mouth half open, his brow furrowed as he examined its intricacies. Laurence's original ring had been a plain band made of gold, about a quarter of an inch thick. But even such simplicity held a lot of sentimental value. Emrys had to make something that didn't immediately remind him of the ring he'd lost.

"It's beautiful," Laurence breathed.

The ring was still a flat band, but it appeared as if it was fashioned of multiple threads, a pattern that included the symbol for eternity that Emrys had long ago taken for his own. It had taken many hours, but he had struggled to sleep. And Galen kept his distance. Emrys had banished every worker from the room so he could work in peace. His skills were rusty, but the end product confirmed he had not lost his ability.

He had engraved words on the inside—*For Providence.*

"I know it cannot replace the one you gave me, but I hope in time it will come to be a symbol of our great friendship. I have faith in you, Laurence, whether or not you have faith in me."

Laurence looked up at him. "You have my support."

He slipped the ring onto the middle finger of his right hand and held it out.

Emrys smiled and shook his hand, the metal dull and ineffective against his soft palm. "I am glad to hear it. Now, you have work to do. I have no doubt you will succeed."

The battle drained out of Laurence and was replaced with genuine appreciation. He bid Laurence farewell, assured that the councilor was now adequately bought and Emrys would have no reason for buyer's remorse.

———

The rebels waited until the evening before giving their answer. The weapons would stay in their possession. They accepted the offer of living on seven and eight unmolested in exchange for keeping the food supply running. It was not a perfect victory, but it was not a stunning defeat. Emrys could claim he was working with all members of Providence to ensure continued survival. Partition was never clean cut, and there would be bleed-through in the days ahead, but for now he was satisfied he had cauterized the wound.

He addressed the citizens from the newly consecrated Temple, repurposing the council chamber to something more fitting of an angel, and decreed how Providence would be divided. He couched it in terms that were more palatable to his followers, though he was certain those on seven who were forced to move would grumble. Especially those who were not committed one way or the other and would prefer to get on with their lives. But if they sat on the fence, they had to accept that borders would move.

After his address, he had a short meeting with Juliet, Laurence, and Kira to hear about the progress with the various projects while Galen was busy overseeing the transition and ensuring no battles broke out. He didn't return to the quarters until late, and even then, Galen seemed reluctant that the day should end.

Despite how much he needed to rest.

His shoulders remained rigid, but his feet barely lifted off the floor when he staggered in. Trellain had reluctantly gone to bed half an hour before, and Micah not long before that. Blessedly, Emrys and Galen were alone.

Even with just the two of them there, Galen bowed his head in greeting, a gesture that Emrys was beginning to despise. It wasn't that he minded it from the Defenders and the Faithful, because he needed their compliance, but to see it on Galen was evidence of a widening divide.

He had to remind himself it had only been two days since his revelation. Familiarity would soften the protocols that lauded one unit to the detriment of another. As long as Emrys continued to remind Galen that fondness was not only allowed but encouraged.

Galen entered his quarters and Emrys smiled. "How are you?"

"I'm exhausted. We finally managed to reorganize everyone. Thankfully, we had no incidents with either the rebels or our followers. Level nine is ours again, and I have had seven and eight segregated from the rest of Providence." Galen stood with his hands clasped behind his back, his chest puffed up like a soldier delivering a status report. "I can't say how long they'll keep the peace or the food supply running, but tonight there should be no surprises."

"If there are, it's a job for later. Sit with me a while."

Galen didn't hesitate, which lifted Emrys's heart high into his chest...until Galen took the couch opposite, rather than the place beside him. As if this was just another meeting. He had to accept it. The pressure he had placed on

Galen was already astronomical, and as much as he wanted more, he didn't want to increase his burden.

"Are you all right, Galen?"

"Of course. A little tired perhaps, but I am excited for what we have achieved and for what is coming."

"I hope you know that it's okay to have doubts about me and what we're trying to do. Doubts help us see where things can go wrong and what pitfalls lay ahead."

Galen massaged his palm. "I have no doubts, Emrys, though I have worries I am not able to serve you as well as you need. I am trying, but I worry my abilities are not enough." He lifted his head, and the dark shadows under his eyes underscored the concern brewing within his green gaze.

Drawn by the need to comfort Galen, Emrys stood from his seat and took the place beside him. He slipped his right hand into Galen's and placed his left hand on Galen's back. "I couldn't have asked for anyone better to lead this. Have no fear that you are more than enough for this job. You were born for this."

Galen gave a weak smile that didn't remain, and no relief swept his held breath out of his body. Emrys had to try harder to convince him.

"You also don't have to do this alone. I am here to guide you and take the heavy decisions. You are a man of Providence through and through, and you know your people. Trust in that knowledge, and trust in your own good nature."

"But that's the thing. Overseeing the migration today, I felt such hate for them. I couldn't understand why they weren't willing to see what we were offering them. Why they would so blatantly deny the truth that you had shown. I wanted them all dead for the distraction they provided, their selfishness in taking our time and effort which could be put to better use." Galen hung his head. "And I hated them for how they were taking me away from your side. Is that wrong of me?"

"I could say you're only human and these feelings should be overcome, but I would be lying if I said I didn't feel them too." Especially how much he wanted to be beside Galen always. "But part of what we are trying to do here depends on faith that they will join us on the right path. I don't like it any more than you do, patience is a hard thing, but the alternative would be too much death, and Providence would not be able to survive."

"And my jealousy?"

Galen's problem had an easy and attractive solution. They could go back to sharing a bed, to making love while Providence descended into chaos, but Galen would take that as a personal failure, and it would drive them apart. Galen wanted to know that it was all right that he deny his carnal desires. Emrys could give him that peace, but self-ishly, he didn't want to seal off that possibility.

"The people of Providence love the Immortal One and the Immortal One loves them, but I, Emrys, love only you. Hold on to that when you see the Defenders close to me or the Faithful fawning around me. You alone hold all of my heart. Will that be enough?"

Galen's eyes brightened, and he kissed him, a perfect kiss that held the promise of so much more if things were different. Galen's lips didn't move, his mouth didn't open, and Emrys did not demand. He reveled in the bittersweet divide between having and not having, an exquisite pain that sliced him from crown to sacrum.

Galen broke the kiss and thanked him with a breath-lessness that verged on the holy. It took the last of his strength, and his head drooped. Emrys encouraged him to lie down and rest his head on his thigh. Such was his exhaustion, or perhaps his need to be close to Emrys, he didn't resist. Galen's head lay heavy in his lap, one hand on the top of his leg. Emrys ran his fingers through Galen's hair and stroked him into slumber. Within minutes, his breathing slowed.

The night passed while Galen slept and Emrys remained awake, thankful that he did not have to succumb to sleep and miss a moment.

Because he had no idea how many more they would have together.

❀ 11 ❀

EMRYS JOINED SCIENTISTS, WORKERS, AND SOLDIERS AS they ventured to the surface, many for the first time in their lives or in the lives of their parents. Juliet came as overseer, while the Five—minus Galen—joined the mission to mark the start of their campaign.

They left through Providence's main entrance, accessible from level ten, passing through a gas chamber that the Scientists had insisted be established to reduce the risk of contamination. They argued that they would be disturbing soil and potentially unknown pathogens that should be kept out of Providence's sealed environment. Everyone had been given the same inoculations as the soldiers who'd already been on surface missions. They submitted to the shower of neutralizing gas; the loud hiss amped up the pumping of Emrys's heart at the progress they were about to make.

Through all his years in Endurance, he'd barely dared to imagine humanity would return to the Earth. His fellow Darisami had not been enthusiastic, and the power plays between Ragnar and Clara meant their focus had been on

86

each other and not the good of the human race. Now, he didn't have to worry about their involvement, only that of ten thousand humans. If he had to, he'd drag them kicking and screaming into the harsh sunlight.

They walked the long tunnel to the large steel doors that separated Providence from the world. An excited buzz hummed through the group. Eagerness shone on their faces, even on Kira's. Whatever apprehensions they had about him and his plans were brushed aside in the eager attainment of their long-held goals.

Galen stayed behind to head off trouble in his absence. Emrys's stomach fluttered at the possibility of being locked outside forever if anyone attempted another coup. The rebels were sealed off and had kept to their bargain of maintaining the food supply, but what of other traitors in their midst?

Part of the reason for taking the councilors was as a guarantee, but what would it matter to Providence if a bunch of elites and a few citizens got locked outside if the city could be free of interference from some *thing*?

Isaiah marched somewhere towards the back with Elaina. Soldiers surrounded them and kept them moving forward.

The doors at the end of the tunnel ground open. Emrys shielded his eyes as the afternoon sun breached the divide and flooded the tunnel. Hot air blasted them. The temperature would take a few more millennia to cool to something he remembered but no one else did.

The ground around the domed roof of Providence's entrance had been cleared of all buildings for a wide radius. The bones of those who had died at its closed gates had blown away.

Kira marched out in front, her Scientists quick to follow as they scattered across the desolate land, less fearful than even the soldiers. Juliet directed the Workers to scope out a location for whatever station would be required. Regardless of the challenge ahead, they were eager to get to work.

But not everyone was enthusiastic, and as he looked out on a barren wasteland, almost unrecognizable from the verdant life he had enjoyed for much of his years, Emrys hesitated on the threshold.

Isaiah stopped beside him. "You're mad if you think this land will support us."

Perhaps I have to be.

He didn't want to show doubt in front of Isaiah—it would only be used against him—but while the worker ants scurried across the dirt, his heart was filled with nothing else. The journey from Endurance to Providence hadn't given him hope, but he hadn't been looking at the Earth in quite the same way. He'd been looking for a home. Sure, it would have been nice to stumble across a group of survivors—a *large* group of survivors—but they hadn't stumbled into their path. And there hadn't been time to search for them, what with the unknown stretching out in front of him, and the month—and the soul he'd harvested before leaving Endurance—dissolving. His survival had come first, humanity's second.

"There is life in the land yet," he said.

"You're right. Under it. Thanks to us being careful. Start sending people out here, you'll send them to an early grave."

"I'd be a little more inclined to believe your concern if I didn't already know you."

"All I do is for the good of our citizens."

"And your ego is stifling them. I give Providence thirty years before it's as dead as the other arks."

"You've no proof of that."

"You're standing beside me. You're all the proof I need. The citizens need something to work towards. Life underground will not serve them well in the long term."

"Then let them decide that."

He blinked at Isaiah. "That's rich coming from you. You shared the same aims as Christos. I know the secrets of his heart, and I know yours too, Isaiah. You had no desire to ever resurface, and you ensured there would be no discussion of it. But no matter. I am merely a catalyst for change, the vessel through which the people's will will be done. The rest comes from them and their drive for freedom."

"The only thing you're a catalyst for is our destruction."

"That will only happen if you disobey me. Providence will not survive another rift. The fractures are too deep, and I am helping to bring them back together."

"You want to help? Then fuck off back to where you came from."

"It's too late for that."

"Why? Because you destroyed Endurance too? I'd like to see it now after you got your hands on it. Maybe one day I will."

Emrys kept his face passive. If Isaiah ever reached Endurance, he'd see how badly everything had gone. "You're welcome to go on a reconnaissance mission, Isaiah. Think of it as a vacation. Might be good for you to wander in the wilderness for a while. Clear your head."

"And leave you to run Providence into the ground?"

"It's already there. I'm bringing it back up to the light."

"It's not the light. It's an inferno."

"Then Elaina's people can treat the burns." He walked away from Isaiah and followed the Scientists.

Isaiah's arguments had wormed their way under his

armor, burrowing in to push them to the surface. He didn't need anyone to give them oxygen. The few scraps of life returning that he'd encountered on his journey fluttered in the winds of doubt and would soon take off into the air with him grasping after them. Was the Earth ready for them?

A nuclear winter had wreaked havoc on an atmosphere already struggling with the effects of man-made climate change, but as ever, life adapted, and mutations abounded. Only the strongest survived, and wasn't he the strongest? Hadn't he adapted?

Pine trees grew in the distance away from the scorched earth around Providence's entrance where so many people must have perished. But the trees no longer glistened green. Their leaves were the color of burnt umber.

The Scientists collected soil samples from different sites, all methodically recorded and tracked and tested. They couldn't keep the enthusiasm out of their eyes or the fumbling of their hands as they sought to gather the answers to long-held questions.

The Workers set off for the nearest structures to see what they could rebuild and what they could salvage. There seemed little of value, but they quickly got used to the newness of their experience, growing accustomed to what was now their expanded reality. They investigated what possibilities lay ahead, how they would have to adapt and do things differently from what they'd known for a generation or two.

When the wind blew and brushed their faces, they stopped, felt it caress their skin like a lover returned, and realized, truly understood for a moment, that they had made it out. That this was where they were meant to be.

Then their attention returned to their tasks, reinvigorated and recharged with purpose.

Isaiah huddled in the entrance's shadow. Trellain stood beside him, no longer the councilor's subordinate, his chiseled chin sticking out and forward, while Isaiah muttered something. Trellain remained unmoved, his belief a rod that kept him in place. What invective was Isaiah dripping into Trellain's ear? How was he ferreting out Trellain's doubts and twisting them to his cause? Isaiah would have to keep talking for a while yet. Trellain's faith was unshakeable.

"Emrys?" Kira touched his arm.

"How's it looking?"

"The soil is damaged, but we've taken samples and will run tests to see how we can improve it. We're also collecting whatever vegetation we can find, but I'd like to set up a permanent laboratory here as soon as possible. We need to know the effects of meteorological elements, sunlight, wind patterns, rainfall, radiation levels, et cetera on the vegetation. Our knowledge is out of date."

"Are you hopeful?"

"I won't know until our research is complete. I wouldn't want to pre-empt the results."

He stared at her, hoping that his silence would push her towards a declarative statement, but she said nothing more.

"What about the plants you've found? Are they encouraging?"

"Without—"

"Without further tests, you can't say for sure." He sighed. "I guess I should be glad you're keen to set up a lab. That gives me hope."

"You would be the last person I think would need it. After all, it's your guidance that's leading us to do this."

"But I can't fix everything. I'm reliant on you and your mortal ways for that."

"Then we should get to work. Do I have your approval?"

"Of course. Talk to Juliet and tell her what you need."

She nodded and walked away.

He wandered, enjoying the chance to stretch his legs and the scurrying activity as the Scientists collected and the Workers assessed. They stayed outside for three hours before the sun dipped and the light turned red-gold. It would be some hours yet before the full moon showed her face. The opportunity for a light show would have to wait. He called them in.

He stood beside Isaiah while the Workers returned and filed past him, bringing with them pieces of metal scrap, overjoyed that they'd been allowed to do it themselves for a change as opposed to relying on what Security retrieved.

The Scientists came next, carrying their samples, including a container holding a four-inch-tall yellow plant, little more than a shoot with two leaves, but healthy and strong. Isaiah stared after it.

"Life *always* finds a way," Emrys said.

And Isaiah shuddered.

❧ 12 ❧

"Excuse me, Immortal One."

Emrys looked up from the screen he was hunched over and raised an eyebrow at Galen's formal greeting. "What did you call me?"

Galen bit his lip. "I'm sorry, Emrys. I don't want to seem disrespectful."

"There is nothing sweeter to me than hearing my name on your lips." *Or more aggravating than hearing that title tripping off them so easily.* "Please, remember that."

"I will try. Owen is waiting outside to speak with you."

He'd promised to speak to Owen after the previous night's address in the Temple when he told the Faithful about the success of the mission to the surface, but circumstances had gotten in the way.

The rebels had removed all cameras on seven and eight, blacking out any electronic window into their operations. This act raised tensions among the military leaders, including Galen, who suspected they were about to launch an attack.

But as the night stretched on and troops were mobilized, no attack came, and a conversation with Warwick gave no indication that one would be forthcoming. He merely said that they deserved their privacy.

That hadn't stopped Emrys from spending the rest of the night and most of the morning watching from the Tower across to eight in the hopes of catching some glimpse of what Warwick was doing.

When Emrys returned to the apartment, he obsessed over the screens, scanning for pockets of trouble. Galen already had it covered, but he did it nonetheless.

Perhaps permitting Owen to come and meet with him was Galen's way of distracting him.

Emrys grumbled but relented. "You'd better show him in."

Galen went to collect Owen, and Emrys dragged himself away from the screens.

Galen marched in with Owen walking a few yards behind. When he was presented, Owen sank to his knees and raised his arms, offering Emrys's own blood-stained white robes.

"Immortal One, I'm here to give back what is yours. I held onto it throughout my imprisonment and after. I wouldn't let them take it from me even when they hit me."

The dark purple and blue bruises on his cheeks and around his eyes made his fervor shine brighter. Any other person would hate those who'd hurt them, but Owen showed none of that, taking his defiance as a sign of his faith.

"Thank you." He placed his hands over Owen's, touching his skin. The boy shivered, with pleasure or pain, it didn't matter which. "But that is for you as a witness and as a believer in my miracles." He could always do with more disciples, and if the young crowd he'd seen surrounding Owen the night before was anything to go by,

Owen would take his faith among them and spread it like a virus. "You will be rewarded for your faith."

Owen grinned wide, staring up with a blazing fire in his eyes. "Thank you for this gift, Immortal One. In return I offer myself. I am here to serve you in any way you need. You only have to say the word. I am your loyal servant."

"If you work in service to Providence, then you are working in service to me."

"But surely there is something I can do for you personally."

If it weren't for the innocent look in his eyes, Emrys would have considered the offer sexual.

Galen stepped forward. The thought must have crossed his mind too. "The Immortal One has already told you what you can do for him."

Owen cowered, his eyes flicking to the fists at Galen's sides. "I meant no disrespect to you, High Priest, or to you, Immortal One. Please forgive me."

Emrys crouched in front of Owen, but the young man refused to meet his gaze. "What is it you think I need?"

Owen raised his face to Emrys, his expression saying he felt blessed to have been spoken to. He licked his lip, saliva glistening on its surface, white foam in the corners of his mouth. "You are already well regarded among people my age. As much as the Five once wished it to be different, we have been longing for a better future, and so your arrival has made many of us happy. But they are wary."

"Of what?"

Owen glanced sideways at Galen, swallowed hard, and hung his head. "I would rather not say."

Emrys gave Galen the nod to leave. He frowned but didn't argue, and Emrys waited until he'd left the room. "Tell me what makes them wary."

"I still don't know if I should say." He reminded Emrys

of a chastened dog, those eyes like liquid pools of pity, his shoulders curling in to brace for a beating.

Emrys held out his hand. "Here, come. Get off the floor and sit with me."

Owen started at his offered hand, blinked once at it, blinked once up at Emrys, then placed his palm in Emrys's and struggled off the ground. Emrys led him to the couch and they sat side by side. Owen gripped the blood-stained robes tight in his fist.

"You have nothing to fear from speaking the truth to me. If it helps Providence, no matter how difficult it is to say, it should be said."

"We think the Five are not committed to your aims." His words came out clearer and more certain than his demeanor would have suggested. The strength of his conviction gave Emrys pause.

"Do you have proof?"

"Only past experience. We do not trust Isaiah, and while we accept that Galen is your high priest, we are not convinced he and his father are not working together to undermine you." Owen ducked his head. "Forgive me, but that is what is being said."

"Do they believe I have chosen wrong in selecting Galen to be my high priest?" His voice was cold, flat, in charge.

Owen's body shrank as his eyes grew large. "No, Immortal One, and we would never presume to know the inner workings of the Divine's plan for us, but he is only human and therefore corruptible like all of us." He shuffled a little closer.

Emrys stayed still but annoyance shimmered beneath his skin. "You are young, so I will forgive you questioning my choice, but Galen's heart is pure, and he works with me in complete concord. He has proven himself many times over, and while you may not see all that he does, you enjoy the benefit of his labors."

"I do not wish to anger you, Immortal One, but I have heard that it was you who defended us when others would have had us slaughtered. I am loyal to you and to you alone. As it is with my friends and followers."

Owen's words trickled fear down Emrys's spine, drawing his muscles tight. He straightened his back but couldn't dispel the feeling that he'd been pulled into a position not of his choosing. Was this a credible threat to the order that Emrys was trying to establish? Had maintaining support for the Five been an oversight that he would come to regret? But more importantly, what was he to do with Owen and his supporters?

"How many followers would you say you have?"

"About two hundred."

Emrys tried not to let his surprise show. Owen had only been released from his cell four days earlier. Could Emrys count that many Defenders?

"And how do you intend to help me and Providence? Do all of you believe in my plans for repopulating the surface?"

Owen's body unbowed, the tension in his face easing. "We do and we would like to participate more. However, there are limited opportunities to do so."

"Are none of you part of the teams?"

"They have all been hand-picked by the Five and their agents, many because of their experience instead of their faith."

"Do you think that unfair?"

"Only if we are never to see the surface ourselves. We understand you need skilled workers, and your ceremony yesterday filled us with great optimism, but we are impatient to receive the same blessings as those whose beliefs are not as strong."

Heaven save him from jealousy! He couldn't have inexperienced people bounding about on the desolate surface. They would do more damage to his vision than the combined hostility of the Five. But if what Owen said was true—and Galen would investigate his claims—his followers would have to be given something to do.

"Would it be best if I found you places among those teams where you can learn from them? Our mission will not be completed tomorrow, and a new generation will have to take their place as we continue to rebuild. Would it not be best for you to learn now?"

"If that is your wish, then that is what we will do. Many of my fellows will welcome it." Owen's expression flashed from the sated softness of a contented hound to that of a wolf scenting blood before he calmed.

He would have to find some way to control Owen and his pack. "And you?"

"I had been thinking it would serve you better if I could expand your mission among the undecided, and perhaps, in the future, the nonbelievers."

"Are my sermons insufficient? Or the messages I put out through my High Priest and the Five inadequate?"

"Again, I do not wish to insult Galen, but he has many responsibilities and cannot give his full attention to converting all in Providence to your path."

"And you think you can?"

"I do. Like Galen, I am a witness to your miracles but, unlike him, my conversion was hard fought. Many of the citizens know of your affection for him prior to your revelation, whereas you and I had never met. Like with the Five, your elevation of Galen to the role of high priest was an easy transition, whereas mine has been a journey that has already enamored many."

Emrys would like to say that pride went before a fall. Or that he regretted not having sucked out Owen's soul when he had the chance. He wanted to knock the annoying little shit back into his place and bruise his faith as badly as his face.

But he recognized his mistake in all this, that belief was a tricky thing and once awakened was impossible to predict. Owen may not have intended his words to sound as threatening as they did, because for all he knew, he was speaking to an angel or some other being with a mission. He was merely trying to stay in the Divine's favor.

But Emrys realized with chilling certainty that he was witnessing the birth of a religion. He could well imagine Owen writing down every one of his words, flexing his creativity to fit the narrative as best he could. Emrys had thought a few well-chosen words, the bestowing of a ritual object, and the showing of miracles would be enough to pacify this group of humans and their need to believe in something, but he had not accounted for their willingness and desire to have more and to localize power within their own hands.

How soon would it get away from him?

And behind it all was the knowledge of where Owen came from and what he had done. Was he still a rebel at heart? Was this a ploy to get close enough to sabotage?

Quick as a flash, his hand locked on Owen's throat, and he squeezed just enough to make it hard for him to breathe. Owen stiffened, his body jolting from the shock, but he didn't try to escape. Emrys's eyes locked onto his pained expression.

"Listen to me, Owen. If you are lying to me, it will be nothing to take your soul. Christos died by my hand for his sins. He attempted to destroy me and in so doing would have destroyed Providence."

Owen's face flushed deep purple, and he struggled to speak, his words coming out in short bursts. "If you do not believe me, Immortal One, then take my soul now. It is yours to do with as you wish. And I would rather die than have you think me a traitor to you or to Providence. I serve you, and I apologize if my words about High Priest Galen have angered you. If you will permit me, you will see the numbers I have gathered in devotion to you, and I will bring you more."

Emrys released his hand, and Owen dropped back into his seat, coughing to clear his throat. His skin gradually returned to its normal pallid color.

To his credit, Owen did not flee from the room. In fact, Emrys's rough treatment increased, rather than diminished, his fervor.

"All right, Owen. I would like to see what you are capable of. Bring your followers to the Temple so I can meet them. The High Priest will be with me, as will other members of my close circle. I will address them and direct them as I see fit, but let it be known among them that they are to abide by the rules I pass down through my chosen representatives, which at this moment, include the Five."

"Even Isaiah?"

What could he say? The Five were meant to work as one unit beneath him, but it must have been an open secret among the citizens that Isaiah was not in agreement with anything that Emrys ordered.

"Directions that come from the Five as a whole or from Galen or me specifically must be obeyed. Tell them that. I already have one rebellion. I do not need another from those who claim to follow me."

"I understand, Immortal One, and I shall make sure

they understand too. In time, I hope we will convince the rebels of the right path in the same way you have, by avoiding bloodshed to bring them back to the fold."

"See that you stick to it. You may go."

Owen bowed deep and thanked Emrys for his time and attention. He backed out of the room. Galen rejoined Emrys.

"I want him watched," Emrys said.

"Already on it. What did he say to you?"

"He thinks the Faithful have been neglected, particularly the young."

"And that is a criticism of me, I expect."

"Not one that I share."

"And yet it holds merit. I hate to admit it, but I have not been able to speak with them as much as I should have while serving as your high priest."

Emrys had lived through thirty-one popes and only a handful of them ever went near a congregation. They had done all right. "You've got nothing to worry about. Your position is secure."

"With you, perhaps, but not with the Faithful. What did Owen offer?"

Emrys filled Galen in on their conversation and the meeting that would take place later that night. "I want you there. We need them to see that you and I are working together so that what one says, the other agrees with."

"Will that be enough?"

"For now. Meanwhile, I want to know what Owen does in between now and then. But do it gently. Those bruises were too much."

"From what Trellain tells me, the boy liked it."

Self-flagellation and hairshirts were all the rage in days gone by. Those bruises made Owen a martyr for the cause.

"Make sure he doesn't get any more."

"I can't guarantee that if he causes trouble."

Emrys sighed and returned to the screens. "Still no success in getting the rebel floors reactivated?"

"None. I think the cameras have been cut completely."

"How did they know where they all are?"

Galen hesitated. "That's what we're investigating."

"Only what? Not who?"

"That as well. I have my suspicions Isaiah is running a backchannel to the rebels, but I've yet to find proof. He's been at this longer than I have."

Emrys straightened at the despondency in Galen's voice. "Would it be better for someone else to take the lead?"

Galen faced him. "I'm not compromised, if that's what you think."

"I had to check. He is your father after all."

Galen's jaw bulged. "And he willingly used me to bargain for your expulsion. His parentage means little."

Would Galen be so firm if he ever had to have Isaiah executed for some infraction or treason? Even if Emrys did give Isaiah a good death, he would be the man who'd killed his father. Could Galen avoid holding a grudge?

"Have you learned anything so far?"

"Not much. He doesn't seem to have a lot to do, and I think he's enjoying that. While everyone's running around making work for themselves, he can stand back and watch us fail."

"That's not like him though, is it? To be idle?"

"No, which is why I'm suspicious. He's making a good appearance of doing nothing, but he's never been one to not have some scheme on the go."

"Then he must be found something more productive to do. Bring him here after the meeting with Owen's followers tonight."

"I'll arrange it. If there's nothing else you need me for, I'd better get back to command."

It was easy to imagine, for a short while, that it was just the two of them and they existed for themselves and no one else. These moments where they could discuss strategy and tactics as if they didn't affect real lives outside the Tower. He wanted Galen to stay so they could talk more, but people were depending on them. Their own pleasure was now a secondary concern. Or at least Galen's was.

He had no doubt that if he asked Galen to remain, he would. If he ordered him to strip naked and give him his body, he would. Anything and everything he asked of Galen, he could have.

But that thought held no allure. He wanted Galen, but as equals. Or as close to equals as possible. Otherwise, it would never work.

"We'll walk out together. Laurence wants to show me the new food systems. I shouldn't keep him waiting."

THE SUBSTITUTE SYSTEM WAS UP AND RUNNING, WITH Laurence looking as if he'd done all the work himself. Sweat plastered his black-and-white speckled hair to his scalp and patches of grease glistened on his skin. Standing amid the Workers who'd headed the project, he looked in character.

The machines produced food much slower than the systems on eight, but Laurence assured him they would improve over time. In the interim, they would feed the population in case of emergencies. Once Laurence could guarantee a secure supply, Emrys wanted the alternatives to become their first recourse. Gradually, what was produced on eight would lose importance. Then the rebels would learn they couldn't ransom Providence's future.

He watched the machines' first full run after testing, then spoke a few words of commemoration and thanked the Workers. He shook Laurence's hand, pleased to see the ring firmly on his finger. Ceremony done, Emrys exited the facility.

Juliet met him in the corridor. Her auburn hair was tied back, her gray uniform crisp and clean. Combined with a determined look that was not just focused on him but on the many steps ahead, it made her the model of efficiency and order.

Whatever she thought him to be didn't interfere with her responsibilities.

"Have you got a minute?" she asked.

He nodded, and she led him deeper into the Factory. "We're planning another mission to the surface tomorrow, but I'd like to make them longer and more frequent. Every day in fact."

He jolted, caught by her enthusiasm and initiative. "Of course, but why?"

"Supplies. I think we have to ration what is used and where. Laurence's project stretched our resources. Necessary, of course, but I've spoken to him, and we've agreed to put everything under harsher restrictions. I also want better security on our stores."

"Talk to Galen about that."

She nodded rather than reply.

"Is there anything you're about to run out of?"

"Not yet but soon. Reclamation from within Providence will only get us so far."

"All right. Take the Workers through the back entrance to enter the city and collect what they can. While you're there, I want them to look over the structures and see what can be rebuilt to start housing people."

"What about the other mission? We're already building there."

"That's for the Scientists; this is for the ordinary population. We must use what we can, and if the city can protect them, then let's do that."

"I don't know, Emrys. From what I saw, the city looks like nothing more than a wreck. I'd be concerned about it falling down on top of us."

"No one moves in unless it's safe, but we'd be foolish not to make the most of what we can."

"What about a reconnaissance mission to an abandoned ark? We could strip them of what we need."

Victory was the nearest ark, and it had been little more than a husk, but it might hold a gold mine. Or preferably iron. But the distance was a problem for mortals.

"Maybe, when things get desperate."

"You may change your mind after you see our stocks."

They stopped outside solid and sealed double doors, the third set they'd passed through, each one requiring security access to enter. People had fought wars over resources, so the precautions weren't excessive. From the quiet of the corridor, they entered a bustling workroom with Workers tarrying to their tasks, transporting stock on trolleys across the Factory floor. They acknowledged his presence but didn't let his appearance slow their work.

The resources were arranged in long lines of lockers. He and Juliet patrolled down one row while she elaborated on what was behind each and what was running low. Even though her role had changed to coordinating the surface missions, she retained a lot of her prior knowledge, and Laurence continued to rely on her talents while he was engaged with the food supply.

"We have plenty of iron and aluminum, but we're low on titanium and lithium."

He didn't pause beside each one as he trusted what she had to say, but it was clear Providence's stocks needed to be replenished.

When they got to the gold cabinet, he stopped. "And the gold?"

"It's always been rare, but it's not required much except for electronics. Kira's Scientists put in the most requests for it."

"You don't make the electronics?"

Juliet scrunched up her face. "No, Kira claims the work is too specialized for the Workers."

"I find that hard to believe."

She snorted. "She deigns to allow us to construct the casings—grunt work, she calls it—but everything else is their domain."

"Want me to talk to her?"

"It's too late now. They've got the expertise, and we're stretched enough as it is. But the point is, they need the gold more than the rest of us."

"How much do they require each year?"

"Fortunately, very little. We're usually able to retrieve enough thanks to our reclamation efforts, but we could always do with more. But so could everyone with everything. Which is why I would like restrictions put in place now. I've been through the access codes and—I take part of the blame for this—we've been far too lax in recent years by allowing so many people access. Most do the right thing, but with our change in focus, we need to do better."

He welcomed any measures that would limit the amount of gold circulating through Providence.

"And Laurence is in agreement?"

"He is."

"Then so am I. Get it done."

She had nothing else to discuss with him so, with a final glance at the locked cabinet, he left the Factory and headed back to his apartments. He quickly changed into his white robes for his meeting with Owen's followers.

Galen appeared in his doorway as he was slipping on his shirt. "Are you ready for this? There are more of them than I expected."

"How many?"

"Three hundred."

Emrys stopped and righted himself. *Owen had said two hundred.* "You're certain?"

He nodded. "Had them counted as they went in and checked for weapons."

"How did that go down?"

"Not so good. They objected to it, and our soldiers got rough."

He swore. "Are they settled?"

"The soldiers are."

"I meant Owen's lot."

Galen gave a twisted smile. "For now, but they're eager for you to appear. Are you sure speaking to them directly is a good idea? What if it upsets the rest of the citizens?"

"Owen's group is the squeakiest wheel, so they'll get the grease. We can't have them splinter."

"I'd prefer to see them broken completely."

"Would you?"

He nodded. "They should be working instead of flitting around causing problems."

"Then we have to find them something useful to do."

"But I don't trust them, not as a group. They're… they're…"

"You can say it, Galen. You have nothing to fear from me."

"They're not the right kind of Faithful."

"Why not?"

"They're unruly. They don't follow commands. They create discord."

"Then we must work harder to keep them in line."

He hung his head and gave an exasperated sigh. "They won't listen to me. I'm afraid I'll fail you on this. Perhaps their faith is stronger than mine."

That would be a dream come true. Then they could finally cross this divide and he could tell Galen the truth.

"As I told Owen and as I'm telling you, you're the only one who truly matters to me through all this. I work for *your* future, not theirs."

Galen blinked at him. "I would have thought their devotion would be more palatable to you and the Divine."

He wrinkled his nose. "That they believe and follow is pleasing, but the work you and others do to further our mission is true devotion." He put his hand on Galen's shoulder, thrilled at being close to him and doing what he could to comfort him. "You and Juliet, even Laurence and Kira, are helping to keep the people of Providence safe and provide them with a future. *That* is the true work of the Faithful. Never forget that."

Galen smiled cautiously. "Thank you, I will remember. But I don't know how you'll convince Owen's faction."

"I'll think of something." Whatever happened, he and Galen had to present a united front. All authority might flow from Emrys, but it had to flow through the tributaries running through Providence. He held Galen's hand, and he squeezed in return as they walked out of the apartments and through the corridors to the Temple. When they reached the closed doors, Galen's hand slipped away. Emrys felt the loss like a knife across his palm.

"I should say good luck," Galen said, "but I don't think you'll need it."

Galen's confidence in his ability bolstered him, but when the doors opened, and the screaming of the fans hit him, that confidence trembled. The noise knocked the smile off his face, and he scrambled to reapply it as he entered the Temple. Their harsh, shriek-like cheering cut jagged edges into his flesh. They thrust their hands towards him, eyes wet with tears and threads of saliva turning their mouths into barred cages from which their fanaticism attempted to break free. They scrambled over one another to get close to him.

Three hundred people bayed for his blessing. The adoration of the citizens at prior meetings had been reassuring, but this... He only had to say the word and they would have destroyed anyone he chose. If allowed to continue unchecked, they would overrun the place.

Galen was right to fear them.

Emrys fixed the smile onto his face with sheer determination while his heart shriveled. The ugliness of religious passion threatened to rip it from him, but he had created this monster, and he had to hold tight to its leash.

Owen occupied a space front and center and was as vociferous in his adoration as others around him. What was more striking, however, was that instead of the gray tunic that was common for most of the citizens, he was wearing Emrys's blood-stained white robes. The tears and tatters exposed his skin beneath. And when Emrys looked at others, looked past their frenzy, he noticed their garments had been torn in a similar way, with three slashes across the front.

Every.

Single.

Person.

At least it made them easy to identify, however chilling the sight.

He didn't approach them. He'd touched their hands and heard their pleas at prior meetings. As they had then, they begged for miracles and demanded to be shown the way to salvation, their desperation greedy.

He took up his position on the dais, encouraging Galen to stand close. More of his Defenders stood around the inner circle and at the exits. They didn't bear arms, but they had batons to beat the crowd back if necessary. He had to make sure it didn't come to that.

He raised his arms above his head and called for silence, allowing their cries to wash over him as they subsided.

"Citizens, thank you for coming. Your devotion to me pleases the Divine and—"

The rest of his words were drowned by their wild screaming, and it took minutes for them to calm. He attempted a grateful smile while keeping a strong rein on his annoyance. Turning a mob was like turning an ocean liner. It took forever.

"I am pleased to see you all here, and I understand, through Owen, that you have things that you would like to ask."

Voices all raised at once, but he called for quiet then selected a young woman with black hair.

"We want to know how best to serve you."

Multiple voices joined in agreement.

"If you serve Providence, then you serve me."

"But how best should we serve Providence?"

"Through work. Many of our citizens are involved in the missions to the surface where they are laying the essential groundwork for our eventual return. While that work takes place, we must continue to keep Providence running and help to shape coming generations for their new home."

"But what if we aren't allowed to help?"

"Everyone can help."

Galen coughed.

He hurried on. "Provided they work together. Listen to those with experience and learn from them."

"But they won't teach us!"

"That's right!" a young man said. "They think we are too young."

Emrys faltered. How could he tell three hundred people who would commit violence for him that any who bar them was his enemy? He couldn't do it. Whatever work they had been doing until then had not been satisfactory, but with no way out, and a controlling council, these people hadn't been able to break their bonds. How to proffer restraint when they had been restrained their whole lives?

"I will personally assign places for each of you. High Priest Galen will take your names, and I will divine where you are best suited to serve. Do you accept?"

They responded with a roar of approval, even if he did catch sour faces at the idea that they would have to submit to Galen. Even so, he smiled at their enthusiasm. This would be one way to keep them separated.

When they died down, Owen raised his voice, and they fell silent immediately. "If it pleases you, Immortal One, perhaps I could provide you with the list of names. No offence to Galen, but we all know how much he is burdened with, and I would like to help ease it."

Emrys dropped his smile. "Thank you for your concern for the *High Priest's* wellbeing, but it is my wish that everyone speak to him directly. His burden is not so great that he would not welcome this opportunity to talk with you all. Is that clear?"

Owen bowed his head. The energy in the room flattened, but no one dissented.

"Do you have anything else you wish to ask?"

"May we see the miracle of the light?" a voice from the back called.

"He is not an entertainer who serves at your whim!" Galen bellowed.

Owen and his followers glared, but Galen stood his ground. Emrys would have liked to shout the same but for the fact that he knew it would only strengthen their resolve to see it. The longer he resisted, the more disgruntled they would become.

"You shall see my light when the time is right." It wasn't a lie. The moon needed to shine from a cloudless sky, and they needed to be on the surface. If he could put them into surface missions, that might happen sooner than they anticipated.

"But haven't we pleased you?" Owen said. "We accept your word as truth, and we are devoted to your cause. Aren't we your chosen? Why should it just be the Defenders?"

"By that logic, should everyone take up arms and shoot me as you did so all can witness my resurrection? Do not presume to know my works or what I choose to reveal to you. Work hard, and you will be rewarded. But for now, you will pass your names to the High Priest, and *I* will decide how you shall best serve Providence. Good night."

He turned and marched from the room in a much less dignified fashion than when he entered. It was quieter too. Their entitlement had affected him more than it should have, but this was a problem of his own creation.

One he was running from.

Galen would handle it, and handle it well, but he shouldn't have had to. Agreeing to the meeting had been his first mistake. He needed to avoid making another.

He left the Temple, and the doors shut him away from the murmuring of their discontent, only to have Isaiah step out from a side room with a smirk on his face.

"Indoctrinating more of the deluded?"

Emrys sneered. "What do you want?"

Isaiah's face shifted like a mask of wax to form something resembling a smile with none of the mirth. It made his cheeks puff up and stretched his lips, but it was a toad's mouth that greeted him.

"I was ordered to meet with you after your little meeting."

Emrys jerked his head in the direction of his apartments and set a fast pace, but Isaiah's legs were longer than his, and he took it in his ample stride.

"I've been told you have nothing to do."

"My son lavishes praise upon me."

"I wonder where he learned that from."

"If you think turning my son against me is a smart choice, then we are doomed."

"You don't need any help from me to do that. Galen has been handling things very well and in better fashion than you." They reached the apartments and entered. He flicked his hand at the chair opposite for Isaiah to take his seat. "So, about your idleness."

"I am never idle."

"No? Tell me what you have been up to."

"You want a blow-by-blow account? It sounds like you are the one with time to spare."

Emrys let silence reign.

"Very well." Isaiah stretched wide his arms and rested them on the back of the couch. "If you must know, there really isn't a lot to do. The wheels of government keep spinning. You took Food away from me and gave it to Laurence. Bravo, well done there. Excellently executed." Sarcasm dripped from his tongue. "And the cleaners keep cleaning. They need minimal involvement from me, but I am always there to guide. The teachers need the most help, though many of their charges seem to have become swept up in your cult. I worry for their education, though perhaps if they're following you, it's already too late."

"It must be difficult for you not to be so involved in every facet of your responsibilities. I understand how enmeshed you were with Security, and you were there a long time—too long—so it is surprising that you haven't thrown your considerable knowledge into the problems at hand."

"I am still learning everything Christos's prior charges are responsible for. That takes time. Don't want to make any sudden changes. You never know what problems might arise."

"I agree, though sometimes the hands-off approach is not the best one." He leaned forward. "You should involve yourself in something sooner, rather than later. And there's no better way of learning how something works than to do it yourself. Perhaps you'd be best to serve as a cleaner for a while. I'm sure they often get overlooked despite the essential work they do."

A muscle pinged in Isaiah's jaw. "I have enough to do. And if I'm to be summonsed to attend the Great Immortal One at his every whim, while maintaining some semblance of authority over a fifth of the population, I can't be burying my head into a toilet."

"Want to bet?"

Isaiah glowered but held his tongue.

Smart.

And it was that kind of smart Isaiah should be pleased to engender in the young.

"But maybe such a singular focus such as cleaning a toilet, though no less important, isn't the right thing for you. Instead, I've taken on board your concerns about the education of the young and the trouble our teachers are finding themselves in. I would like you to spearhead a review of the curriculum."

Christos had valued the importance of information and considered his team, particularly the teachers, of vital importance to Providence's ongoing survival.

"I've spoken to many people and have found that their knowledge of life before the Fall is shrouded at best and opaque at worst. That will be rectified."

"You want me to change history?"

"Reveal it. And I want you to ensure Providence's children have the knowledge they need for their future."

Isaiah's mouth moved like he sucked on marbles. "I have more to worry about than a fucking curriculum."

"I'm sure a man as talented as you can multitask, but I can divine the truth behind your reticence and that you would like some assistance. Don't worry, you won't have to do this alone." Emrys plucked a name out of Christos's soul, a problematic teacher who had not always agreed with Christos's blinkered view of history. He gave it to Isaiah.

"Her? She's a crank."

"She knows more than you or Christos gave her credit for." He had no idea if that was true, but he had to sell her somehow. "I will also be giving you a member of the Faithful to help guide you." Galen could give him a name from one of Owen's cohort to aggravate Isaiah until Judgement Day.

"I work better alone."

"None of us work alone, Isaiah. We always need help from somewhere, even I."

"Especially when people find out how much of a fraud you are."

He smiled through the comment. "I expect you to work on the curriculum with great enthusiasm. You'll send approval through Galen. You may go."

Emrys valued education, even when it had been used as a weapon for centuries to divide and conquer, but right now all he intended for it to do was keep Isaiah occupied and reduce his opportunities to cause trouble.

The councilor made for the door, giving no word of acceptance one way or the other, but it didn't matter. He would soon have a whole team eager to bind him in meetings for hours on end. He had some qualms about letting one of Owen's fanatics loose on the councilor, but the two might make a good match.

Or end up killing each other.

Both options had benefits.

❧ 13 ❧

In the stark whiteness of Kira's lab, the plant's pale-yellow leaves radiated. Not literally—thankfully, not literally—but they radiated with life. Emrys crouched to be at eye level to it, his breath held and his mouth half-turned up in a wondrous smile.

This was the true miracle. Since its collection seven days before, the plant had grown six inches taller and sprouted an additional two pairs of leaves along its new branches. Thin, spindly, fragile, he had never seen anything more beautiful.

"You're pleased?"

Emrys brushed away the tear that had collected in the corner of his eye and looked up at Kira. "What did you do?"

"Enriched the soil, moderated the amount of UV it received, and sang to it."

He raised an eyebrow. "Sang to it?"

She gave a tight smile. "A joke. One of the research papers I dug up from the archives suggested it helped."

"And it didn't?"

"We haven't tried. We'll keep that as a last resort."

Another joke, judging by the tightening of her lips.

"Whatever you did, it's amazing. I wouldn't have expected such growth in such a short space of time."

"It has come at a great cost. This is the strongest we have. We've lost twelve so far, and another five aren't looking healthy. We're caring for an extra twenty-three with varying results. We're not yet certain of the optimal conditions, but based on our discoveries so far, I'm doubtful that we can replicate it on a large scale."

"You're not giving up, are you?"

"No, merely managing expectations. We have one plant that I'm confident in. Those results are not encouraging, especially not being able to upscale it to a whole field."

"But we have time, Kira. It doesn't have to be immediate. Repeat the experiments using new samples, refine the process, improve on any failures." He stood up. "But this is a great moment in our mission. It must be celebrated."

"I would prefer to wait until it survives another week."

"I understand your reticence, but the people must see it. It will be given a special focus at our next meeting." He hadn't been sharing enough good news lately. The citizens were restless. The perennial worry about a rebel faction among them kept everyone in an alert state that would lead to burn out. The plant would be like a breath of fresh air, one that it could make on its own.

"But Emrys—"

"We must take our wins where we get them." And if the people were as enamored with the plant as he was, the joy at seeing it should last for months.

It reminded him of the first time he'd ever seen an electric lightbulb, the way it glowed as if by magic with its coil burning bright. He'd burned with the same intensity, a buzz that ignited his heart. Finally, something shone brighter than him.

"I want the healthiest put on display in the Temple permanently."

Whoever wanted to see it could visit, day or night, as a reminder of what awaited them on the surface and of what they could achieve. The others would remain in the labs and their techniques improved to make them grow hardier, better, faster.

"We can't guarantee it'll stay alive if the conditions change."

"If it wilts, replace it with another."

"If all you want is a prop, the Scientists can make you one. This is wasteful."

"The citizens must see the real thing. There's a whole world up there, and if you have this many samples to work with, you can find more."

"We intend to, but please don't make promises that *we* can't deliver."

He straightened. "Kira, I understand you not wanting to pre-empt results, and you would rather any failures to be kept hidden rather than shared, but——"

"All I'm asking is for you to wait until we can at least create another like this. Surely, that's not unreasonable."

Her argument knocked his excitement, enough to make him wary. He stared at the plant and a deep hollowness widened inside his chest, down through his stomach and beyond. A feeling of impotence that he was beholden to Kira and her Scientists' abilities. If the people should see this plant die, he would be blamed. None of his so-called miracles would amount to anything if he could not ensure the earth bloomed once more. If only the Darisami had such power.

If only *he* had such power.

"Very well, Kira. You have one more week, then I want it placed in the Temple. Agreed?"

"Thank you, Emrys."

"Now, if that's all?"

"There is one more thing."

Of course there is.

"The Tornshirts you've given us—"

He held up his hand. "I've heard your complaints before, Kira. I'm not interested."

"But they don't know anything."

"Then teach them."

"They refuse to learn. All they want to know is how everything helps the Immortal One's plans, then accuse the Scientists of deliberately slowing progress. They're sullen, they're rude, and they don't integrate."

He cocked his head. "You expect me to fix this problem? These are *your* people as much as they are mine. Surely some of your Scientists belong to Owen's factions."

There were enough of them that statistically every department and activity should have at least one Tornshirt. Not that that's what they called themselves. Owen's people referred to themselves as the Reformed. But no matter how many times Owen tried to get that name to stick, as far as Emrys and many others were concerned, they were the Tornshirts and always would be. If they took offence to it, they could change their uniforms.

He had also heard that the Defenders who served under Galen, Trellain, and Micah, were colloquially known as the Golden Goons, and the Tornshirts hissed it with no less acrimony.

"As if my scientists would be so—" She stopped herself.

"So what?"

Her lips thinned into an approximation of a smile. "All I'm saying is that the Tornshirts are ill-suited to the work we do here. They might be better serving elsewhere. It would allow us to get on with the mission you have entrusted to us."

"No. They stay. Figure out a way to make it work. That's what you do."

He sympathized. The Tornshirts' fanaticism made it almost impossible for common sense and analytical thinking to flourish, which is exactly what was needed. But he had to be fair in how he distributed them, and even then, Science and Security had gotten away with a smaller portion than Service, Labor, and Health.

"But when we have so much—"

"Everyone has a lot to do. Managing *your* people is part of the deal. Sort it out. Understood?"

"If they refuse to learn and our work suffers, I can't be held responsible."

"You can and you will. This is the new order, Kira. Deal with it." He glowered at the scientist. She met his ire with disdain.

Trellain appeared in the lab.

"Yes, I know, Trellain. I'm coming." Owen had requested a meeting, but it suited Emrys to make him wait.

"Forgive my intrusion, Immortal One, but it's not about Owen. We have a situation on the surface."

Emrys straightened. "What is it?"

He flicked his gaze at Kira.

"You can speak freely in front of the councilor."

"One of the Tornshirts is refusing to come back inside. They're making things difficult for the rest of the team."

Fucking Tornshirts. Emrys curled his lip, and his grimace worsened when he caught the shadow of Kira's self-satisfied smile.

"Which team?"

"The Workers in the city."

He growled. "Get Owen and meet me there."

Trellain bowed and ran out.

"I'm surprised you're not expecting Juliet to handle it." Kira's lips and cheeks plumped with smugness.

Emrys rolled his shoulders and left without saying anything.

He hurried to the back entrance and ascended to the surface alone. He emerged into the empty warehouse with the late afternoon sun burning red through the broken windows. Through the open door at the end, he could see people blocking the way, and the closer he got, the louder their shouting became. He had yet to be noticed so he could approach unobserved and get an unfiltered view of what was taking place.

Battle lines had been established between the Workers and the Tornshirts, though no fists had been thrown. The insults and jeers were just the prelude. When he appeared behind the backs of the Workers, a Tornshirt across the way spotted him and dropped to the ground. Others followed until all of them fell silent. The Workers were slower to respond. Even when they did see him, they stayed standing but parted to allow him through.

"What's going on?" He took up a position in the No Man's Land between the two groups, keeping his attention on the lowered backs of the Tornshirts.

Juliet rushed up to him. "Jacob is refusing to come back inside. When we tried to force him, the rest of the Tornshirts—"

One of them lifted their heads and spat at her feet. "That is not our name. We are the Reformed, and we are the true followers of Emrys the Immortal."

Juliet's face tensed. It looked as if she had to use every ounce of strength to stop from rolling her eyes. "When we tried to force him, they intervened, and all refused to come inside. We've been out here for an hour trying to get home."

"Stand up, Jacob." Emrys released the full weight of his authority into his voice.

A short, solid man of about twenty rose to his feet.

"Why won't you return?"

He pinched the ends of his fingers, one after the other and back again. "I can't go back there, Immortal One. I have seen the sun and the promise of new life you have shown us. To return will kill me."

Jacob's words pricked the skin between Emrys's shoulder blades. He couldn't blame him. Every time he went to the surface, it got harder and harder to go back. Free of recycled air, getting an injection of vitamin D—though he wouldn't be surprised if they all got skin cancer—and being able to roam more than a few yards without hitting a wall were intoxicating, no matter that things weren't ready for them to stay there permanently.

"Have I decreed that you can stay?"

Jacob ducked his head and withdrew, his chin dropping to his chest. "No."

"Then why have I been summonsed here?"

"I am sorry, Immortal One. I did not mean for you to be disturbed, but I cannot go back underground. Not when you have showed me the Promised Land."

Only Jacob's delusions could allow him to see beyond what was actually there: a crumbled, destroyed city that lay as evidence of humanity's decline. How he could see hope in the broken walls and shattered concrete was a testament to the need for them all to believe in something more.

But could he allow Jacob to stay? He wanted people living on the surface but not without proper planning and more than a shred of a possibility of success. Otherwise, they would quickly become despondent, worn down by the surrounding desolation. It would leach into their souls and lay waste to their future. Jacob couldn't stay. Not yet.

A shuffling in the dirt behind him turned Emrys's head. Owen and Trellain had arrived, and the Tornshirts' leader looked at Emrys with trepidation before casting his fury at Jacob.

"Owen," Emrys said. "Your man here says he doesn't want to go back inside, against my orders."

"Forgive me, Immortal One. If you allow it, I will handle him."

Emrys nodded.

Owen stepped forward. "The Immortal One has given us his instructions, and we are his to command, Jacob. You have shamed yourself, the Reformed, and me in disobeying." He ordered four of the Tornshirts to pick Jacob up.

"Please, Owen. I didn't mean to. I can't go back in there." He cried and trembled as his comrades surrounded him. "Please! Please!"

His begging cut into Emrys like a rusty knife, the hysteria in his voice keen and infected. He screamed as they hauled him up, and he kicked out at them, trying to break free, pleading for Emrys to help him. He was sorry. He was so sorry.

"You will not be allowed to return until you have served penance," Owen shouted.

Jacob's screams got louder and echoed around the empty buildings, bouncing off the broken walls and the rusted metal, ricocheting directly into Emrys's heart.

Owen turned to the remaining Tornshirts, and they hung their heads. "Let this be a lesson to us all."

"Praise to the Immortal One," they replied in unison.

Like a gong, the chant shimmered through Emrys, leaving behind a headache right behind his eyes.

Owen turned to Emrys and bowed his head. "I apologize, Immortal One, and willingly accept any punishment you see fit to bestow upon me. Jacob's failures are my failures."

The display of Owen's power over his people was greater than Emrys had over his. He had to ensure he didn't appear too conciliatory or else Owen's influence would only increase, but neither did he want to treat him too harshly and risk Owen's followers turning against him. He had to be harsh but grateful.

"I am pleased that you have taken the initiative to handle this situation, though if it happens again, I will be forced to keep the Reformed from the surface until they can be trusted."

"You have my word that it will not happen again."

"Good." He turned to everyone. "Now, the day has ended, and you should be proud of the work that all of you have done for your fellow citizens. We are making great progress and that is thanks in large part to you. One day soon we will be ready to live on the surface, but that time has not yet come. Nothing would please me more, but we must not rush." *Thanks for the advice, Kira.* "Let us return to the city. Tonight, we will share a meal together."

This pleased the Tornshirts, but the response was not so vociferous from the Workers. Even Juliet scrunched up her nose.

He thanked them all for their work and returned to the warehouse with Trellain beside him. Once inside, Owen trotted up to join him on his left.

"I'm sorry about Jacob, Immortal One. I understand if your displeasure continues, but if not, might there be a chance we could still meet?"

Trellain gave the Tornshirt the side-eye. The request for the meeting had come through the proper channels, with Owen seeking out Galen and offering all sorts of platitudes to the High Priest. The crux of the matter: Owen was dissatisfied with where he had been placed. He hadn't come right out and said it, but Galen had deduced from the layers of effusive waffle that that is what he'd wanted to discuss.

Since the meeting in the Temple, Galen had found nothing to suggest that Owen was anything other than genuine in his belief and his willingness to serve the Immortal One. He ate and slept with the Tornshirts, and where he'd been put in Service, he kept to his own kind. He even isolated himself from anyone even remotely connected with the rebels on seven and eight, beyond those who'd converted.

"Very well. We can discuss it on the way." They entered the elevator and began the return journey to the city.

"First, let me thank you and High Priest Galen for what you have done for me and the Reformed. Barring this afternoon's unpleasantness, I hope that we have been able to show you how willing we are to aid your mission. Though even then I think you will agree that Jacob's lapse is in no small part a demonstration of the depth of emotion we have for you."

Jacob notwithstanding, the Tornshirts had caused few disruptions beyond asking a lot of questions—about the surface and the future and the nature of the soul. Emrys answered as best he could. Any issues among the Tornshirts Owen handled as adjudicator. The sight of Jacob thrashing while being carried shot through Emrys's mind. How many other similar actions had he not witnessed?

"Yes, thank you, Owen. Their work and devotion have been exemplary."

"I'm pleased to hear that. Me especially, considering my past and how wrong I was. I am glad that we have been able to show that we are eager to work for your common goals."

Trellain's breathing grew heavy, almost a rumble.

"So why did you want this meeting?" Emrys said. "Surely, not just to hear how pleased I am, which I have made a point of mentioning to the congregation in the Temple."

"And that praise has truly warmed our hearts as we wish only—"

"Out with it, Owen."

"I would like to suggest an alternative position for myself."

"Which one?" He was wary of giving Owen too much of what he wanted, but it was apparent that despite trying to separate the Tornshirts and lessen Owen's influence, he had maintained his hold over the group. Emrys would have to be careful in how he handled this. Or else, with the end of his thirty days approaching and his need to feed on a soul becoming unavoidable, Owen might become the first martyr of Emrys the Immortal.

As soon as he thought of it, he wished he hadn't. The complexities and complaints that would stem from that were too much to contemplate. He'd have to harvest elsewhere.

"I wish to be one of your Shadows."

Trellain snorted, which earned him a glare from Emrys as well as a look of pure malice from Owen.

"I know I am not as strong as the ones you already have around you, but their muscle isn't all that you need."

"And what else do I need?"

"You need the citizens to see you with people who aren't part of Security."

"I take my advice from all quarters."

"But the three people you are most often seen with are

from Security. The Gold— The Defenders, as noble as they are, don't engender much encouragement from people from other walks of life."

The elevator slowed, and the doors opened. Galen and Micah were standing there waiting for him. The gold cross on their sleeves seemed to glow.

Galen took in Owen with one disdainful look. "Is everything all right, Emrys?"

Owen ignored Galen. "As I was saying, Immortal One, a bit of diversity can only help you."

Emrys waved his hand, and the five of them walked down the corridor. "Diversity such as yourself, Owen? When we met, you shot me. Are you saying you didn't want to be like the Defenders?"

Galen and Micah fell back with Trellain, murmuring between them as Trellain got them up to speed. It was distracting, but Emrys forced himself to pay attention to Owen.

"I was merely cannon fodder for the foolishness of the rebels' faithless leaders. I should never have been handed a weapon, and I don't ask to have one now."

"Then what good as a bodyguard are you?" Trellain said.

"And why does the Immortal One need you if he cannot be hurt?"

"To protect him from the likes of you."

"And yet here I am."

"Trellain, I'll handle this. Owen, he does raise a point. Why would I have you as a Shadow if you aren't able to serve as one? These men are here to ensure that the citizens don't get hurt in the crush to be near me."

They reached the door that would lead into Providence proper and didn't stop as Owen's demands dogged him. He would have liked to leave the fanatic behind with a few sharp words, but the demonstration of his sway over his followers gave him cause to refrain. They marched across the raceway.

"That will happen regardless, but if I am there, one of the so-called Tornshirts as our detractors like to call us," Owen sneered at the three Defenders, "then it shows you truly listen to us. And considering our numbers are growing more each day, it's only right that the *Defenders* share their access to you or else it may be construed that we are second in your affections."

The sneaky fucker…

The last thing he wanted was to have Owen underfoot all day. It was bad enough having Micah and Trellain there as it was, and he quite liked them most of the time. But Owen's rising importance as a cult leader was not to be denied.

Emrys reached the door to the Tower. Owen had made his request, and he would have to wait for his answer. "I will need some time to think this over. You raise many reasonable points, but it is not a decision I would like to make rashly." Emrys turned away.

Owen touched his arm, and Emrys slowly swiveled back and glared at the offending hand. Owen retracted it, but he didn't veil himself in subservience. "With all due respect, Immortal One, this is not something that can be delayed. The Reformed expect an answer tonight."

"Insolence!" Galen said. "You cannot dictate when the Immortal One speaks."

"I only mean that it has been a topic of discussion among them, and I am speaking to you now because it has become urgent. If I do not give them an answer, then I'm afraid they may turn on me."

Emrys blinked at the lie—and Owen's audacity at wielding it. Owen had more than enough influence over that rabble. Maybe he should take his soul now…but that would only give rise to complaints against him. After all, he was merely an angel and even they could be corrupted from the Divine's plan.

"Very well, Owen. You shall serve as my Shadow along with Trellain and Micah."

"And Leya."

"Who?"

"She is one of the Reformed, very devout, and, helpfully for you, a woman. It will even things up a bit."

Emrys ground his teeth. "I want to meet her first."

"Of course. You can meet her when you dine with us tonight."

Galen's eyes widened.

"And then we can move into your quarters tomorrow, much as Galen, Trellain, and Micah have."

"You presumptuous little fuck," Micah said.

Emrys didn't bother reprimanding him, but he wouldn't have Owen in his rooms. "You and Leya can have the quarters opposite."

"Thank you, Immortal One. The Reformed will be very happy. And this way, I will be able to more readily pass information on to you from them. For example, Haley has told me that while she and Greta are hard at work on the new curriculum, Isaiah rarely attends. But I imagine the Defenders have already told you this."

Emrys narrowed his eyes at the Tornshirt and entered the Tower without a word. He'd see the acolyte later, a much less pleasant proposal than before. If that were possible. Despite Emrys's harsh treatment, Owen appeared no less fervid in his belief. It was a fanaticism that turned Emrys's stomach, and he was glad to be out of sight of it.

They were soon back in Emrys's quarters, and Galen,

Trellain, and Micah vibrated with their barely contained complaints.

"I know what you're going to say but go ahead."

They talked over each other, freed from the confines of propriety to outline how Owen and the Tornshirts could not be trusted, that it was too risky having him close, and any other number of reasons why it shouldn't be allowed.

He agreed, but apart from killing Owen and imprisoning the Tornshirts, he didn't see a quick way around it. He also saw its merits, now that the initial fog of fury had lifted. He was too close to the military and they had far too much power, though even that was stretching thin. So many of the citizens were under surveillance, it was hard to find someone who wasn't.

And yet Isaiah had managed to slip through.

He waited until they'd released their invective. "I understand your concerns, but you do not have to worry about me. Unfortunately, Owen is right about Security and the need to share some of its power. The Workers are beavering away in the background, while Security is the most visible part of my ministry, particularly you three."

"If we have disappointed you, Immortal One—" Micah said.

"No, it's not that at all. You are my Chosen and my Defenders, but I cannot rely on you forever. In time, there will have to be others within my congregation. For now, Owen is serving that need."

"He's grasping for power," Galen said.

"But he won't be able to seize it. Leya and Owen will attend me from tomorrow. I want one of you with them at all times when in my presence. That should do something to quell any complaints of favoritism. And another thing: lose the guns. It's not a good look."

"As you wish, Immortal One," Trellain said.

"And Galen, I want to know what Isaiah is doing every minute of every day, understand?"

"It's not like we haven't been trying, Emrys."

"Then try harder."

"Short of locking him in a cell, we can only do so much."

The position he found himself in, cornered by Owen and circled by Isaiah, made his neck itch.

"He's been far too slow with the task he's been given. Tell him he either finishes it by the end of the week, or he'll be stripped of his power and imprisoned. That might be threat enough to keep him in one place."

"We can try, but I wouldn't count on it."

❋ 14 ❋

THE PLANT WAS A HIT WHEN IT WAS DISPLAYED A WEEK later. People began lining up well before dawn to be the first in line to see it. Security was tight and the crowd controlled to form a single slow-moving line. Dead dictators lying in state never got such a passionate viewing.

The Tornshirts were the most ardent in their adoration, but the difference between them and any other citizen was minor. Everyone wanted to see the plant. Everyone wanted to see some evidence of life.

Two guards flanked the plant, while another four ensured the line of admirers flowed. They were each granted about thirty seconds to stand in front of it before they were encouraged to continue. From reports Emrys was given, many rejoined the line.

He stayed through most of the day, basking in the reflected glory and admiration that the plant inspired. It would suit Providence well that people associated him with the miracle of life they witnessed. It gave them hope and him legitimacy. They thanked and praised him, and he reasserted his campaign promise to see Providence return to the surface.

Trellain appeared at his side. By that time, Emrys's hand had long since lost the ability to determine when it was clasping someone else's and when it was not. Phantom fanaticism dulled his senses, and his smile had molded into place. He retained their joy, but Trellain informing him that Isaiah was ready for their meeting knocked the top off his high.

He ordered Owen and Leya to remain in the Temple to oversee the Tornshirts and left the Temple with Trellain. Micah stood guard outside the door of one of the nondescript meeting rooms beneath the Temple, saluted as Emrys approached, and opened the door for him to enter.

If he expected Isaiah to be flustered about being summoned to this private meeting, he didn't show it. The councilor reclined in the chair, much as he had done during the meeting where he'd ordered Emrys to kill Laurence. His arm rested on the table, his fingers drumming atop it, and when Emrys entered, Isaiah delayed turning his attention in his direction. When he did, his movements were as fluid as a sun-warmed snake.

But Emrys wouldn't be rattled by the passive mask of fanged superiority.

"Do you know why I've called this meeting?" Emrys sat opposite Isaiah, leaned back in the chair, and interlaced his fingers over his chest.

"Who am I to know the inner workings of the Divine's mind?" Isaiah's cheeks plumped.

He would not let Isaiah rattle him. "Quite. You were given the task of revising the school's curriculum. It was due today. Has it been completed?"

"No."

"Why not?"

"These things take time. A couple of weeks is not nearly enough to rewrite years of history."

"Then what progress have you made? Because I have been reliably informed your devotion to the work I have given you has been lacking."

"The Tornshirt and the quack have it in hand. I guide where they ask for guidance, but otherwise leave them to do the work. I find more gets done that way."

"And what do you do with your time?"

"I have Service to run. I cannot be expected to devote all my time to working on one project."

"Nevertheless, that is what I wanted. I was also clear that if you didn't have the curriculum finished by the end of this week, your position would be forfeit. It is now the end of the week, the deadline is here, where is the curriculum?"

"I've told you we need more time. You don't want us teaching the children something that isn't well thought out, do you?"

Emrys cracked the knuckles of his left hand, then his right. He unlocked his fingers and slid the palms of his hands across the surface of the table as if he probed for the most vulnerable parts of Isaiah's arguments. He chose one. "You know, Isaiah. Considering you've chosen to disobey an order, I could have you stripped of your position and put in a cell. No one would mind. In fact, a lot of people would celebrate your downfall."

"You can try, but your position isn't as secure as you delude yourself into believing. Providence is unstable and removing me would destabilize it further—particularly if it's over something as trivial as school curriculum."

Emrys smiled but it felt tight. "That wouldn't be the reason, and you know it."

"But that would be the reason others would believe.

You'd have parents upset that you were playing politics with their education. You'd have my supporters angry that I was removed. And you'd have a large swathe of the general populace think of you as a petty dictator."

"As opposed to the petty dictator many already consider you to be."

"I would be nothing compared to you. Especially as you have already killed one beloved and long-serving councilor without strong cause."

Emrys traced the infinity symbol but it morphed into the one for harvest.

"By your silence, I take it you agree. Now, I solemnly swear that I will continue to work on your pathetic pet project to twist the minds of the young to your propaganda, but I cannot be expected to devote all my time to it. There is a city to run, and right now, it is in both of our interests to ensure we have our attention firmly where it needs to be."

Emrys leaned back. "And where exactly is your attention now?"

"Believe it or not, I am helping to calm the many complaints against you."

Emrys laughed, sharp. "I find that *very* hard to believe."

"About as hard to believe that you're an angel?" Isaiah raised his eyebrows. "You can trust me or not, but daily I am listening to grievances about your leadership."

"Fomenting them more like."

"I assure you, I am not."

"Then what do you tell them?"

"That everything will be fine. That they should have faith."

"Faith in who?"

"In Providence." Isaiah sighed. "I have to live here as well, Emrys. It does me no good for it to collapse, so I will do what I need to ensure it survives and weather the tumult that you have caused. Now, if that is satisfactory, I'd like to get back to work."

No. It was not satisfactory. But as much as he would have liked to remove Isaiah as an issue, Emrys hesitated. What unforeseen consequences would he put in action if he removed him? His surveillance would be upped. The pressure would be increased. He would bow before Emrys.

"Very well. You may go. But I warn you, I won't play these games for long. Even the Divine's patience can break."

Isaiah smiled the smile of a winner and stood. He walked around the table towards the exit but stopped before he opened the door. "By the way, the curriculum for the lower school is almost complete. You can check our progress on the servers. The only section I'm missing is the one about the creation of the universe. Perhaps you would like to provide your unique insights into it. I can set up a meeting, and you can tell us *all* about it." Isaiah chuckled, opened the door, and left.

Isaiah had him there. No doubt he'd placed a large note in the science curriculum calling for Emrys to provide details, knowing his integrity would be at stake. Could he really expect greater transparency and truth about the world before the Fall, while peddling lies about the creation of the universe, the planet, and humanity? But what else could he do?

"How'd it go?" Galen appeared in his eyeline. Had he been standing there long?

Emrys took his hand away from his mouth, ripping off a chunk of nail. "About as good as could be expected. He's still a councilor. He still hasn't finished the curriculum. I still don't know what to do about him." He told Galen what Isaiah said, and Galen agreed to increase the surveillance, but whatever Isaiah was doing, they were overlooking some aspect. "Do you think I've done the right thing by letting him stay in power?"

"I hate to admit that he does have a point about the perceived pettiness of it. We'd know the truth, as would some others, but it wouldn't be enough."

Emrys let his head hit the back of the chair and released a long breath of air. "What happens if, during your surveillance, you find evidence of him committing treason?"

"We'd put him on trial."

He looked at Galen. "And?"

"What do you mean?"

"And if he was found guilty, what would the punishment be?"

"Well, it's usually death."

"And if I executed him?"

Galen's words faltered on his lips and an unease passed across his eyes. He couldn't hold Emrys's gaze. He dropped his chin.

"You don't have to answer it, Galen. I can see what it would do to you."

"But if it's to help Providence—"

"It would hurt you. Despite everything he's done to you, it would hurt you."

"It would." He said it with such weariness, such sadness, such longing.

"Then I promise you, I won't harm him, but we must remain vigilant to his schemes. Because I'm worried that there's a lot we don't know, and the future is not yet won."

Dark clouds hung heavy over Providence. Emrys could smell the rain coming—God, how he'd missed it— but the storm built without release. He wanted to stay until it broke over him, feel the rain drench him and wash him away. No one would deny him, but something about its gathering anger made him wary of its force.

He was meant to be standing there for propaganda purposes only, forcing himself to be seen being calm. That morning, the alternative food supply systems had failed. Laurence and his crew were attempting to get them back online.

Galen had gone to investigate and confirmed it was not an accident but an act of sabotage. Emrys suggested he leave it to someone else, but Galen insisted. He had taken Owen's criticism of the Defenders—and by association, of Galen himself—to heart, thinking that what was required was more involvement and not less.

Emrys let him run with it, trusting that he and Laurence would do the right thing. He did the rounds of Providence, to calm anyone who needed calming, but such were the restrictions on people going in and out of the Factory that most citizens were unaware of what had happened. Meanwhile soldiers were put on high alert in case the rebels interfered with production on seven.

As the hours stretched and Emrys completed his tour, his anticipation for news, whether good or bad, forced him outside or else he'd hover over Galen's shoulder. On the surface, he could breathe freely. Even so, he remained tense and alert to any crackle coming through Trellain's radio.

The storm on the horizon didn't ease his agitation. The Workers and Scientists slowed as they watched the rolling clouds and wavered in the stronger wind. Some requested to return inside, fearful of something they had never experienced, and he allowed it.

Kira remained. As did Juliet. And Owen and Trellain, but they would stay wherever he was, or wherever the other was. The acrimony between the two did nothing to ease the tension in Emrys's shoulders, a tension that had only grown more over the past few days as he attempted to keep the factions together.

Perhaps harvesting would help. He had thirteen days until he needed to feed again. He had been neglecting Elaina lately. He could organize a visit to the hospital and find someone on the cusp of death, someone who would be grateful for a peaceful escape.

"Can that hurt us?" Owen asked.

Trellain tutted. "Where's your faith? The Immortal One will protect us."

Emrys was growing tired of their sniping. Trellain should know better. The soldier had gone through enough training to understand when to hold his tongue and when to speak. But Owen was not without blame and often baited him, testing his faith and devotion. Leya did the same to Micah. At least those two were out of his sight, down in the Factory helping Galen.

"Providence provides the protection you need. I cannot hold back the storm. And if we are to grow crops, we need the rain."

Though whether it was acid or not, he wasn't certain. The Scientists hoped to test it.

Emrys could stand out there for hours, free of the confines of Providence but not completely free of its intrigues and responsibilities. With Trellain and Owen by his side, he was constantly reminded of the frictions between the two cults. And staring out at the limited progress that the Workers and the Scientists were making was an indication of how far they had to go.

Some structures had started to appear, and there seemed no end to samples and readings that the Scientists took, but compared to the frenzied work below ground, they were sloths compared to ants. He couldn't hurry them or make the Earth any more likely to turn in their favor, but the gathering storm raised an energy he didn't know what to do with. It hummed through him in fearful antic-ipation.

Trellain's radio squawked and shattered his maudlin mood. It wasn't Galen's voice, but he could make out the frenzied shouting as commands went back and forth over the radio, calling for help. Trellain looked at Emrys as the full import of what was being said came through.

An explosion in the Factory. A plea for medical aid.

The tinny scratchy voice sliced a jagged line through Emrys's heart, and he was running down the tunnel into Providence faster than Trellain and Owen could keep up.

Galen had to be all right. If he wasn't, any injury that had befallen him was Emrys's fault.

The gas chamber slowed him down. He wanted to

smash the glass apart as its doors ground closed. He shouted at the inanimate object to hurry up, even as it cleansed him.

No alarms sounded as he re-entered Providence proper. No smoke assaulted his nose, but the panic coming through the airwaves had been real. Emrys rushed to the edge of the balcony and peered down to the bottom floor ten levels below. The elevator would be too slow, so he climbed onto the railing and dived off.

He cut through the air as the levels passed in a blur, holding his body as still as he could while the velocity of his descent conspired to make him flail. Only through sheer will could he keep his limbs close together while his heart shrieked at what this would do to him when he hit the ground. It didn't matter. He would recover. All he had to do was get to Galen.

He angled his body and landed on the raceway on the fourth floor. Unable to shed his speed as he met the immovable ground, he crashed into the wall, ungraceful and tangled in his arms and legs. He grunted from the impact and struggled to stand, slightly dazed, but unwilling to stop. He staggered to his feet and pushed through the soldiers who'd come to his aid. He barked orders at them to get out of the way and hurried up a level so he could join the throng of workers and medics as they ran into the pandemonium of the Factory.

Acrid smoke assaulted his lungs as he entered alongside stretchers. Lights flickered and alarms sounded as they were directed by soldiers and workers deep inside the Factory. But instead of turning towards the rooms that had been commandeered for food production, they continued straight into the workshops and storerooms where the bulk of the Factory's efforts took place.

He stopped sharp. Rubble lay strewn across the Factory

floor while gaping holes had been blasted into the walls. Medics rushed to the wounded while soldiers controlled the crowds, but Workers refused to stand down and pitched in to lift rubble off their injured comrades.

A soldier recognized him and came over, saluting, the flash of the golden cross on the arm of his uniform. "Immortal One, it's not safe for you to be here."

"Where's Galen? Is he all right?"

"I'm not sure, Immortal One. We haven't heard orders from him yet."

"Was he in here when it happened?"

"I don't know. We will search for him. If you'd like to wait here—"

Emrys marched into the fray and searched with the rest of the Workers, ripping off his white robe to make it easier to move and using his considerable strength to help lift whatever he could lift, to overturn whatever he could overturn.

What had done this? *Who* had done this? If Galen were injured, there wouldn't be a soul left in Providence when he was through with them. He'd turn the whole place into another Endurance, picking off souls as he saw fit, whenever he wanted. What right did they have to freedom after this?

As he dug through, helping free one person after another, he jerked to a stop as his eyes fell on Micah. He was trapped beneath a collapsed piece of wall, his right leg crushed, most of the fingers on his left hand missing.

"Micah," he said loud and firm. "Micah, can you hear me?"

But his vision was fixed, his breath shallow and halting, the death rattle already in his throat. It was hopeless. A violent rage swept through Emrys. He'd liked Micah. The soldier was gentle and friendly and innocent.

Even as Medics ran to help, Emrys knew there was no hope for recovery. He'd seen this kind of death before. It was sometimes drawn out, and it sometimes came with pain, but it was always fatal. Micah deserved a peaceful death.

He held onto Micah's bare hand as they dug him out. While their attention was on extracting him, he formed the harvest symbol in his mind and released it down his arm with a prayer of thanks for his service.

It struck Micah's soul and separated it from his body. His grip tensed, and Emrys drew his soul in as quickly as he could so as not to prolong his passing. Micah's soul swept into him, and he caught snatches of Micah's joy at finding Emrys, of having something to believe in, and the comfort it had given him the last few weeks. At least Emrys had given him that.

Micah died in their arms, and Emrys let his hand go as they took his body away. A tear rolled down his face at the beauty of what Micah had shown him at the end. So quick, so fleeting, and yet so precious.

And someone had taken it from him.

Replenished, he returned to his search for Galen, uncovering body after body while other teams got the fires and smoke under control. Order was restored. And gradually, over the din of it all, Galen's voice cut through. Emrys stopped. Was he dreaming it? He wiped the sweat and grime off his face and listened.

It wasn't some plea. He was shouting orders to the Soldiers and Workers. He was alive.

Relief pushed Emrys from his post. He found Galen, covered in ash and dirt, but alive and healthy. Emrys ran to him and tackled him into a hug, lifting him off the ground and crushing him to his body.

"What the? Emrys?"

"You're alive," he whispered, more to himself than to Galen.

"I'm fine. You can let go now."

He didn't want to but knew keeping Galen from working would cause trouble. He unwound and set Galen back on the ground.

"Sorry. I was worried."

Galen smiled at him, one of those rare, brilliant smiles that Galen had given him at the beginning, before all this, unguarded and welcoming, and emotion spiraled through Emrys's body, suffusing him with soothing warmth to replace the scorching heat of destruction.

"You almost had cause to be. Look." Galen spun him around and pointed towards one of the holes in the wall. "I was on the other side of that when it happened. Laurence too."

"Is he okay?"

"Shaken but standing."

"This was an attack, wasn't it?"

Galen nodded. "Considering the force of the blast, it can't have been an accident."

"And the food supply?"

"Still down but not as damaged as all this."

"You think the two are connected?"

"I'm not sure. We'll know more once we've got things under control and investigate."

Galen had done a good job of that already, assuming command over Soldiers and Workers and Medics in this portion of the Factory blast site. Emrys wanted to take him away and lock him up somewhere safe so he'd never be in danger again, but the realities of their situation refused to allow such an indulgence of selfish fancy. A soldier interrupted them to say that the rest of Providence was now aware of what was happening inside the Factory and unrest was imminent.

"We'd better get out there in case something else happens," Galen said.

Emrys was torn. He wanted to stay beside Galen and help the recovery efforts, knowing he could do far more than many, but unless a camera broadcasted his every movement, he had to be out and reassure as many people as possible. His tour that morning had merely been a rehearsal.

***

EMRYS DID WHAT DUTY DEMANDED. HE ADDRESSED THE citizens via the public announcement system and gave them only as much information as they needed to keep from getting in the way. He refrained from casting blame on any particular group, waiting to see if the rebels knew of what had transpired. He made no mention of rationing but considering they had reduced their demand for the supplies from seven and eight, the rebels would notice the increase.

Not that many people had much of an appetite.

Galen and his security forces ensured civil unrest remained limited while allowing the Medics efficient access in and out of the Factory. By the end of the day, all injured had been rescued and all corpses retrieved. They were to be cleaned and dressed, and the next day would be laid out in the Temple as martyrs. Micah would lay in the middle. Whoever had done this would see the full impact of their cowardice.

When he'd been given the news of Micah's death, Trellain held back his weeping and threw himself into helping beside Emrys. Owen had begged to be excused to ensure that the rest of the Tornshirts were holding true, leaving with no word of consolation for Trellain, but instead gave a promise to Emrys that whoever had done this would be brought to justice. Emrys was glad to be rid of him and would have preferred Leya to go too, but she remained. At least she helped with the cleanup.

Once all the people had been rescued, it was time for the Factory to be secured. Providence had been constructed soundly and the explosion that had ripped through this level had not caused much structural damage. They were not in danger of having the upper levels fall down upon them.

He bade Workers to go home, many running on the fumes of their adrenaline, exhaustion evident in the gradual slowing of their footsteps and the reduced speed with which they worked. Some refused, but others wept when he stopped them and offered comfort. They had lost friends and family with the death toll at thirty-six and rising.

Those who wanted to stay were permitted to do so and continued to work beside him until they had nothing left to do. Reconstruction would have to wait for the morning, and he wasn't skilled enough to begin it on his own. He ordered Trellain to bed, and it was a sign of his exhaustion and grief that he did not argue, but he did not stay in the apartment. He wished Emrys a good night, or what was left of it, and sought the comfort of other Defenders with whom he could mourn for Micah.

Emrys was back in his room, pulling off his boots, when Galen returned. His high priest strode into the room as if he had not been on his feet all day. He was covered in ash and dirt, his hair disheveled and his eyes highlighted with deep shadows like he'd been socked. Emrys couldn't say whether he himself looked any better.

"How's Providence?" Emrys asked.

"Quiet. Finally."

"And the rebels?"

"Even quieter. It won't be long before they realize, if they don't already, that we're now entirely reliant on them for our food. I'm sure by now they understand that if they fuck with that, then we fuck with them." Galen laughed, a little too sharply, a little too maniacally.

Emrys held out his hand. "Come here."

"I can't. I just came to get a second change of clothes."

"Galen, come here," he said more firmly.

Galen had to stop, but he fidgeted, shifting his weight from one foot to the other, and his attention kept being diverted when nothing grabbed it. His gaze darted to the window and out to the other levels. He was running on pure adrenaline, and at any moment, he'd crash.

"Sit with me for a while."

"I've got to get back out there."

Emrys smiled. Of course, he wouldn't be so easily led. "Very well. If that's what you need to do, I suggest you have a shower first. You've got to look good for your troops."

Galen looked down at himself and wrinkled his nose. "You're right. I stink too."

Emrys took Galen's hand and led him into the bathroom. Galen pulled off his shirt, while Emrys sank to his knees to undo Galen's boots. He made him sit on the edge of the bathroom sink and brace. The moment Galen sat down, he sagged as all the energy that had been keeping him upright drained. He pitched forward, but Emrys caught him and leaned him back against the wall so he could continue with the job at hand.

Galen rallied a little, apologized, and made to leave, but Emrys forced him down. It didn't take much effort to stop him. He pulled off his boots and socks, then unbuttoned his trousers.

"Think you can stand?"

Galen grunted, a half-smile that fell fast, swept away by exhaustion. He rested against Emrys who stripped him naked. He definitely didn't smell fresh, but he still smelled good, of hard work and sweat and honor.

Emrys kept his trousers on and half-carried Galen into the shower. He turned on the water and stepped under the flow with Galen in his arms. The spray gave him back some strength so Emrys didn't have to hold him up, but he kept one arm around his waist all the same.

With his free hand, he washed Galen's hair and scrubbed the dirt and sweat from his skin, his hand slipping down Galen's chest and over his body, trying to be perfunctory, while inside his desire screamed for the man.

Galen lifted his arm so Emrys could wash his pits, holding himself up against the wall so he could get to all of him, then turning so Emrys could wash his muscled back.

Thank God Emrys kept his trousers on, soaked as they were, because his erection strained to break free.

"There. I think I've got all of it."

Galen turned back around. "Not all of it." He closed the distance between them, his hands coming up to Emrys's face, and kissed him with a ferocious need. Emrys hugged him tight, feeling the thick hardness of Galen's arousal pressing against him. The dreamy languid way Galen kissed him showed he had little energy left, but what he had, he packed into his affection.

Emrys held onto him, using all the strength he had to keep Galen in contact. He kissed him desperately.

Galen broke, the water cascading down his face. "I want you, Emrys. I want you now. Is that wrong after what's happened today?"

"Never." The word dragged guttural from his throat. "I was so afraid you'd been injured or killed." Emrys stripped down from his trousers, freeing himself.

"I was lucky, but throughout it all, while I was helping everyone, all I thought was it could have been me and I might never have got the chance to be with you again." Galen kissed him again, deep, desperate, devout.

"What about not wanting to complicate things?"

"I can't not be with you any longer. It's too much. Maybe I'm weak. And if you tell me no, then I will accept it, but I can't spend another day not being able to touch you, to kiss you, to tell you how much I love you."

Emrys picked him up in his arms and carried him out of the shower. Water dripped off them and onto the floor, landing wet and soaking the bed, slick and slippery as their bodies writhed against each other. In their frenzied embrace, as Emrys kissed Galen from his mouth to his neck to his chest and belly, body heat raised to dry them. And whatever exhaustion Galen felt was shoved to the side as he opened himself up for Emrys. He entered him, the length of Emrys's shaft slipping inside Galen up to the base, deep and tense.

And home.

❧ 16 ❧

"What happened to Micah?" Galen lay in the crook of Emrys's arm, his hand splayed across Emrys's chest, a comforting pressure that surrounded his heart. Morning had come and Galen had stayed and Emrys was glad. He felt, more than ever, that it was the two of them against their foes.

Micah's killer had to be found. His *real* killer, the one that had made it necessary for Emrys to ease Micah's suffering.

"He died. But I was there when he went."

"Oh, I know that. I meant..." Galen paused, his fingers tracing a line down Emrys's sternum. "I meant, what happened to Micah after he died. What happened to his soul?"

He opened his mouth but found he had no ready-made answer. Five hundred years living as a Darisami, of taking at least six thousand souls, and he couldn't say what happened to a soul once he'd ingested it. He never really knew if what he harvested was a person's actual soul or a copy of it or a collection of memories and energy. He wasn't even sure if souls actually existed or if they had somewhere to go. Did souls have some natural home to go to once they left a human's body? And if so, were Darisami a prison that trapped them in internal torment? He had tortured himself through the centuries with these questions and never been satisfied with an answer.

But what to tell Galen? He had trotted out some trite explanations for the citizens, but he wanted to give Galen something real.

"The Divine has taken everything that Micah was, every memory, every emotion, every deed, and enfolded it into its endless love. Micah's soul lives on in the heart of the Divine and keeps it pumping. There is no waste, there is no loss, and there is no pain where Micah has gone."

"Did he…did he suffer at the end?"

"No. He was at peace, and he died thankful for the hope we gave him, for the purpose and the future." The words caught in his throat and he forced down the tears. He hadn't meant to get attached. "Has that helped?"

"Yes. Very much so." Galen melted against his side. "About last night…"

Emrys tensed. He knew he should have carried Galen to his room before he woke so as not to cause him embarrassment. Then they would not have to have this discussion. What was said under the influence of emotional and physical exhaustion was not to be trusted in the harsh morning light after a good sleep.

"Do you regret it?"

"No!" Galen sat up. "Absolutely not. It was…" He sighed into a smile, one of the beautiful unguarded ones. "It was wonderful and welcome. At least for me. I hope it was for you too."

"The same and more. But you have concerns?"

"Only that you understand I expect nothing. You have

a city to oversee and a civilization to save. I don't expect to come first."

Emrys brushed Galen's fringe aside and let his fingertip trace a line down his cheek. "First and last. You should know that."

Galen took Emrys's hand and kissed his fingers. "I know how difficult this all is, and it doesn't look like it's getting any easier. Just know that I don't expect more. I am here to serve you and Providence. My needs don't come into it."

"And what if I want to focus on your needs?"

The corner of Galen's mouth hitched up. "Who am I to refuse the Divine?"

Emrys pulled Galen down for a kiss. The weight of the weeks behind them were replaced with the weight of Galen's body. He felt reinvigorated, thanks in part to Micah's soul but also to the clearing of the hurdles between them. Already that morning, Galen had shown himself to be easier with his affection, and that gave Emrys energy to face the trials that he knew were coming.

"We should go," Galen spoke against Emrys's lips.

"I wish we didn't have to, but you're right." He kissed him again, and they got out of bed. Emrys grabbed his old uniform from the wardrobe and dressed while Galen grabbed his clothes and marched out into the common space. The quarters were empty. But as Galen reached his room, Juliet barged in, auburn hair disheveled and clothes stained. Guilt ran its oily finger down Emrys's back. How long had they been secluded?

"Good morning, Juliet."

Her gaze bore into him. "I think you need to come see this."

"What's happened now?"

"It's the stores. They've been ransacked."

Her words punched Emrys in the gut.

"Ransacked?" Galen re-entered in a clean uniform, boots in his hand.

She blinked at him before turning back to Emrys. "Robbed. Pilfered. Whatever you want to call it, shit's been taken."

The speed with which he moved had the two of them hurrying to keep up. Galen was already calling for soldiers as they exited onto the raceway and down to level three.

They hurried into a Factory teeming with activity. Workers were already there and at their essential tasks while others were scuttled in and out of the destroyed sections. He asked about food supply and Juliet said it was being worked on. He caught wary glares from Workers unafraid of him or his soldiers. He couldn't blame them. He had brought this down upon them and they had lost companions because of it. He would have to work hard to regain their trust and support, if such a thing were possible.

They burst into the stores where Laurence was assessing the damage with subordinates. Doors that kept the supplies secure had been cut or pried open and their contents snatched.

"What's happened?"

Laurence bid him good morning. "We believe the stores were broken into soon after the explosion on the other floor. While the rescue effort was in place, much of the security allowing access was disabled to make it easier for Medics to come in and out, which meant that the stores were unprotected. That shouldn't have made much of a difference because the individual cabinets were all locked but…well, that didn't matter."

Emrys's stomach fluttered, wanting to investigate the cabinet holding the gold, but he had to restrain himself in case it raised suspicions about why he should be so keen to focus his attention there.

"What's been taken?"

"A large supply of lead and steel, some copper. About as much as they could take."

"They?"

"There would have been multiple people to carry it all. As you can see, they didn't leave us much."

Plenty of cabinets remained untouched, leaving behind tin and aluminum, silicon, and silver. "Anything else?"

"The gold. They took all of it."

Emrys's heart dropped into his stomach. "Show me."

Laurence led him to the busted and empty cabinet. Everything that could be taken had been taken. "How much was in there?"

"About two hundred ounces. Our whole supply."

"Any leads?"

"We've sent a dispatch to Security—"

"Galen will make sure it's prioritized."

"Of course, but I think that the main focus should be on finding out who caused the explosion, don't you? The resources are one thing, but we can salvage more. People have died."

Emrys's mind raced to where the gold could have gone and why it had been taken. There could be some banal explanation, but rational thought was severely rationed when the one thing that could actively kill him was loose in the city.

He looked at the golden knife on Galen's belt. Perhaps whoever had taken it wanted to create another in its image. And for that he'd have to look at Owen and the Tornshirts.

"I agree that it's a lower priority, but what could these materials be used for that would warrant the destruction of the Factory as a diversion?" Emrys said.

"We don't know that's exactly what has happened," Laurence said.

"It's a pretty sound argument, though. Find the stolen supplies, and we may find the culprits."

"We could have every room searched," Galen said.

"Not yet. But ramp up the investigation. I want to know every single person who came in and out of here over the past twenty-four hours and what they've been up to since. Understood?"

Galen nodded and excused himself.

"And Laurence, your focus needs to be on getting food production running again."

"That's not—"

"That's an order, Laurence. I don't want any excuses. By now, the rebels must know how exposed we are, and it won't be long before they press it to their advantage. But if they try to negotiate, it will end badly for them."

"Very well."

"Good. I will be calling the councilors together for a meeting later today. Make sure you're there with some good news."

Laurence nodded and strode off. He no longer held a cane, and no longer limped.

Juliet was the only one still beside him.

"Why do you trust a man who lies every day?" he said.

"I trust you, don't I?"

"Very amusing. But do you think I am right to trust *him*? He gives the impression of the helpful type who's only got the good of Providence in his heart, but is my faith misguided?"

"If you're talking about the cane and the limp, he does it to put people at ease and to catch out those who would take advantage of him and Providence. You could do much worse than trust him."

"Perhaps. Time will tell. Now, about the surface——"

"I'm not going out there again. Not while the Factory is in this state. I need to be here to help rebuild. I hope you won't try to stop me."

"As if I could. On the plus side, if you're here, then I am guaranteed the work will get done. I know the Workers have put a lot of faith in me, but I'm trusting you to let me know if there's something I need to do to hold onto it. I'll speak to the people again today, and their sacrifice shall be lauded. They'll be martyrs."

"Make sure there aren't any more." She nodded her farewell and went to oversee the rebuilding. He knew this was where she needed to be, but to have her focus turned from the surface made him anxious. How many of her Workers would want to stay above ground now so much had to be done below? He would make their reconnaissance and recovery missions a top priority, turn it into an act of valor for Providence's recovery. The Tornshirts would love that.

But would the Workers?

<hr>

Emrys forced himself out among the people to calm them as much as he could, but his mind was elsewhere.

Would the rebels attack?

How many more injured Workers would die?

Could they eat without fear of being poisoned?

Where would the next assault come from?

Would it be laced with gold?

He wanted to be everywhere and nowhere, and the people he met noticed they didn't have his undivided attention. He gave up and left them alone. He went back to his apartments and poured over the screens, trying to be patient while he let others do what they did best.

If only he could have split a soul with all of them, he might have been able to keep better abreast of developments.

He gave an order for the Five to attend a meeting late that evening and waited for the time to come.

He waited so Laurence would have enough time to assess the damage.

He waited so Galen would have enough time to uncover the culprits.

He waited so Elaina would have enough time with the injured and the recovered.

He waited so Kira would have enough time to collate her data.

And he waited so Isaiah would have enough time to communicate with traitors.

When a Defender came to tell him everyone had assembled, he was out the door before he'd finished his sentence. Trellain and Leya ran to keep up.

Emrys marched into the chamber, but instead of taking the empty seat and projecting an aura of calm control, he paced. The frenetic energy tripping his nerves kept him moving. He'd been inactive for too many hours.

The councilors and Juliet were slow to stand and greet him, but he disregarded their reluctant deference in favor of expediency.

"Laurence, update."

The councilor looked even more frazzled than he had earlier in the day. Grimy, too. "To put it simply, it's fucked."

Emrys flinched at the councilor's choice of words. "Irreparable?"

"Essentially. It's broken beyond repair, but not through

brute force alone. Whoever did this altered various camshafts, pistons, and fanbelts to the point where they were on the verge of failure. Then they just had to wait until the pieces worked themselves to death. It could have been done earlier that morning or the night before or anytime over the previous week and deteriorated without us being aware. And then when we were, it was already too late."

"Can you build an alternative?"

"No. The last one was made from the backups that we already had down there. The rest of them are on seven."

"Can't you build them from scratch?"

"You've seen the state of the Factory. Essential work only."

"This is essential work."

Juliet placed a hand on Laurence's arm. "What Laurence means is essential work that existed prior to the current change of priorities. We don't have the capacity for building a whole new apparatus. I'm sorry, Emrys."

He ground his teeth together and pushed his frustration out through the bottom of his boots. "How long until the Factory is back to normal?"

"Months, if not a year."

"If at all," Laurence said. "We've never had such a catastrophic event so replacing what was lost will take time. We lost Workers who knew those machines best. The archives will have some results—"

"I'm afraid they won't," Isaiah said.

All eyes shifted to him.

"I've had the Servers look into the original records. I admit I should have been working on that ridiculous curriculum, but you were insistent on knowing what the founders had left for us. The truth is not much remains uncorrupted."

Emrys narrowed his eyes at the councilor. "You expect me to believe that the plans that this place is built on have been destroyed?"

He spread his hands. "Believe it or not, they're no longer there." Even though Isaiah delivered news that was harmful to Emrys's reign, no celebration enlivened his voice.

"How about I suck the soul of you and find out if you're telling the truth?"

The people around the table stilled, but Isaiah didn't flinch. "It won't make any difference. The plans will still be gone."

He turned to Galen. "Look into it"

Isaiah laughed. "Along with everything else I'm currently being investigated for? It's a surprise there's anyone left to be a soldier."

"You're walking a very thin line, Isaiah," Emrys said. "Providence has been sabotaged, and those responsible will pay the ultimate price."

"Yes, I'm sure they will."

Emrys's cheek twitched. He resumed his interrogation of Laurence. "Do what you can to get everything working again. It's only a matter of time before the rebels take advantage of our exposed position. Galen, have they been in contact?"

"They remain silent and compliant, but our forces are standing by."

"I want to know the moment they try anything."

"Understood."

"And what of the investigations? There must be some link between the attacks and the rebels."

"We're still chasing down everyone who's been in and out of there over the past twenty-four hours, but we've got no way of knowing when the attacks were planned or bombs placed. It could have been at any time over the past two-and-a-half weeks and by anyone, including the Workers."

"Or soldiers," Juliet added.

Emrys slapped his palm on the table. "Whoever they are, they're traitors, and I want them found. What about the resources? Surely they must be easier to track."

Galen scratched the side of his neck. "That's… ummm…well, that's been a bit easier. Sort of."

"What do you mean?"

"Well, they just showed up."

Emrys blinked at him. "Where?"

"In the arsenal."

"What?!"

"We're investigating, but from what the cameras show, multiple soldiers at different times brought the metals into the military complex and left them stacked in the arsenal."

"How is that possible?"

"They used Christos's access codes to gain entry and wore helmets and head coverings to bypass recognition."

"This is a major breach, Galen."

"I'm aware, and we're—"

"Investigating?" A smirk slashed across Isaiah's face.

Galen glowered at his father. "Christos's codes have been revoked, and I accept responsibility for that oversight. I've got people on it but have had to limit those we can trust. My gut tells me that they're Security, and I'm looking into as many of the people as we can, but there's over two thousand personnel so it's taking time."

"But that doesn't explain why they'd take those supplies and leave them," Elaina said. "What purpose does it serve?"

Laurence leaned forward over the table, interlaced his fingers and tapped his thumbs together. "Clearly, they wanted us to know that the rebels aren't limited to living on seven and eight."

"Has everything been returned?" Juliet asked.

"Everything except the gold."

Emrys tried not to react, but his body went rigid and his slowing pace stopped altogether as if someone had pumped his muscles with lead.

Or gold.

He clenched his jaw until it hurt. He couldn't breathe deeply enough to relax so he had to wait until it passed.

What did they want with the gold? Did they know how much damage it could do to him? Or was there some other explanation? Galen still wore the knife, but if gold were so precious, how soon would it be before they attempted to steal it? Had bestowing it upon Galen made him vulnerable to attack? A lot of power flowed from having given it to him, but would it be better for Emrys to take it back?

"Emrys?" Galen broke through his torturous musings.

"Yes. Fine. Keep searching." Emrys sat stiff-legged on the empty chair. He hovered his hand over the top of the table, wanting to draw the eternity symbol on its surface, but also wanting to not show his panic. "It's much more important to find out who did this than to retrieve the gold."

"But it is baffling, don't you think?" Elaina tapped her finger to her earlobe.

"Not so much," Kira said, the first thing she'd said all meeting. "It's a test. Most of the resources were too heavy to move around but the gold…well, there wasn't so much of it that hiding it would be hard. And while we're all looking for it, who knows what other havoc they might wreak?"

"Agreed." Emrys closed his hand into a fist and rested

it on the table. "But if we find the gold, we find the traitors. I'd like to commence room to room searches."

Isaiah laughed. "And you'd better be sure your soldiers are ready to put down an uprising. It's true we don't give the citizens much privacy, but we at least observe the sanctity of their rooms."

"These are desperate times," Emrys said.

"Oh yes, while soldiers are looking for gold for the Emperor and his consort, the people are starving. What a good look that will be."

"Careful, Isaiah, or I'll think you had something to do with it."

"Paranoia has always been the mark of the despot."

He ignored Isaiah and turned back to Galen. "No room searches. Yet. There are other ways to catch the culprits." And he'd feast on souls if it helped. "Keep up with the investigations. Elaina, how many are in the hospital?"

"Of the forty-three brought in, twelve have been sent home. Sixteen are being treated for burns and smoke inhalation and can go home tomorrow. Ten are in serious or critical condition. Five more died."

"Add their names to the list of martyrs. Kira? Juliet? Surface progress?"

"I'll defer to Kira on this. I recalled all Workers to help with recovery and rebuilding."

"Send them back." He delivered his words in a rush.

"Be reasonable, Emrys. They lost friends and family. They want time to mourn."

"Then find others who don't. The work must continue. It's more vital than ever that they go to the surface to recover resources."

"But the supplies have been found."

"But you'll need more for the repairs."

"They won't like it."

"Then impress upon them that it is their patriotic duty to their fallen comrades that they go. And I want you out there too."

"And if I refuse?" Her words came out clipped. She blinked once but was otherwise still.

He rose out of his seat, inflating with their evasions and excuses and insubordination. "Don't test me, Juliet. I understand you're feeling guilty about what happened—"

She puffed out a breath of incredulous air that blew away her mask of controlled anger. "Guilty? Why should I feel guilty? I never put any of this in place."

"I didn't say your guilt was justified, but you want to keep control over the Factory when your place is on the surface now."

"If I go back out there, they'll feel abandoned. My authority will be questioned." She maintained her seat even as he leaned further over the table. He was aware of how much more power she displayed but he was unable to stop himself.

"Your authority comes from Laurence. He's still there. He can work harder for the privilege of serving on Providence's council and ensuring its greatness. Understood? Kira, update." He collapsed back into his chair, frustration shedding the control he needed for a graceful return.

"Slow. We have no qualms about continuing our work on the surface, but we are drawing to a close with what we can usefully collect. The lab experiments continue, but I am concerned about the quality of the soil and how they interact with the seeds we have in the bank. The properties have changed over the past sixty-five years—actually longer as the seeds were collected at least ten years preceding the Fall."

"You must push harder. I want to see results—*promising* results."

"You can't rush science, Emrys. We're still learning. It'll be some time before we can attempt to grow anything on a large scale."

Of all the information he'd been given so far, it was Kira's laid-back attitude that got to him the most. It shouldn't have. He knew how long these things could take. He couldn't rush them, and he wanted them to have the time to get them done. Science was meant to be apolitical, unbiased, and proceed at its own pace.

But as irrational as it was, the promise of replenishing the Earth was the greatest prize. He shouldn't have been surprised that in such a short space of time there had been limited progress, but it stung. If he didn't have any successes to show the people, all he had was a long list of problems. He could go harder on the religious rhetoric that there were enemies—demons, even—in their midst, but the Tornshirts would probably have a field day with that. And flood the radioactive fields with blood.

"So, what progress have you made? Give me some good news."

"I wouldn't want to pre-empt my results."

He growled, a rumble that leapt out of his throat and caused everyone to pull back.

Everyone except Isaiah. "Surely, considering Kira and Juliet's failure and Laurence's inability to keep Providence provided with food or working parts, it is now time to abandon this dangerous fantasy before Providence itself becomes uninhabitable?"

Emrys opened his mouth to answer, but a ruckus outside the closed doors silenced him. He stood, fearful of an attack. Trellain and Leya turned to protect him. The doors opened. Owen and a group of Tornshirts wrestled a

Defender into the room. Shouting and bellowing continued in the corridor.

"Silence!" Emrys roared, bringing the groups to an awareness of his presence, but once gained they started to shout over each other. "Quiet, all of you!" He marched over to the door and shouted at the groups amassed outside. "Disperse!"

Galen appeared by his side, as did Leya, and he left them to corral their forces while he turned to Owen.

"What is this?"

"We have found the culprit, Immortal One?"

Which one?

He looked down at the soldier who'd been forced to his knees, his hands tied behind his back, his nose broken and face bloodied. Emrys racked his brains for the soldier's name but couldn't place it.

"John?" Galen returned to Emrys's side. "Let him up."

Emrys gave them the nod. "Owen, why have you brought him here?"

"We have evidence that this Golden Goon is responsible for destroying the food supplies."

"What evidence?" Galen said. "You Tornshirts wouldn't know a real traitor if you fell over one."

Owen glared at him. "On the contrary, *Captain*. Thanks to the Reformed, who were working diligently in the Factory, they know what was done and how this Golden Goon was responsible."

Subtlety was not Owen's strong suit, and his repeated use of the phrase 'Golden Goon' was deliberate, an attempt to drive a wedge between Emrys and Galen, but he was wise to it. It would take more than a Tornshirt's word to cast doubts upon a soldier.

"Layout your evidence, but it had better be solid."

"It is, I assure you, Immortal One." He indicated the

brown-haired woman standing beside him. "Sofia was assigned to the Factory with Ingrid, Naomi, and Sam. Their diligence to the cause and their work was recognized by councilor Laurence—was it not?"

Laurence nodded. "And they were assigned to assist with food production, but mostly because their skills were limited elsewhere."

"Nevertheless, they have eyes and brains, and it is only through the selfishness of other Workers that they were denied the chance to grow. No matter, however, as they have served Providence proud today."

"Get on with it, Owen." Emrys dug his fingernails into his palm.

"As you command, Immortal One. The three of them worked in food production, but not at the same time. They noticed this Golden Goon paying regular visits to seemingly assess the progress and ensure supply."

"Is this true?" Emrys asked of Galen.

"Yes. John is a trusted member of the Security forces and one of the first to recognize your divinity, Emrys. He is a commander of two units within our forces. He is above reproach."

"You mean he's a friend of yours and doesn't deserve scrutiny," Owen countered.

Heat flushed up Emrys's back and skull. "Stick to the facts, Owen. You're trying my patience on what has already been a trying day."

"Forgive me, Immortal One. These Reformed saw the Golden Goon multiple times throughout his visits inspecting the machines as he went but always accompanied by another Worker. And yet, on two of his visits, they witnessed him alone, both on the day before the sabotage and the day of destruction."

"Why did they not report this to anyone?"

"It was not until after the disruption occurred that they conferred with each other. The Reformed have gathered as much information as they could about the events of that day, drawn from the many eyes they have among the population, and it was only when they mentioned witnessing the same thing that they considered John to be a suspect."

"Just because he was there doesn't mean he is responsible," Galen said, but not with as much force as he once would have.

"He refuses to give a reason for being there."

John glared up at them, a snarl in his voice. "I don't answer to you filthy Tornshirts. You're all mad. Every one of you."

"Then answer to me, soldier." Emrys bent at the waist, close to John's face until he couldn't look away without appearing guilty. "What were you doing there unaccompanied?"

"I wanted a better understanding of the systems without getting the filtered version from the Workers." Defiance shone in his eyes, but the muscles surrounding them quivered with the force of his concentration.

"Preposterous," Laurence said. "As if you, a soldier, would know the first thing about those mechanics."

"I admit, my understanding is limited, which only goes to prove I wouldn't know what to do to sabotage anything."

Owen laughed. "As if an idiot never broke anything."

John glared at Owen, but he had a point. You didn't need to know how everything worked to break it. Look at what Emrys had done to Providence.

"Do you have any other evidence?" Emrys asked.

"Sam witnessed John in the Factory late the night before. He was wearing a Worker's uniform."

John tensed. "That wasn't me."

"It was. Sam would know better than to lie. And so should you."

"Have it checked out," Emrys said to Galen. "Meanwhile, take him to a cell."

"But Immortal One, I have done nothing wrong," John said.

"Then go willingly and trust that the truth will set you free."

But John did not go willingly and was dragged out of the room while shouting for Emrys's mercy. Galen ordered Trellain to oversee John's processing until the meeting was finished and he could attend. The Tornshirts left but Owen remained.

"Immortal One, I know you will find the Golden Goon guilty of treason and in light of it, I feel it only fair to warn you that there may be others within their ranks who feel the same about you and what you are doing for us. My brothers and sisters are ready to protect you with our lives. We don't ask for any extra favor, though in the light of such an event, it would seem that your trust in the Golden Goons may be unwise."

"You little cunt," Galen said. "You think the Immortal One is blind to your games."

"My impertinence comes from a place of love and faith while you have allowed your soldiers to grow fat on his largesse. When the truth is revealed about your Golden Goon and his treachery, the citizens will no longer support you as his Chosen people. You may give the Immortal One guns, but we give him our hearts."

Galen moved to strike Owen, but Emrys ordered him to stop. "Owen, thank you for your work in bringing this to our attention. It will be investigated, and if it turns out to be true, your efforts will be rewarded." Owen's eyes brightened at the promise. "But I caution you to not stir unrest against the Defenders for it angers me, and a move against them is a move against me. Understand?"

For the first time since he'd shot Emrys, Owen paled. It wouldn't do to offend his god, even if he thought he was justified. But the fear worked and removed some of the tension in the room.

"Of course, Immortal One. I apologize if I have displeased you. I live only to serve you."

And yourself.

Emrys waved him out of the room. That left Emrys alone with the councilors and Juliet. Isaiah couldn't keep the grin from his face, but most of the others looked appalled.

Emrys tried to lighten the mood. "Well, it seems we have our work cut out for us, doesn't it? Have no fear, Owen's accusation will be examined."

"And if John is guilty?" Elaina asked.

"He'll be executed. Along with any co-conspirators. It seems I have been too lax in demonstrating my powers and the seriousness of what we are doing. No one here should consider themselves above my law, and if necessary, I will take a life for every one that has been taken needlessly. Ensure your factions are aware of this. They are either for me or they are against Providence." He focused on Isaiah. "Is that clear?"

The councilor didn't look away. "Crystal."

✼ 17 ✼

Galen crept into the apartment at around three in the morning, but Emrys was awake. He'd been locked in a state of paralysis, staring out the window at the facade of a peaceful Providence while events transpired to pull him apart. Deep in the middle of it was a conspiracy he couldn't define.

Galen did not display any of the manic energy he'd possessed a few nights before. He was focused. And grim. No smile broke across his lips. No joy sparked in his eyes.

"What did he say?"

"Nothing." Galen's teeth didn't separate. He pulled off his shirt stained with grease and blood. How long had the day lasted?

He marched into his room, and Emrys followed. Galen pulled another uniform from his wardrobe.

"You're not going back out there. You need to rest."

He put on the clean uniform. "I need to find out if what Owen said was true. Providence depends on it."

"Others can continue in your place."

"But how can I trust them? What if Owen is right and John is a traitor?"

Emrys didn't have an answer.

Galen's eyebrows flicked up. "You see? I'm right to worry."

"But if you're exhausted, you won't be able to see what you need to see. Rest, please. I'll go."

"No! I have to do it."

"But why?"

"Because this is my fault." Galen pointed his finger to the ground. "I let this happen." His voice punctuated his blame.

Emrys took Galen's hand but he pulled it free. Emrys tried again, resisting Galen's resistance. "Listen to me. We don't yet know if what the Tornshirts said is true."

"But it sounds like it, doesn't it?" Galen squeezed his hand. He held on. He held on to Emrys. "I can see by the worry in your eyes that you think it holds merit."

"We will find out in time, but you can barely keep your head up now. Rest, at least for a few hours. If John is the culprit, then let him stew in his guilt."

"Until then, whoever helped him continues to undermine me." Galen's jaw snapped shut. He breathed out his mistake. He was beyond exhaustion. "Us. I meant us."

Emrys guided Galen to sit on the edge of the bed. "I agree that time is important, but you will not achieve much more tonight. Providence has been locked down tight, so if anyone moves against us, we'll know. Right?"

Galen didn't answer.

"Right?"

Galen pinched the bridge of his nose, massaged that tiny spot as if dispelling the tension that had collected there would solve everything. "How should I know? I allowed this to happen so what confidence can you have in anything I say? I'm not cut out for this, Emrys. I never was." He broke from the bed and paced the room.

"I don't doubt your abilities, Galen."

"Maybe you should." Galen refused to look at him. "Owen's already proved himself far more capable than I in protecting you *and* he's ten years younger than I am *and* he has no training."

"You think he's better than you?"

"Yes."

"You don't seriously think that. Not after everything you've done."

"What have I done?" Galen exposed his hand, extended his fingers, examined his record. "Guns stolen from the armory. Rebels annexed two floors and now hold a knife to our throats. We've been sabotaged twice. And people are dead because of me."

"Galen, they're dead because of the choices others have made, including me. I don't expect perfection. This is a hard thing we're doing. There were always going to be casualties."

"But they're my fault."

He dug his nails into the palms of his hands, but it wasn't enough to rival the pain he'd caused Galen. "No, they're mine. You wanted to storm the rebels and clear them out, but I stopped you. That was a mistake I have to reconcile with. And it was my mistake to not expand my ministry further so we didn't end up with factions."

"So, you don't trust the Defenders?"

"That's not what I'm saying."

Galen's face hardened like hot metal plunged into water, his position set and resolute. "It sounds like it. You think we've monopolized you and isolated you from the rest of the people."

"Everyone has equal access."

"But that's not true, is it? How many other Faithful have you fucked? I know Owen's gagging for it. Perhaps you should give it to him like you gave it to me."

Emrys braced too late for Galen's blow, his heart taking the full brunt of its force.

Galen was exhausted and emotional, that was all. He didn't mean these things. He'd regret them in the morning and wonder why he'd said them. Emrys had a duty to stand by him and ensure they made it to that new dawn together. But speaking was difficult. "I have no interest in Owen."

"Then perhaps that's another mistake. He would make a far better partner in all this."

"This jealousy doesn't suit you. I understand that you're tired and upset about John—" Emrys approached Galen but he cut across the room.

"I'm upset about the fact that you have chosen wrong in choosing me, which means you're fallible. Because if you knew anything about me, you'd know this isn't who I am. I can't lead, I wasn't made for it, and if you believe that, then what else are you wrong about? What else have you lied to me about?"

More than you'll ever know.

But how to restore his faith, not only in Emrys but in himself? Emrys saw Galen more clearly than he did. He saw how good he was and how he strived to do the right thing for Providence without putting himself first.

"I didn't lie to you about what I saw in you. You are more than enough for me and for Providence. You only have these doubts because you are a good person. You see the pain that we can cause, and you do what you can to avert it. You do right by your people and by me because you know how painful it can all be otherwise. Hell, you're exhausted because you serve everyone else before you serve yourself. Only you can't see it."

Galen's lips thinned and he went very still. "That doesn't make me a good leader. It makes me a failure."

"If that's what you want to believe of yourself, go ahead. I can't convince you otherwise but know I'm not the one pushing you away. I'm not the one making this difficult."

"Another thing for me to take the blame for." He picked up the gold knife in its sheath, pulled it off his belt, and dumped it on the bed beside Emrys. "I can't wear this now. I hate the sight of it for the reflection it shows me. Give it to Owen. I'm sure he'll be thrilled."

And Galen quit the apartment.

❧ 18 ❧

EMRYS STOOD AT THE EXIT TO PROVIDENCE AND SURVEYED the decimation. The storm had broken during the night two days later. The new structures housing the Scientists' experiments proved too flimsy to withstand the force of the gale. Meteorological instruments had been smashed into fragments. All that wasted effort was strewn about before him.

Scientists and Workers picked over the remains like scavengers in a garbage dump. Juliet and Kira directed recovery efforts, holding back their disappointment and their I-told-you-sos, at least until they returned to the safety of Providence. News of this failure—of *his* failure—would spread.

Owen stayed by his side. The Tornshirts might hold true, buttressed as they were on uncovering John and his conspiracy, but when the missions would inevitably halt, how long would their faith hold?

"Is any of it salvageable?" Emrys asked.

"We've lost everything we built. We don't have the materials or the skills to create something that would withstand another storm like that." Juliet kept her voice taut, except for a few errant notes.

"But you will in time."

"That's time we don't have. Not with the state of Providence as it stands. All materials need to be used to repair the damage done and not on building a second city that can be ripped apart in an instant." Her voice took on a hard, high edge, like a jagged mountain peak. "We must be reasonable or else we run the risk of total collapse." A Worker signaled for Juliet, and she left him with Kira and Owen.

"And Kira, you're of the same mind?"

"Science remains committed. We want to continue gathering the data we need to make a full appraisal, though I will say, and you know how I hate to pre-empt the results, we were already beginning to doubt the quality of the soil."

"And now she speaks."

"The soil is incompatible with life as you once knew it. In time, we may be able to genetically modify them to make them suitable, but I am not optimistic."

"Are you ever?"

"I've read extensively on what scientists were able to do before the Fall, but we don't have their capacity or skills. Perhaps if we had your many centuries in which to learn, we could do it, but as for our ability, we are limited as mere mortals."

"You'd be surprised what mere mortals can achieve. I should be pleased that you wish to return to the surface from time to time. At least some progress can be made."

"Very much so. And no doubt the Workers would like to continue their sojourns to collect scrap, especially after the depleted supplies. That should make you happy."

"Happy while the rest of Providence is tearing itself apart beneath me."

He was due to interrogate John. He'd given Galen plenty of time to come up with an answer, the latest report being that he refused to speak given he didn't recognize the Tornshirts' authority or their faith. He didn't respond to his High Priest's questions either beyond proclaiming his innocence.

"Come on, Owen. We need to go."

He turned and left, Owen passing close by Kira and sneering at her as they moved off. But the Tornshirt's display didn't faze her. She called out to them and ran over.

"Emrys, I hope you know that no matter the effect on the other factions, I am thankful for what you have allowed me to achieve. It has been a dream of mine for many years."

She smiled, a thin weak thing like it didn't get used very much, a shriveled muscle that struggled to work. But the words touched him. She held out her hands, and he placed his in hers. She clasped them in something resembling friendship or gratitude or deception then let him go. Owen cut across her and sneered again, but she paid him no mind, and the two of them walked back down the tunnel.

"I don't trust her," Owen said when they were alone.

"You don't trust anyone." Emrys wished he hadn't responded, but the sight of Owen—and the flash of bare skin through the torn garments of his followers—was a nervous tic, something he couldn't help responding to.

Owen had driven a wedge between him and Galen, and while he would have been perfectly within his rights to order the sniveling weasel from his company, Owen's faction numbered over a thousand. Galen couldn't confidently say he commanded as many Defenders, even as the head of Security.

"I trust in you and the Reformed. I don't care what anyone else says. You will lead us into a great future on the surface. And the Reformed will be there with you all the way."

Emrys held his tongue and his disgust. He didn't want any of them. It was fast becoming clear that his presence in Providence was more harmful than helpful. He'd been a fool to think that he could escape the fact that his touch brought death to everything. The drive to escape Providence before further calamity struck was getting stronger. But what could he do about Galen? He wouldn't leave without him…and therein lay the problem.

Owen left him in his maudlin silence.

They reached the gas chamber and entered together. The doors closed, and the gas streamed in. He breathed it in, hoping it would flush his soul of poison and doubt, but when it stopped, he was the same as before. The doors on the other side opened, and they proceeded into Providence's main hall.

No new tragedy had befallen the city in his absence. At least one that was not immediately visible. No one had set fire to the city. No gunshots. No screaming. One brief moment without problems before he threw himself into the next one.

But as he and Owen walked towards the elevator to ride down to the military complex, Emrys's chest and throat burned, a tickle that grew to a scratch that grew to a clawing. He cleared his throat but the feeling intensified. He coughed hard, but each breath scraped through his grazed windpipe.

"Immortal One, are you all right?"

He tried to speak but could only cough, and once he

started, he couldn't stop. He doubled over and was forced lower to the ground. He waved away Owen's help, but soon he couldn't even do that as he had to grip his sides and stop his body racking in agony.

Owen shouted for assistance, and soldiers ran to help. They barked into the radio for medical assistance, but the commotion faded as the pain whited out his mind.

What was happening? Had the Workers disturbed something poisonous? But then why wasn't Owen having this reaction?

And then he understood.

The only thing it could possibly be.

He'd inhaled gold.

"Get. Me. To. My. Quarters." He forced his words in between heaving great lungfuls of breath in the hope he could clear his lungs, but he already knew it was too late.

Emrys? Nimue's worry streaked through his mind.

He was going to die. The gold particles had entered his blood stream. They traveled up to his brain and would soon kill him.

He had one chance to save himself. He reached for Owen—

EMRYS CRACKED HIS EYELIDS APART UNDER THE WEIGHT OF several tons of bone-shattering pain. Agony thrashed through his head, goring his insides with a torment he hadn't known since he'd been made Darisami. His throat rasped raw like it had been stripped with acid. He opened his dry mouth. For the first time in centuries, he craved a glass of water.

He turned his head a fraction to the right, afraid of aggravating the pain further. He lay in bed, surrounded by medical machines and their tinging sounds, their leads attached to his finger and his chest.

Why hadn't he died? The gold would have circulated into his brain, but there he was, awake, if not healthy.

His brain must need to be damaged, hence the efficacy of the knife. Everything else merely made a Darisami ill. He had that to be thankful for. He had less gratitude for the fact that someone had discovered his weakness and pressed it to their advantage.

He reached out for Nimue, but he couldn't make out her presence through the headache. She was gone. He'd heard her voice when he collapsed, but now… No voice. No presence. No support. He was alone again. Had the time limit on the connection expired, or was it the effect of the gold? Whatever the reason, Nimue couldn't help him now.

Juliet slept in a chair in the corner. What time was it? How long had he been unconscious? He cleared his throat, partly to test if it started a coughing fit and partly to wake her. He didn't cough, but his throat stung like a third-degree burn scrubbed with steel wool.

"Juliet," he whispered hoarsely. "Juliet."

She stirred, rubbed her eyes, and bolted to his bedside. "You're awake!"

"How long have I been out?"

"About two days."

He swore. A lot could happen in two days, especially in a place as broken as Providence. "How's the city?"

"Not good. There have been rumors of your illness, but Galen's tried to quash them. One side thinks you've abandoned them, another that you've died and are preparing to retake control. Owen is imprisoned—"

"Owen? Why?"

"Galen thinks he poisoned you. He was the only one who was with you when you got sick, and they found gold on him."

Emrys tried to growl, but the burning in his throat stopped him. How could he have known about gold's effect?

"Is he alive?"

"For now. But the Tornshirts are demanding he be released. They've staged a protest, and there have been clashes with the Golden Goons, but that's not the worst of it."

"There's more?"

"The rebels cut off the food supply yesterday. The city has been rationed, but riots have already broken out in the messes as people try to stockpile. Laurence is working as hard as he can, but there's no alternative system, so Galen has ordered an assault on the rebels."

He cursed again. "That can't happen. We need to reason with them."

"They think you're dead. There's no time to negotiate. Providence is about to starve. I don't know how you're going to fix this."

Neither did he. Perhaps it would have been better if he'd died.

"What happened to you? I didn't think you could get sick."

He hesitated. He didn't want to tell her the truth, but she'd make her own assumptions, and considering how much his status must have dropped while he'd been unconscious, it would do him good to have someone on his side.

"I didn't think it was possible either, but here we are."

"Kind of jeopardizes the whole divinity thing, doesn't it?"

He grimaced. "I need to speak to Galen."

"He's busy. He's come by often to see you, but there are too many fires for him to put out. Literally, in some cases."

"What of Trellain?"

"He's helping Galen. As much as both of them want to be here, they're facing too much opposition. He's ordered that no Defender or Reformed is to appear in your chambers as some attempt to keep the peace between the two factions, but it's not holding. Any Tornshirt who steps out of line is seized and thrown in a cell. I'm only allowed in because I'm the closest thing to a trustworthy person around here."

"Lucky you."

What was he meant to do next? He needed to find out if Owen had actually poisoned him and if so, to what end? But that would take him away from seeing the people and calming them. The Faithful needed to know he was alive while the rebels needed to know he would not stand for them breaking their agreement. He had to get better, and the only way he could think of doing that was to harvest.

"I need to get out there." But when he tried to move, his body resisted, and he broke out into a sweat.

"You need to rest."

"I can't. Too many people will die if I stay in here."

"You're in no position to go anywhere."

But he ignored her and tried again, pulling the oximeter and pads off his body. He pushed back the sheet, gathering all the strength he could muster. Doctors and nurses rushed into the room at the sound of the monitors' alarms and demanded he get back into bed, but he pushed them aside even as the symbol flared inside his head.

He needed a soul. That was the only thing that would restore his strength.

He could have taken a soul from any of them, including Juliet's, but he needed to make it worthwhile. A rebel would do, but he couldn't get one without putting himself into danger. He could take Owen's and learn the truth, but he was too valuable as the Tornshirts' leader. Then he remembered John, sitting in a cell and refusing to talk.

Guilty or not, he could make repayment for the mess he'd caused and the damage he'd brought to Galen's position.

"Get me to the cells."

"But Emrys—"

"That's an order, Juliet. All of you, get me to the cells

now. Have Trellain escort me if need be, but I'm going to the cells *now!*"

It took far too long for Emrys to get out of the Tower. Galen couldn't come, having locked himself away with his commanders to organize their imminent attack on the rebels. Emrys gave an order to stand down, but it didn't go through.

Trellain appeared with a contingent of Defenders, loyal through and through—or else very good actors—and praised the Divine for his resurrection. Emrys was ready to rush out of his quarters, but his body was too weak for that, and Juliet cautioned against him being seen in case it emboldened the rebels further or created a panic more than the one that had already set into Providence. They took him to the almost-deserted bottom level and a long circuitous route to the cells.

John lay on his bed, bloodied and bruised, curled up on his side with his eyes wide and staring. Had Galen done this? Had another of the soldiers? But even as they approached, he sensed his cohort's unease. John was one of them. He could not be a traitor. But the job that Galen had done on him had not been about finding the traitor but about working out his own failings. If John were innocent, Galen would hate himself forever.

For Galen's sake, John would be found guilty.

They wheeled Emrys up to the glass. When John noticed him, he crawled off the cot and sank to the floor with his head bowed. He didn't speak, but his manner said enough. Meanwhile, Emrys's body screamed and a shiver wracked him, setting off spasms that shook him from head to toe. He waited until it passed.

"Open the door and wheel me in there with him, then I want you to leave us alone."

"But Immortal One, are you strong enough?" Trellain said.

"Strong enough for this."

He could imagine the looks passing behind his back. What would the Immortal One do with their brother? Should they comply with his orders? But the door opened, he was wheeled in, and the two of them were trapped together.

Trellain, Juliet, and the others left, but he waited until he was certain they were alone.

"Look at me, John."

"I am not worthy, Immortal One. I have failed you."

So, they were playing that game.

"How have you failed me?"

"My faith has not been strong enough for High Priest Galen or for you. I have been accused of a heinous crime that I did not commit. I have been punished for it, but clearly I am not deserving or else you would have protected me."

"Tell me what happened. Why were you in the Factory?" Emrys knew John was going to die, even as rusted needles pinged through his veins, but for his own conscience, he'd rather harvest a guilty soul than an innocent one.

"I was given orders to check on the progress of the project and to ensure it remained safe. High Priest Galen gave me those orders personally, and I took it as a matter of pride that I had been recognized for my faith."

"Then why were you there alone?"

"Because the Workers are not as committed. They don't believe in your divine project the way we do."

"And what way is that?"

"That it is what we have been promised. They merely see it as work to be done, a new task to set their mortal understanding to."

"And you disagree with that?"

"I do not trust it."

"Is that why you were sabotaging the machines? To test them?"

His eyes lit up with the idea. "Yes, I changed one minor thing which I knew would not affect their working so they could catch it and fix it, but it is clear that the Tornshirt scum took advantage of my actions." He raised onto his knees and clasped his hands in prayer. "Please, Immortal One, you must believe me when I say that it was they who have caused these problems from the very beginning."

"I have just come from those Tornshirts, and Sonia has confessed to exactly that."

He flinched, caught out and suddenly wary. "She does, Immortal One?"

"Yes. She admitted to being jealous of your excellent work and sought to discredit you. On the basis of her confession, I was prepared to sign her execution, but I wanted to wait to hear you confirm it. Now the deed is as good as done. You have done well, John, and your faith has kept you strong." Emrys held out his hand. "Stand and take my hand, knowing that you have my trust."

John frowned and staggered to his feet, the beatings he'd undertaken making him wince, and in a daze, he slipped his palm into Emrys's.

At the touch of skin to skin, Emrys formed the harvest symbol in his mind and released it. As weak as he was, he was strong enough to hold onto the treasonous bastard. The symbol made contact.

John's soul was his.

Slowly, painfully, he drew in the soul, holding John in

his thrall as he sank back to the ground. "I'm sorry, John, but your lies will always be your downfall, and no matter how strong you think you are in withstanding Galen's interrogation, there is no secret unbarred to me. Every co-conspirator I find in your soul, I will destroy until I have purged Providence of this threat. For that, I thank you. You shall be a martyr for Providence. Take comfort in that knowledge as you betray your friends."

John tried to speak, but the seizing of his soul stole his ability to talk. There was no escape. His eyes widened further at the inevitability of what was happening to him, but Emrys had no desire to watch the life leave his face. He needed those secrets.

He closed his eyes and dragged John's healing soul into his body. Piece by piece, he unpicked John's history and hunted every last traitor.

❧ 20 ❧

Names and faces shuttered through Emrys's head. The list of traitors stretched too long for his liking. Thankfully, Trellain and the group of six soldiers who accompanied him had not appeared in John's memories. When they returned to him, they praised his recovery even as they shied from John's corpse.

Emrys's revitalized body felt like his own again, refreshed and powerful—except for the jittering in his nerves, like piranhas whipped into a feeding frenzy. He had hoped to call off Galen's assault on the rebels, but his recovery was heralded with the sound of orders to charge.

They didn't have much time.

And nowhere in John's memories was there any indication of the gold's source. Owen was locked up in a cell nearby, but first he needed to get to Galen.

They ran, and Trellain outlined Galen's strategy. There would be a two-pronged attack, with soldiers advancing from across the raceway while others would break through the back channels and stairs. The elevators would not be used as they would create cages for soldiers, but whatever way they attacked, they were at a disadvantage as they had no current information about what they faced.

How big was the rebels' cache of weapons? How much destruction were they willing to wreak? How many more lives would they sacrifice? And would they sacrifice their own before Emrys got his hands on them?

They entered the main area of Providence to a siren blaring through the speakers. Citizens were ordered into their quarters while gunfire popped through the air high above. They raced across the gangway and ascended the Tower to level eight. A group of soldiers in body armor and helmets advanced carefully across the raceway. The space between shots shortened as the staccato of gunfire increased and made an almost run-on sound.

All around the Tower, battle raged as bullets blasted concrete, ricocheted off steel, and shattered glass. Deep inside the maze of quarters and offices and food production units there came more muffled sounds of assault. The soldiers' progress was slow but steady, and as far as Emrys could see none had suffered a hit. Even so, his heart rode high in his throat. He had to get out there to help.

So why did he hesitate?

"Immortal One, you should stay and let us go."

He couldn't let any more people die on his behalf. "No, Trellain, you are staying here. All of you. That's an order."

The soldiers gathered behind the barrier set up at the end of the gangway. The rebels kept their distance, far back from the balcony so they wouldn't be exposed to any shots angled from above. The soldiers waited, but they couldn't wait too long. The time was now.

He took Trellain's gun. Feeding on souls would be quick and painless but flashing a gun in the face of an inexperienced person could make them drop their own weapon without a loss of life. And he wanted to save as many as he could.

He tightened his grip, took a deep breath, and ran. He charged behind the soldiers, ordered them out of the way, and leapt over the barrier towards the rebels. They fired, but he was quick enough to dodge their bullets. He advanced towards their position, the symbol flaring at the front of his mind, ready to put this to an end. But rebels quaked at the sight of him, dropped their weapons, and surrendered.

Soldiers appeared at his back and tackled the rebels to the ground, cuffing them and confiscating their weapons. Unsated, Emrys ran for another position, shooting one of the rebels in the leg as they attempted to retaliate. He swept up their weapon and kept running as the blare of gunfire decreased.

Before Emrys had done a full sweep, the battle on eight was over. Those rebels they could find were rounded up and cuffed. Even deep within the warren, the gunfire had ceased. A quick report from his soldiers was that the number of dead was in the single digits.

Was that it? Had they won? The rebels must not have had as much weaponry as they'd feared and had even fewer people prepared to use them. People were marched out, men, women, and children, and he soon learned that the leaders had abandoned the people and bunkered down on level seven, a more heavily fortified position.

He asked for Galen, but he was immersed in the attack one floor down. The rebels sent word that if Emrys's forces didn't pull back, they'd destroy food production. Galen was going hard and fast to limit their ruination.

Emrys took the elevator, knowing the danger involved.

The elevator slowed and stopped on seven. The doors opened, and an untrained finger fired into nothing. The bullets ricocheted off the back wall and narrowly missed Emrys's head on the rebound. Shouts followed.

Now or never.

Emrys stepped out from the protection of the elevator wall and charged the rebels. He ran at them, and they squeezed their triggers. Round after round entered his body, the bullets embedding in his chest, making him bleed and stoking his anger. Rapid fire and the force of the impact kept him back as his body danced with each hit to his shoulder, his legs, his arms, his head. He didn't go down. Not yet. He wanted to at least make it out of the elevator.

When he couldn't stand any longer, he collapsed and crawled.

I can survive this.

I can survive this.

I can survive this.

He repeated the thought for every bullet that entered his body. Had he made a mistake? They couldn't kill him —could they?—but they could slow him down. He was just as susceptible to physics as the next thing in creation. More bullets, more fire, more wounds, he inched forward, chunks of him blown off under the assault. Shouts as the rebels called for backup and approached and shot him again.

He couldn't go any farther. He played dead and hoped he wasn't dying. His body howled, shuddering with each wave of agony.

"Who's a god now?" Warwick's voice wormed its way through the blood clogging his ears. Hearty cheers followed. "String him up." Warwick kicked him in his bleeding stomach.

He didn't have the energy to brace and protect himself, didn't even have the energy to breathe. He only had enough energy left to live. What must he look like to them? Did he look dead? Did they think they'd won?

Rough hands hoisted him off the floor. How many? Twelve hands, six people. Which ones could he touch? They carried him towards the balcony where they'd hang his corpse for all of Providence to see. The symbol flickered in the front of his mind, pain making it difficult to summon and maintain, slashing it to smithereens with each rough jostle of his corpse. The one constant in his immortal life, and it was failing.

He clenched his jaw and grabbed the symbol. He pried open his eyes, keeping his gaze dead while stretching to the edge of his peripheral vision. He needed only the barest touch of skin. Three men carried him on each side, and his hand was close to the middle two. He raised his arm and brushed against their naked forearms, releasing the symbol with the barest push and—

The souls were his.

He drew them in as quickly as he could while the two men stumbled and fell to their knees. He sagged between the others, and they cried for help. But no matter what they shouted, he harvested their souls with speed. The light touch of their essence was like the first drink after an endless march through the desert: refreshing, lifesaving…moreish.

The two souls twined through his body, healing him on their journey and filling his head with the breath of angels. They mended his wounds, but he needed more.

He *wanted* more.

He woke to a cacophony as the men screamed. He bound to his feet, healed, and strode towards his next victim. They pointed their guns at him and let off their rounds, but their wild shooting mattered less to him and more to their own people as their shots went wide and the bullets made fatal holes in their flesh.

He lunged for the nearest one, symbol blazing, and swept his hand over their skin, the symbol free, and the soul his. He kept moving as the soul swept into him, taking the next and the next, snaring the six souls of those who would have been his pallbearers.

Each one made him want another. The leadership and the rebels kept back and fired more bullets, but their numbers were reduced, and he shrugged off their attack. Shouting from behind and around filled level seven as Galen and the soldiers advanced under the distraction he'd provided. Stuck between a rear flank attack and the vengeance of a wounded monster, few rebels died in a blaze of glory. Outnumbered and outgunned, they were brought to heel.

Except for the leaders.

Warwick and his band formed a tight circle and kept their guns out as a wall of soldiers advanced from one side and Emrys from the other.

"It's over, Warwick," he said. "Put down your weapons, and this ends now."

"It's not over until you're dead."

"That's never going to happen." He advanced.

Warwick raised his gun.

"You can keep shooting me, but that will make things worse for you and everyone here." He stopped when the gun's muzzle pressed against his chest. "You'll have one shot then you'll die, and I'll still be here. Put the gun down and surrender."

The man's hate flared in his eyes and emotion tested his common sense, but after the seconds stretched and the souls flooding Emrys's body worked their magic and restored him, Warwick's death wish faded. He lowered his gun. The others followed suit.

Soldiers secured them while Galen hurried over to check Emrys's wounds.

"I'm fine, Galen." Though feeling Galen's hands over his body, even if only as part of an examination, almost made getting shot worth it.

"You're covered in blood."

"But the wounds are gone, see?"

"And before? We couldn't wake you."

"I'm much better."

But remembering John's soul brought with it the list of names he had to pass on. As he looked for the traitors among the Defenders, suspicion doused the relief at seeing Galen again.

Galen beckoned over a soldier who brought him a new tunic. The sight of all that blood must have unsettled them. He turned Emrys towards the elevator, his part of the mission over.

"We'll secure the prisoners in the cells. It'll take a little while but…" Galen's voice lowered. "What do you want to do with them?"

"They'll go on trial."

"And then?"

He meant would they be imprisoned, set free, or executed.

"I don't know, but right now we have a bigger problem to deal with. I interrogated John. Owen was telling the truth. John was a traitor, and there are others. Others who I think are up here right now." Helmets made it impossible to determine who was friend and who was foe.

"Who?"

As he was about to give him names, a scuffle broke out

behind them. Galen turned first, stepping in front of Emrys, as three of the rebels fought with their captors, brandishing guns that should have been confiscated.

Galen barked an order for them to be restrained, but in the brawl, shots were fired.

❧ 21 ❧

EMRYS'S HEART LURCHED AGAINST THE INSIDE OF HIS CHEST as Galen collapsed to the ground, a hand over his stomach, blood seeping through his fingers. Soldiers hurried to Galen's aid, but all Emrys could do was stand and stare.

Frozen.

A soldier called for a medic.

Still, he couldn't move.

Galen's eyes searched for him while the soldiers made quick work of pressing down on his wounds.

"You're going to be okay." Trellain spoke fast.

Galen nodded, but he wasn't calm, as he stuttered short breaths.

Emrys still couldn't move.

Galen's skin shifted to a pale shadow of white.

Could he make Galen a Darisami? He knew the symbols and their order though he'd never worked them himself. He'd never been tempted. As much as he valued his immortality, he had never wanted to curse another person with being forced to feed on the souls of others. Had never wished it on his enemies. Had never wished it on his loved ones. But faced with the prospect of losing Galen…

The first symbol blazed in the front of his mind.

"Where's the damn medic?" Trellain shouted.

Galen slipped back and closed his eyes.

"Stay with us, Galen."

One held pressure to the wound, another put their fingers to his throat.

They waited for a miracle.

He could bring Galen back from the dead.

Galen's breathing got shallower, the gaps between exhale and inhale getting longer. They were running out of time. Could he do it? Could he condemn Galen to eternal life?

I can't go on without him.

Emrys took a deep breath and crouched down. His hand reached out to Galen. He would be saved.

"Step back, everyone." Medics intruded with a gurney and swarmed Galen's body. Emrys was forced out of the way. They pulled back Galen's tunic, quickly assessed the wound, and applied bandages. He was hefted onto the gurney and whisked away in seconds.

Leaving Emrys behind.

He tried to hurry after them, but Trellain and his soldiers intercepted and asked for his orders. They said Galen would be fine. He'd be taken care of. He'd be saved. The elevator doors closed, and Galen was gone.

Behind him, that petty squabble kept going, the fight of a small group of people who thought they still had the right to resist. Rage boiled in his blood and melted his inaction. He marched into the fray, pushing aside his own soldiers and charging the rebels.

Startled faces met his as he picked apart who was whom and found the one who'd shot Galen. He still held the gun. Emrys confronted the young man, his murky hazel eyes widening.

Emrys wrapped both hands around the man's neck and squeezed, squeezed, squeezed. The rebel's eyes bulged, skin blushing purple, mouth spluttering for breath. He clawed at Emrys's hands and gouged into Emrys's skin, but he couldn't free himself. Emrys lifted him, and the rebel kicked empty air.

Pure molten hate washed through his muscles and hardened in his hands. He crushed the rebel's windpipe, poured all his restored strength into finishing this one little worm who had shot the man he loved. With a little extra pressure, he cracked the rebel's neck, and his body went limp. But Emrys squeezed, squeezed, squeezed until he crushed meat and bone into a bloody mess.

He dropped the body. The rebels that had flanked this pile of wasted flesh fell to the ground beside him and quaked. Silence prevailed except for the heavy breaths streaming through Emrys's nostrils, his chest heaving, unable to keep back the guilt that he hadn't acted to save Galen.

Warwick broke the silence and spat his insults, mocking him for his love. Their poisoned words snapped him into action, and he stalked towards the rebel leaders.

One more soul…

But why stop at one? He could take all their souls. A massacre of the Unbelievers that would live forever in infamy. In a thousand years, it would become a tale about demons who'd tried to take over heaven or about the wicked who'd attempted to thwart God. But right now, he wanted a blood bath. He wanted their souls to cleanse him of his indecision and dissolve his mercy.

He glowered at Warwick, the rebel's eyes defiant except

for the flicker of fear that dashed across them whenever Emrys moved his hand.

He leaned close to Warwick's ear. "I'm not going to kill you here. I'm going to make sure the whole of Providence knows about your treachery, and *then* I'm going to kill you." He straightened. "Get these traitors out of here. I want the whole of level seven cleared in the next hour."

"And what of…" Trellain indicated the one who'd shot Galen.

"Take his corpse and incinerate it. There is to be nothing left. Then take his ashes and scatter them on the wind outside Providence as a lesson to all that they may wish to spend their lives underground, but their true home is on the surface."

Emrys marched to the elevator and descended to the medical level. He may yet save Galen from death.

Rumor abounded throughout Providence of Emrys's assassination, but he would not leave Galen's side. He watched Galen's surgery, against the advice of the medical team, against the advice of Juliet and Trellain and Laurence and Elaina who said that Providence was collapsing. The rebels had to be processed. The Tornshirts were making noise about Owen being locked in a cell. Emrys had a conspiracy to uncover and the knowledge of his weakness to gold to ferret out. So much to do…

Yet none of it mattered until Galen was safe.

As the seconds passed, he traced the two symbols that would work the Transfiguration over and over in his mind until he felt he'd carved them into his skull. He had to be ready to intercede if Galen's life looked about to end. He watched for any sign of tension among the team as they entered Galen's body and removed the bullet, stitched up the muscle and the veins and arteries, and sewed him back up. They pumped him full of antibiotics, then took Galen, with his heart rate returning to normal, to another room.

The doctor talked while Emrys followed Galen. He told Emrys that it all looked good but that it would be best to keep Galen unconscious for a few days. Risk of infection was a problem, but otherwise they were confident of a full recovery.

Emrys held back his relief. He didn't want to tempt fate. He'd been playing god long enough that if one actually existed, they might decide to knock him back into place. He clasped the doctor's hands in thanks, noting the way she tensed at his touch. He could live with the fear, especially if it kept people in line.

After Galen was settled, Emrys remained. It wasn't long before Trellain found him and delivered his report. Everything was going to hell. As much as he hated to leave Galen behind, he had matters to attend to.

A guard of five assumed position outside Galen's room. Emrys scrutinized them to ensure none were the traitors that John's soul had betrayed.

Once they were alone and marching towards Owen's cell, he gave Trellain the list of names. Trellain struggled to believe that twelve of their soldiers could be so deceitful. Eight of them were Defenders, holding rank and access.

"What do you want me to do to them?"

"Wait until tonight when they're off duty and in their rooms. Gather a force of people you trust and take the traitors while they sleep. I'll interrogate them once they're in a cell."

"You mean…"

"I will kill them. Their souls will give me the names of the next traitor. I'll be lenient if they confess, but it had better be a good confession." He stopped and put his hands on Trellain's shoulders. "I am trusting you with this mission. You have served me well, but I understand the difficult position you find yourself in. Tell me now if you cannot do this, and I will relieve you of its burden."

Trellain didn't hesitate. "It is my honor to serve you. Your enemy is my enemy."

He could hate himself for how he manipulated Trellain's faith.

They continued to Owen's cell, passing chambers filled with rebels. Some sneered, most cowered. They would be dealt with in time.

When he saw Emrys, the Tornshirts' leader dropped to the ground and clasped his hands in prayer. "May the Divine be praised. I knew you could not be harmed." Tears welled in his eyes and his skin turned blotchy. "They thought I had hurt you, but it would be impossible for me to do so. You would know, once you saw me, you would know I couldn't do it and here you are."

Owen seemed genuine. The bruises and the cuts were real, and he offered no confession. Owen was a talker, unable to keep anything back, whether to his advantage or not, so under extreme pressure, the chance of him holding his tongue was small.

Perhaps that honesty was why the Tornshirts found him so appealing.

And why Emrys couldn't stand the sight of him.

He could fix that…but not without breaking many things.

Emrys entered the cell and sat on the chair provided. Owen continued to kneel.

"Tell me what happened when I became ill."

Owen's jaw dropped. "You can't believe I did this to you. Oh. Oh. Oh." He grabbed hold of locks of his hair and beat his fists against his head. "I promise—" Tears sprung to his eyes so fast it was like he'd burst a fire hydrant. "I promise I never did anything to harm you. Please, Immortal One. You must believe me."

Owen's pleading hacked into him, but Emrys's heart only bled for Galen.

"I didn't say you did anything, but I need to know what you think happened."

He sniffed and scrubbed at his face. "We were outside. On the surface. And you were fine. We both were. But when we re-entered Providence, you began to cough. You collapsed, and I called for help. Seeing you injured broke my heart, and I was afraid of what might happen to Providence if you left us."

Emrys wound his hand through the air to speed him up. "You were arrested."

"I didn't resist, as much as I feared for my own life. I thought they might assassinate me to secure their influence, but I knew you would protect me." He paused. "Eventually. If I pleased you."

"Why do you think I became ill?"

He dropped his head. "Because of our squabbles with the Golden Goons—I mean, the Defenders. We have angered you and the Divine. While I have been imprisoned here, I have had time to reflect on how we have made things harder for you, and I have resolved that the Reformed…" He breathed. "That the Tornshirts must make amends. If you have chosen the Defenders, then we must be more like them to earn your favor."

That wasn't exactly what he needed, but it was refreshing to hear Owen take some of the responsibility for the city's friction.

"I am pleased to hear that," Emrys said. "The only

enemies we should have are those who seek to tear Providence apart."

"Yes, Immortal One. We agree."

"What of gold, Owen?"

"Gold, Immortal One?"

"Yes, gold."

He looked truly puzzled. "Like the gold knife High Priest Galen wears?"

"Or the gold that was stolen from the stores."

"I confess we have been unable to locate who stole it or where it has gone. Is it of great value to Providence's future?"

"You were found with traces of it on you, as was I."

Owen's eyes widened. "I promise you, I have no idea where it came from, but if it was found on me, then I can only presume it was to frame me for a crime I did not commit."

"Traces were found in your quarters."

"But that's impossible. I have never touched gold in my life. Please, you must believe me."

Emrys didn't want to raise the idea that gold was so dangerous to him. The more he focused on it, the more his detractors would wield it against him. He could suck out Owen's soul, but his pleading seemed sincere and desperate, and he had been imprisoned long enough. Whatever happened next would reveal whether Emrys had chosen wisely.

"You're free to go."

"Oh, Merciful One. Thank you. I promise I will stay true to my word. The Tornshirts will never again give you cause to doubt their faith or wish them away." Owen kissed Emrys's hand.

He rose, and Owen followed. Emrys stopped at Trellain. "Owen can leave and resume his position as one of my Shadows."

Trellain opened his mouth to object before remembering he was a soldier.

"Tell the Defenders he is to pass by unmolested so he can go about restoring order among the Reformed. See it is done, Trellain."

Owen beamed at Emrys and thanked him again. Emrys bid them both goodbye and returned to Galen's bedside.

He was only checking on him before returning to the city to help quell further unrest, but once he arrived, he didn't want to leave. He stayed and watched, lost himself in the rhythmic breathing being done on Galen's behalf. Juliet sat with him. She didn't speak, and he was grateful. All he wanted to do was hold Galen's hand and heal him. He wished there were some way—other than making him into a Darisami—that he could pass on his own strength to make this right.

But even angels had limits.

Hours passed but in the underground city, in that bright room, he had no way of telling how many until Trellain came.

"Forgive me for interrupting, Immortal One. The citizens demand to see you. They've heard that the rebels have been routed, but rumors abound about your wellbeing. They need reassuring."

Trellain spoke true, but Emrys couldn't leave.

Juliet squeezed his arm. "Emrys, you need to speak to them. Galen will be fine. The doctors have said so."

"But they've been wrong before. They don't know."

"Then get this over quickly so you can come back. Don't leave them wondering."

But it wouldn't be quick. He'd have to tell them all

what had happened. And he'd have to have a trial and stamp out the resistance before he then went to work on the Defender traitors. It was going to be a long day.

"Are the corpses in the Temple?"

Trellain nodded. "They're lined up on the main floor. There are, uh…there are a lot of them."

"Then people will have no doubt as to the lengths we will go to ensure peace. Have the leaders brought under guard to the antechamber. They'll be put on trial for all to see. How long will that take?"

"Half an hour."

"Do it. Then I'll speak to the citizens."

"As you wish, Immortal One." Trellain marched from the room.

Emrys massaged Galen's hand, the rough skin of his palm rasping against the raw muscle of his heart. The rebels' actions had exposed how little use Emrys really was. He'd ridden on a wave of tricks and hysteria. Would he be swept out to sea when the tide turned? Swaying the hearts and minds of every individual in Providence took time and effort he didn't want to spend, not while Galen's life hung in the balance.

The alternative was to rule Providence absolutely, become the whole of the Law and destroy resistance wherever it rose. And why should he not do so when the result so far had been the deaths of innocent people?

But that path required Providence live in a state of terror. Hearts closed, minds shut, and loyalties died when fear ruled. He'd achieve nothing. He'd be standing behind them with a cattle prod urging them on, but they wouldn't want to go. The mission to the surface would never succeed. Galen would die. Emrys would perish.

"Do you think I should show mercy?" His thumb

rubbed over Galen's knuckles. *Please wake up.* He looked up when Juliet didn't answer. "Well?"

Despite his prompting, she took her time responding. She sat with one leg crossed over the other at the ankle, her hands clasped in her lap. "You will do what you think is best, but I think you should show mercy and compassion to those who were so easily led astray. The example you set determines how those below you behave."

She was right. In the times before the Fall, when wars had torn countries and people apart, conflict had only resolved when reconciliation ruled instead of recrimination. Bloodletting never washed anything clean. Bloodletting only made more stains.

"What about Warwick and the other leaders?"

She bit her bottom lip and looked down at her hands, one thumb pressing down on the other. "You've already made up your mind about what will happen to them."

"But you don't disagree?"

"Not after the trouble they've caused. They've put us on a road to starvation. They no longer deserve to live in Providence."

Her pronouncement reverberated in his spine.

When Trellain returned to tell him everything was ready, Emrys knew what he would do.

EMRYS ENTERED THE FULL BUT SILENT TEMPLE. THE PLANT had been pushed to the back of the room, no longer the center of attention. Citizens gazed in horror at the bodies on the floor, twenty-five of them, their arms folded across their chests, dried blood on their clothes and skin.

Twenty-five corpses.

Twenty-five martyrs to the rebel cause.

The cameras were rolling when he took the stage. The councilors, barring Galen, stood in their places. He'd meet with them soon. The matter of his poisoning remained an open question.

But perhaps what he was about to do would help close it.

He'd dressed in white trousers but left his upper body bare so no one would have any doubt that he was whole, and the bullets had left him unscathed.

Galen will have a scar.

He faced the people gathered. "Citizens of Providence, the rebels have been defeated."

Cheers erupted in the chamber and barreled into him with unexpected force. His eyes closed against the onslaught, and he allowed himself a small, benevolent smile before raising his hands for silence.

"But I am here to beg for your forgiveness. The actions we took were regrettable, and the deaths of these twenty-five people weigh heavy upon me. I had hoped to preside over a peaceful Providence. However, there are those who did not want that to happen. I tried my best to be reasonable, but events transpired against us, and we were forced to act to save the city." He paused and held their attention.

"We advanced. Our soldiers secured level eight with little difficulty. However, the rebel leaders, those weak men and women who treated the lives of these innocent people with such disdain, hid on seven. I did not wish to risk the lives of our soldiers more than I had already, so I entered the battle. You may have heard rumors that I have been unwell, as the pain of the factions tearing Providence apart wrought havoc on my body, but I knew I had to fight on. For you. For Providence.

"On reaching level seven, I was attacked, but I survived because I believe in what we are doing and where we are going. And because of my faith and my love for all of you, we have prevailed, and we are stronger than ever before."

Cheers blistered his ear drums.

"Not one of Providence's soldiers lost their lives in this battle, and the casualties on the rebels' side were minimal. However, it is my wish that those who are responsible for this crime, for the danger they put you and all of Providence in, and for their continued resistance against the will of the people, should be brought to justice."

The crowd screamed for rebel blood. The Tornshirts were the most vocal, egged on by seeing Owen standing so close to him once more. When it reached a pitch, he nodded for the soldiers manning the doors at the back to open them. Warwick and the other four leaders were marched in and stopped in front of Emrys. The crowd pelted them with boos and screams, their lips bared and teeth flashing. The mob rose to its feet, hands turned to fists, humans turned to hate.

He let their outrage flow until there came a natural lull in their cries and he raised his hands for silence. Spectators had to be pulled back into their seats, and the fury that had been unleashed took time to subside.

"I do not wish to see more death befall Providence. There are too few of us as it is; we cannot afford to tear ourselves apart. That is why I would absolve the people who followed this group of five of wrongdoing."

Shouting drowned out what he was going to say next. A mob was a tricky thing to manipulate, but he had to, for their sake as well as his own.

"I know at this time it may seem forgiveness is impossible and unwelcome, that to embrace someone who has wronged us is unwise. But I ask for you to give the people who did not have the chance to follow me the opportunity to do so now." He let his voice soothe them, setting a gentle course for them to drift along with him.

"Twelve hundred souls lived on seven and eight. Twelve hundred of your siblings who had not understood the truth of my appearance but are now free to accept and follow." He picked up pace, his voice becoming firmer, the rapids getting stronger.

"I ask, with your permission, that they be granted the same rights as you and returned to the fold of our family. Many were led astray without knowing what they were doing, led astray by the wickedness of these five people in front of you."

His words became a wild torrent, buffeted by his arguments and his demands, thrashing them within the white spray and churn. "It is this group's blasphemy and their denial that have led to division and death. *They* are the ones who gave the orders to resist. *They* are the ones who denied others their right to everlasting life and an eternity through me. *They* are the ones who would have let you starve!"

"Kill them!"

"Hang them!"

"Make them suffer!"

The leaders took the brunt of the citizens' savagery. Many of the twelve hundred were locked in their quarters on seven and eight while others were imprisoned in the cells. All were easily cast as dupes or too terrified of these wicked men and women to speak out. Emrys could see their future reintegration and their gratitude for his protection.

As for the five before him, he wanted hate and terror poured into them. He wanted their deaths sanctioned.

"Their guilt is certain, their confessions shown through their deeds and treachery." He didn't wait for a lull, raising his voice as fast, as loud, as unrelenting as a maelstrom. "They should be punished, but it is not my place to pass their sentence. Galen Rhodes, councilor, leader, and my high priest, was injured in the battle through an act of dishonor. He lives, but my heart is wounded from the acts of these traitors. I cannot remain impartial, and so I turn to the members of the Five present to pass judgement."

He turned to the councilors, Isaiah glowering, Kyra passive, Elaina torn, and Laurence stony. He'd cornered them, at once affirming their place as leaders within Providence but giving them a warning. One group in judge of another. What Emrys wanted was clear. What the crowd wanted was clearer. To give any response but the one demanded would put them on the wrong side of this war.

"Councilors, what is your answer? Will you allow these traitors to walk free of their crimes, or should they suffer the same fate as those they have wronged?"

Cheering and shouts for the group's death rose, whipping up into a storm that made it hard to hear himself think. Two of the five rebels trembled. Soldiers moved in close to stop them running.

Laurence raised his fist, extended his thumb, and sliced it across his throat.

Death to the rebels.

Hysteria swept the crowd.

Elaina repeated the gesture.

As did Kira.

Isaiah hesitated.

Warwick glared up at him. Whatever assistance the councilor had given to the rebel would not save him. Isaiah had nowhere else to go. Vote with the others, and he risked Warwick exposing him. Vote against them, and he would be a traitor.

Isaiah's thumb slashed across his throat.

The hysteria raised higher, gathering sound and emotion until it filled the chamber.

Warwick shouted and charged the bench. He tripped over a corpse and the soldiers pinned him to the ground. For the spectators, this couldn't have worked out better. The Five had made the decision, not Emrys, and all responsibility was assigned to them.

The soldiers dragged Warwick back. He cursed the Five, but his cries were drowned out by the crowd clamoring for his life. This couldn't go on any longer. The rebel leaders had to die so twelve hundred could live.

"The Five have spoken, and these traitors must pay the ultimate price for their crimes. But in my mercy, their deaths shall be quicker and more painless than the ones they would have given you through starvation."

The harvest symbol flared inside his mind. He raised his hand high above the head of a black-haired man with brown eyes. His hand flat, he placed his palm on the top of the man's head. The rebel jerked as the symbol shot down Emrys's hand and cleaved the soul from the body. With a rapid inhale of breath, Emrys sucked it in, barely capturing more than his name—Aaron—and a fleeting scream of terror.

The soul whirled through his body, brushing against the sides with its feather touch, whipping up a cool breeze that shivered beneath his skin and tingled at the back of his skull. He breathed deep and heavy, fighting against the rush that would have him freeze in bliss. He had to move on. He couldn't linger as long as he wanted or else the horror of what he was doing would be too visible. The longer he took, the sooner the mob mentality would run out.

The soldiers caught the corpse as it fell. The crowd praised him for justice done and demanded more.

Emrys went to the second, a woman, light brown hair, green eyes. When he placed his hand on her head, she didn't look away. Only when he sliced the soul out of her did her eyes roll back into her head. She fell into waiting arms.

The rush intensified. Sweat broke on his brow, his clothes dampened with the exertion of fighting ecstasy. The crowd kept cheering, but he tried to ignore it, wishing he could do this in private, in the dark, where he had time and space.

He moved on to the third, a man, and raised his hand. The woman next to him broke and ran. The soldiers chased her and dragged her back. While the crowd was engaged elsewhere, he brought his hand down onto the head of the trembling young man and reaped his soul, drawing it in as fast as he could.

He staggered onto the fourth, the young woman, as she fought and spat and raged. Soldiers held her tight. This young woman with eyes of fire who defied the insanity of all this, who didn't believe he was an angel any more than she believed in gods of the past. He took her soul to give her peace, and it curdled in his stomach.

The crowd quietened as he made his way to Warwick. He breathed like an enraged bull but stood his ground, willing to take his punishment.

"Any final words?"

"You are no angel, and we are not the end."

Boos and hisses followed, but Emrys admired his clarity. He raised his hand and brought it down on Warwick's thick hair.

Unlike the others, this would not be quick.

He released the symbol. Warwick's soul unlocked, and through a massive stretch of will, through a need to take this soul fast and then another and another, to feed the greedy beast within, Emrys pushed through to a place of calm.

He closed his eyes and sank into the depths of Warwick's soul. The sound of the crowd slipped into the background as he slipped into Warwick's recent past and his hate for Emrys with his glowing skin. He wanted Emrys to pay for killing Christos, and he would do anything to have his revenge.

And to do that, he allied himself with Isaiah.

They met prior to the lockdown. Warwick had had bombs planted in the Factory that first night, the altercation out front a distraction that kept the Workers engaged while an act of sabotage could be worked and wielded at the right moment. He witnessed other meetings and other promises to work together, each more damning than the last.

Isaiah was done for.

Emrys extracted all he could within a reasonable time-frame, then sucked up the dregs of Warwick's soul. It was done.

He struggled to open his eyes and swayed on his feet as his balance suffered from the influx of souls. He forced himself to look upon the crowd, and the sight of their bloodlust assaulted his vision. The souls' shadows fluttered across his vision, blurring them like he peered through fogged glass. He wavered, the rush too much, the souls too many.

The nausea too overwhelming.

The councilors glared down at him, but they had done what he'd demanded and always would. Isaiah had the audacity to look him square in the eye, but the destruction of yet another of his schemes had left him exposed. He'd deal with Isaiah privately before giving him his own trial.

Emrys dug deep to rebuild his borders, to separate his

own life from those of the ones he'd taken. He ordered the thirty corpses to be incinerated.

"Citizens," he called, and silence followed. "The evil that has infected Providence has been destroyed and what was once broken has now been repaired. We are united in our goals and in our mission. The wisdom of the Five has brought us here, and I have cleansed us of the wickedness that infected our city. Let us have no more death and no more fighting because we are weaker when divided and stronger when we work together. Now that this unpleasantness is behind us, we should all proceed together hand in hand to a brighter future for all."

He'd have to tell them another day about the destruction of the surface.

They clapped and cheered their approval, and he stepped off the dais to shake the hands of those in the front rows. Some were cautious of his touch, but most were unperturbed. Touch was important, or else they would live in abject fear for the rest of their lives. He took his time meeting with them, cast a glance at Isaiah, and swept away to Galen's bedside.

❧ 22 ❧

Emrys strode into Food on seven later that night. Owen and nine Tornshirts accompanied him while Trellain was overseeing the reintegration of twelve hundred people who had to be found places to sleep.

"How's it looking?"

Laurence appeared even more tired and worn than he had over the past few weeks, the effect of long days and short nights, of having to do more physical labor he would have had in years taking its toll. He had deputies and managers—as competent as Juliet—but the councilor's integrity and his close contact with his faction had not come about by chance. It had taken years of working side by side.

Which was why Laurence was in Food, greased and sweaty and exhausted.

"The machines are all intact."

"All of them?"

"It appears so. The team is going through them piece by piece in case there's something the rebels did that'll cause trouble later, but I'd say we could have it all up and running for the morning."

"Why didn't they destroy them?"

Laurence shrugged. "Human decency?"

"I doubt it. Why didn't they press their advantage?"

"Maybe they didn't have time before you attacked."

But they had. They could have ruined Providence. True, they would have been committing suicide, but in war, why wouldn't they? Isaiah would know. But getting it out of the councilor would require harvesting his soul, and Emrys wasn't ready to do that. Not while Galen slept.

"Ditch everything that's not sealed. If they didn't break the machines, they may have poisoned the food."

"That would be a lot of wastage. It may necessitate more rationing if we did that. How about I get Kira to test it?"

A muscle in the back of Emrys's neck pinged. "Talk to her deputies. I have Kira working on something else."

"What would that be?"

"Nothing for you to worry about. Get the scientists to help you, but if they can't guarantee the food is one hundred percent uncontaminated, get rid of it. Better a hungry population than a dead one."

"Understood."

Emrys turned to leave, leaving two Tornshirts behind. Laurence called out to him before he got to the door.

"Yes, Laurence?"

He came over, eyeing the Tornshirts as he passed. "Why are the Tornshirts staying?"

"They are your Shadows."

"My what?"

"Your Shadows, Councilor. I have learned of worrying things. You must have someone close to you I can trust."

"Am I untrustworthy?"

"I choose to trust you, and your work has been exemplary, but the Shadows are as much for your protection as my own."

"This is outrageous. If it's not the Golden Goons spying on my every move, it's the Tornshirts sticking to my heels."

"Pretend they're not there. I'm sure you have nothing to be troubled by, and at the least they will be able to transmit messages to me quickly so you may continue to focus on serving Providence."

"This is a gross overreach, Emrys. You're treating me like a traitor." If Laurence had had his cane, he would have been grinding it into the floor. Even without it, his hand opened and closed into a fist.

"But you're not one, so don't let it bother you. The other councilors will receive the same."

"Even Galen?"

"He has Tornshirts there for his own protection too. And theirs. If anything happens to him, Owen's life is forfeit. Isn't that so, Owen?"

"It is, Immortal One. And gladly offered in bond."

"You brainwashed imbecile." Laurence words came out in a canine-toothed snarl.

The Tornshirts stiffened. They didn't carry knives or guns, but they'd been fitted with clubs. No doubt they'd be in trouble against anyone better armed or better trained, but their uniforms and evangelical zeal gave them an edge that Emrys would press to his advantage.

"That's enough, Laurence. Get on with your work. I cannot treat one councilor different from another."

"And if one of us is found guilty, will all be charged?"

"That depends on who knows what when, and whether they intend to tell me about it. Understand?"

"Perfectly." Laurence glared at the two Tornshirts and returned to his work.

Emrys left Food and ascended to level nine. The great migration of the former rebels continued. Some noted his passing, and that of his entourage, but mostly the people were focused on finding new homes. They weren't allowed back on seven and eight until the floors had been thoroughly checked for explosives, and he wanted their numbers scattered so they couldn't create another ghetto. Isaiah's Servers had been pressed into duty finding accommodations for them and were working efficiently without their councilor's oversight. Not that he would have been of much use even if he weren't locked in his quarters. He'd be seen next after Kira.

Emrys's access granted him entrance into her locked apartments. When the door opened, she was sitting at the table.

"Good evening, Councilor."

She didn't rise when he entered but turned her cool gaze towards him. "What is the meaning of this, Emrys? Why have I been marched off to my quarters? My Scientists need me."

"You'll be back at work soon, provided I like the answers to the questions you're going to give me." He took up the chair opposite her while the Tornshirts entered her apartments and searched her small quarters.

She rocketed to her feet. "What's going on?"

"Sit down, Councilor. This will go a lot quicker if you don't make a fuss."

Her glare pierced him with the precision and power of an electron microscope. "What is the meaning of this?"

"I am searching for who attempted to assassinate me."

"Surely you can't think I had anything to do with it."

"Why can't I? You are a councilor, after all. One of the

Five. You fought your way to the top only to have me come in above you, an agent of the Divine whose existence you no doubt question. Why shouldn't I think you tried to kill me?"

She sank down on to the chair while the search continued. "I had nothing to do with you getting sick. If anything, I would have thought Owen was your main suspect. He was there when you became ill."

"Just because he was there doesn't mean it was his fault."

"And so, because I wasn't there, it means it was mine." She smirked at the reversed logic. "Aren't you meant to be immortal? Or is there something you're not immune to?"

He leaned forward. "And what would that be?"

"You tell me. I'd love to know. For science."

He sat back and traced the figure eight on top of his crossed thigh. The Tornshirts knew what they were looking for but not exactly why. It wouldn't take much for them to piece it together, but they would be less likely to use it against him.

"I've had Trellain pull up a list of all your access points throughout Providence."

"That's an invasion of my privacy."

"If you have nothing to hide—"

"Don't use that old argument against me. I've done my reading. I know how police states and dictatorships used it against their citizens to keep them in line. You want me to figure out how to make the surface inhabitable again? Then leave me to do my work in peace."

"We are at war, Kira. For all our survival. Your privacy means nothing. While we're in here, Tornshirts are searching every place you've been in the past two weeks. If they find what I think they'll find, you will be executed for treason."

"And if they don't? What then? Will I ever be free of suspicion?"

"Only if you give me good cause to believe otherwise. Two Tornshirts will remain here after their search is completed."

She blinked and pulled back. "Why?"

"They are your Shadows. I am giving them to every councilor, including Galen, for their protection as well as Providence's. They will be there every minute of every day to ensure you are working with us, not against us."

"I refuse."

"Then you can go in a cell. I have had enough of pandering to the whining of spoiled children. My belief in Providence's future is sound but my faith in any of you is weak, and I see no reason to let it cripple me or Providence. The Shadows stay until I have cause to relieve them of their duties."

"And what would that take?"

"Loyalty."

"I am loyal."

He snorted. "To yourself. Like all the councilors. Which is why I'm appealing to your own sense of self-preservation. There is a rot in Providence, and it starts at the top. How far it extends, I've yet to find out. And if you know, you should tell me before then or else the consequences for you will be unpleasant." He got up from the chair and bid her farewell. Owen, Leya, and two more Tornshirts came with him, leaving the other four to continue their search.

Isaiah was next. After the council meeting, instead of being confined to his own quarters on five, he'd been escorted to a room in the Tower. Spacious and empty except for a bed, it had no windows and no communications in or out. When Emrys arrived, Isaiah was hammering on the door. When it opened, he stepped back rather than charge forth.

"What is the meaning of this?" he bellowed.

Emrys gave a cold smile and entered the room, locking them in alone. What he was about to say he didn't want the Tornshirts to hear. He went over to the bed and pointed at it like a master ordering a dog to its place.

"Sit."

Isaiah didn't move. "I demand you tell me what's going on."

"You and I are going to have a chat, then I'll leave, and you'll stay here."

"I'm a prisoner? On what charge?"

"Conspiracy, aiding and abetting, treason, murder, theft…I could go on. I'm sure no matter what crime I announce, you've committed it. So, sit. Or I will throw you to the floor."

Isaiah narrowed his eyes and wrinkled his nose like an angry Rottweiler but did as he was told.

"Good boy." Emrys couldn't resist. "I suspect it must have pained you to order Warwick's execution."

"Being your puppet is not my idea of ruling with honor."

He laughed. "And yet you think nothing of being the puppet master to others." He held up his hand. "No need to respond. The question was rhetorical. But back to Warwick and the others. How did you feel about giving the order for their execution?"

"About as well as any of my fellow council members must have felt. Are they in the rooms next to me? Under other false charges?"

"No. However, thanks to you, one of them is lying in hospital."

He flinched. "How is my son?"

"I am surprised that you care considering it was your actions that led to him getting shot."

"I had nothing to do with it."

He sighed. "Isaiah, this would be so much easier if you'd admit how you helped the rebels."

"That's preposterous. I may not like you, but I'm not about to support a group of misfits who threaten Providence."

"Isaiah, I know all of it. I looked into Warwick's soul and saw your conversations with him."

"You're deluded. There were no conversations. He's a rebel and I no more wanted them to succeed than you did."

"You told him he had your full support. You said you'd provide him weapons. You said to threaten the food supply. All of it comes from you."

"On what proof? If you had any, you'd be bringing it before the council and the citizens to condemn me. I know you don't do well with giving people actual proof, but you'd at least need that for your plans. And conveniently the one man you say I spoke to is dead. How do you expect to hold onto any legitimacy if you condemn me on hearsay?"

Emrys's eye twitched. Isaiah had him there. Could he gamble bringing Isaiah before the citizens to lay out his crimes when he had no hard proof except what he'd gleaned from the soul of a dead man? People would believe it, but would they accept it? And was there enough trust in Emrys to do right to make sure everyone knew it?

"Proof exists, and once I have it, you will be tried and executed."

"Until then you'll keep me locked up? Providence is falling apart around you, and you intend to hide me away until you find proof of nothing? Paranoia is the worst trait in a leader."

"No, that's cynicism. To think that everyone is less than you, that nothing is better than something and that disobedience is better than compromise. Your days are numbered, Isaiah. Your only chance to survive is to confess, and only then will I consider a reprieve."

"If living under your rule is the result, I choose death."

"Then so be it." Emrys's smile was made of wire.

He left the councilor locked in the room and stationed two Shadows—the largest and meanest looking Tornshirts he could find—outside his door. He returned to Galen's bedside and waited for Elaina to be shown in. He hoped that the confusion of the rebels being reintegrated would continue long enough to provide him cover while two of the Five were incarcerated. He wouldn't have long before questions were asked—and before Elaina and Laurence tired of their bondage.

"Good evening, Elaina."

"Good evening, Emrys. What have you summoned me here for?" She eyed the two Shadows standing on the other side of Galen's bed, watching her.

Galen was unconscious, though his skin looked healthier than it had when Emrys had left. Or perhaps that was the rose-colored tint he was putting over the situation. He wanted so desperately for Galen to be awake, to provide a firmer hand on the rudder while he sailed across a sea that was smashing Providence apart. He couldn't tell whether he was guiding them to safety or onto the rocks.

She approached Galen's bedside, and sadness splashed her eyes. What treachery did she work? What knowledge would the doctors who'd tended to Emrys during his illness pass on? Of all the Five, she was the one who made Emrys feel most vulnerable.

"Elaina, I know of the friendship you and Galen shared when life in Providence was…different."

She nodded.

"I hope that history and that depth of feeling overrides any ill will you feel towards me in ensuring Galen receives the best care."

"The doctors are doing their best, Emrys. They treat everyone equally."

"I hope so because I'm sure I don't need to tell you how important Galen is…to Providence."

"You do not. My involvement in his care has been limited, but I am confident in the abilities of my people and of their impartiality in his treatment. If Galen can be saved, they will save him."

"Thank you."

"Though it strikes me as strange that this is something you are incapable of fixing for yourself. Or are your powers only limited to taking life, not restoring it?" She raised an eyebrow.

He half-smiled at his impotence exposed. He could heal Galen—while damning him to a life as an immortal soul-eater. He'd only take that action once every other option had been exhausted.

"If I restored Galen to his full health, he would be forever changed and not necessarily for the better. I prefer to leave some things to mortal means. But either way, Galen will survive. I hope we both agree on that."

"He is a patient first, your lackey second. My team knows my feelings."

"Do they know all of them?"

"No one truly knows another's soul."

"That's not true. Warwick's soul, for instance, revealed a lot about his collaboration with Isaiah in the recent rebellion."

Her eyes widened. "Isaiah? He wouldn't have."

"Wouldn't he? You have worked with him for many

years. And you were there when I first arrived in Providence and made our pact to serve as your assassin. I know he helped them, and I am gathering the proof. As yet, I don't have any of your agreement with his plans, but if I find any, it will not go well for you."

She pursed her lips. At least she had the strength of character to not go flying off at his accusations. "Whatever my agreement with Isaiah and Christos's plans in using you as an assassin, they do not extend to sanctioning a resistance. I am a healer. I see value in removing tumors but not if it means killing the patient."

"Am I a tumor?"

"You are a parasite, but unfortunately one that cannot be removed without killing the host."

The Shadows hissed at her, and she flinched, seeming to have forgotten they were there. Which is what he had hoped for.

"Isaiah's collaboration with the rebels is news to me. I had nothing to do with it."

"I'm glad to hear that. But until things have quietened down, you will be accompanied by these two Shadows."

"I am to be put under guard?"

"For your protection as well as Providence's. They will also be your direct channel to me when you need to relay any information."

"Such as?"

"Anything that could be useful to Providence's good health. Do you understand?"

"Better than you'll ever know." She glared at him then rolled her eyes at the two Shadows before she left the room. The Shadows followed.

Emrys sat by Galen's bedside, worry gnawing on his insides. He didn't like putting these leashes on the councilors, but he'd do it so he didn't have to wrestle with wolves.

He held onto Galen's hand and stared at the equipment telling him that Galen was alive but could tell nothing more than that. All the while the symbols for turning him into a Darisami rotated in his mind. Would he do it? How long would he wait before he attempted it? He could make it into another miracle—the Resurrection of Galen—or even an Ascension, but the thought of it seized his heart in an awful grip. Galen would know how much he lied, and he'd lose him anyway.

So, he waited.

Owen and the other Tornshirts—his guards as well as Galen's—left him to his peace. The hours ticked by until Trellain came to tell him the first round of traitors had been rounded up and awaited his judgement.

❧ 23 ❧

Emrys struggled to walk in a straight line. The souls of the previous two lying Defenders swam through him like strong wine. If he wasn't careful, he'd become addicted, drunk on the power, drunk on the souls, drunk on the idea that the wine would never stop flowing.

Forgetting that a blight had hit the vine, the grapes had shriveled, and he was onto his last few barrels of vintage.

But if they weren't going to answer truthfully, how was he meant to get to the truth and save Providence?

Emrys braced himself against the wall, took a few deep breaths, then entered Matthews' cell. The black-haired Defender broke down and pressed his body low to the floor.

Again with the bowing.

Again with the love and adoration.

Again with the lies.

"Do you know why you're here, Matthew?"

"I can only assume it's some kind of test of my faith, which is solid. You are our leader. You are the Immortal One, and everything I have is yours."

Emrys sighed and a growl rumbled in his throat. These kinds of platitudes had begun to aggravate. "What do you know about the explosions in the Factory?"

"They were the work of the rebels."

"Anything more specific than that? You are one of the Defenders' commanders. You have access to a lot of information. I've seen you in conference with Galen. Don't be modest. Tell me everything you know."

He stammered. "Of course, Immortal One, and I am honored by the trust that High Priest Galen puts in me. I live to serve—"

"Can we hurry this along? It's been a long day, and my patience is wearing thin."

"Yes, Immortal One. Forgive me, Immortal One. The rebels sabotaged the alternative food supplies, and while they were being repaired, they set off an explosion in the Factory which killed about fifty people and injured many more."

"And what was your involvement in all this?"

"My involvement?"

"Yes, what did you do? To help the situation."

"Oh, I helped with crowd control and coordination of recovery efforts. High Priest Galen should be able to confirm. When he wakes up."

"No doubt. So, you were in the middle of it all when it happened?"

"You could say that. I was there but not for all of it."

"Which part then?"

"The...the explosion. I was...I was called to the food supply area and was in there when the explosion happened."

"And which room specifically did you run to next?"

"The...the workshop, I think. I followed High Priest Galen."

"Mmm. Well, I'm sure he can confirm that when he wakes up. Provided he wakes up."

"I'm sorry, Immortal One, but what is this about? I was brought here in the middle of the night by my own comrades and given no explanation as to why. Have I offended you in some way?"

"Your name has come up in connection with the investigation into the explosion in the Factory."

"How?"

"From a Defender called John. You know him?"

"Yes, he's one of the commanding officers. We've worked together."

"Collaborated would be a better word."

His brow tensed, jagged lines marring his forehead. "I'm not sure I follow."

"Do you also know Luke?"

"Of course. He's another of the Defenders."

"Are you close?"

Emrys knew the truth. That the two had been close since childhood.

"Yes, we're friends."

"How good a friend is he?" Emrys leaned forward and stared into his eyes, holding his gaze with extreme prejudice.

Matthew's neck flushed. "I've…I've known him all my life."

"You are close? Like brothers."

He swallowed hard. "Yes. Like brothers."

"That's what I thought. That's what Luke thought, too."

"He's…he's here as well?"

"Was."

Matthew blinked, and the weight of his friend's passing crashed upon his face, crumpling his expression into something that reminded Emrys of a paper bag, empty and disposable.

"He was part of the plot to destroy the Factory and undermine my rule in Providence. And he implicated you as well."

The fight returned to his face. The Defender returned to his name but only in defense of himself. "He wouldn't. I had nothing to do with it. Nothing at all."

"And yet, I know the truth. Now, it's too late for Luke but not for you. You can either tell me everything you know, and I'll let you live, or you can keep lying to me and your life is forfeit. Which is it to be?"

"Please, Immortal One, I don't know what you're talking about. Luke would never be a traitor. He loved you. He believed in what you were doing."

"And you? What about you, Matthew?"

"I trust you. I would never do anything to hurt you."

"And yet there you were, tucked into Luke's memories as a co-conspirator. There you were, helping him steal supplies from storage. What I want to know is who else was involved and what did you do with the gold once Luke gave it to you?"

"I tell you, Immortal One, I had nothing to do with it. I wasn't involved. Please, you have to believe me."

"Why? Because you say it is so even when I know the truth? I've given you the chance to save yourself, why don't you take it?"

He sniffed back his false tears and stood, broadened his chest, and lifted his chin. He stared into middle distance, like a soldier, like a Defender. But who and what was he defending? "Because this is a test of my faith. My life is yours to do with as you see fit."

What bluff was this? Emrys knew the truth Luke's soul had revealed. The gold was passed from Luke to

Matthew for delivery to somewhere else. And yet, Matthew refused to believe he could know. Or perhaps he thought him weak and unable to do this in cold blood.

Matthew thought wrong.

Emrys formed the symbol in his mind, locked his hand tight around Matthew's throat, and squeezed. He brought the soldier to his knees so he could look him in the eyes. "This is your last chance. Tell me what I want to know, and you can live."

He released his grip to allow Matthew breath to speak, but the fire lit in his eyes as his skin turned red. "I'd rather die."

Emrys smiled. Pushed to the edge, Matthew's desire to face off against this foe, to be the strong man as he died, was too great and gave Emrys all the justification he needed. He closed his grip, released the symbol, and took his soul.

He closed his eyes, ignoring Matthew's attempts at freeing himself, and delved into the memories of his soul, seeing his conversations with John and Luke, watching as the gold was passed into his hand, and following him as he moved through Providence with his special package up to the fifth floor where he entered a chamber and…

Left it there? A thought dashed through his mind. Matthew had no idea who it was being left for, only that he hoped it would bring about the downfall of Emrys's theocracy. His hate burned deep, similar in style to John's and Luke's, a jealousy born of being overlooked in favor of Galen and how the High Priest would one day get his comeuppance, dying alongside the fiend from the wild.

The hate with which Matthew's thoughts burned, so deep it was etched onto his soul, shocked Emrys into losing control of the soul. When he regained it, the memories were hard to latch onto and no useful names came to him, if ever Matthew knew them.

He broke his grip, let the body fall to the ground, and sucked up the remains of the soul in half a second. Matthew's hate mixed with Emrys's own frustration, and he kicked the corpse in the ribs. The bones snapped.

Still no proof of who coordinated it.

Still nothing to tie the plot to Isaiah.

The councilor was still locked up, but it was clear that the rebels weren't the only ones he should have been worried about. He'd glimpsed a network, tugging on one end of a web, but the more he pulled on it, the less certain he was that he wasn't instead trapped on the sticky thread and all this tugging was alerting him to the spider he couldn't see coming.

EMRYS DIDN'T BOTHER WITH THE INTERROGATION ROUTINE on the next three soldiers. They were all penitent as he entered, but he'd grown numb to their lies. He walked in, placed a hand on the back of their exposed necks, and took their soul without a word.

More names and faces revealed themselves as their involvement in the plot, shallow or deep, was exposed. None of them knew of any who were higher than those he'd already killed. Whatever instructions had been given were passed only between themselves. There was a barrier that he could not breach.

Perhaps the next batch would be more revealing.

None had known anything further about the gold, though one had been trusted with transporting the rest of the materials to the arsenal, along with another soldier, and leaving them there as per instructions, no matter how bewildering. Isaiah had to be involved, but nothing revealed him.

Emrys disliked having to take the souls so soon one after another, but time was of the essence. He also disliked having to slow down. It was too easy to savor the sensation of the divine. The rush of their souls—no matter how tainted with hate and fury—was intoxicating. The more he took, the easier it was to drift like a boat on a pond in the ripe full heat of summer. Languid, luxurious, decadent. His grip faltered, and he struggled to maintain focus through heavy indolence. He couldn't take anymore, and once the fifth body fell, he gave names to Trellain and left the cells.

He wanted to lounge in bed beside Galen and sleep off his somnolence, but he could not rest. How much time had passed since Galen had been shot? How long had he spent recovering? Time meant nothing now, and Providence reflected the same.

He could not tell whether it was day or night. People were out and about, more than should be in the middle of the night, but then again, perhaps the same amount that would be around in those hours between breakfast and lunch or lunch and dinner. He wanted to see the sun. Even the moon. Anything to escape this interminable nothingness.

Owen and Leya joined him once he exited the military complex, having waited dutifully for him to return. They weren't welcome inside and truthfully, he didn't want them there. He was starting to hate their attention. They had seemed only too enraptured with the power of his touch. They had screamed the loudest for the rebel leaders to die while behind them stood a much more subdued crowd. Had they looked on aghast at what he did? No, there had been plenty of support, but once away from the effects of the mob, what thoughts crept in to undermine him? What questions festered in their hearts that would make it all too easy for a conspiracy to bloom?

How easy it was to change people's loyalties.

He went to the fifth floor and into the room down a deep corridor where Matthew had taken the gold in its locked box. He entered, and it was the same as Matthew's soul had revealed. An empty room, not even an apartment, with a table but no chair. No shelving. Nothing. Just an empty room and no sign of the gold.

He hadn't really expected to find it there, but he'd expected something, some clue as to why this room and to where it had been taken after that. He cursed and left, looking for security cameras that might have remembered who had retrieved it.

He returned to the military complex, leaving the Torn-shirts outside, and received a less than enthusiastic salute from the soldiers he encountered. By now, word would have gotten around about him imprisoning unit leaders and Defenders. They didn't glare, but they were wary, frightened.

Good. He would let them know what it was to quake in fear. It might remind them to whom their loyalty was owed.

He entered the command center, commandeered an officer who could pull up the security footage, and asked for everything relating to the room. He rewound to seven days prior and watched Matthew deliver the gold to the room then leave. Emrys got closer to the screen, hoping his nearness would reveal the culprit faster, but when someone did come into view, the flash of a black uniform, the video stopped, and whatever happened next was scrubbed until the time of the attack on the rebels.

Emrys growled. Who was that? And who had deleted the video? "Replay it."

The video played again.

Again, the gap.

"Widen the search. I want to see who goes in and out of that corridor around that time."

It took the officer a while to find the necessary footage. Emrys towered over her, his muscles hardening. Someone in Security, perhaps even in this room, perhaps even the one who was helping him now, had aided this plot. Where would it end? How many souls would he have to harvest to find the truth?

She racked up the videos and played them, but no soldier appeared. They could have walked down one corridor in civilian garb, gone into a room, and emerged in their uniform. Or worn a helmet. He stayed too long, pouring over the footage, getting more agitated as the seconds passed and people zipped in and out. Certain he would miss something, but equally certain he wouldn't find it. Whoever had done this had deleted the important part.

"Who has access to the surveillance footage?"

"Most officers ranked lieutenant and above. I'd estimate at least a hundred and fifty people."

He suppressed another growl. "Find out who deleted that footage. Get help if you need it, but I want to know within two hours. Understood?"

"Yes, sir." She pulled up to the screen and got to work.

But could he trust her? What would she provide him with? If anything? Or would he soon read her name in another's soul?

❧ 24 ❧

"You must be mistaken. Look again."

"I promise you, sir. I have gone over everything three times and come to the same conclusion each time." The officer stood before Emrys, having been searched by the Tornshirts before entering Galen's hospital room.

"Then there must be another explanation." Emrys approached her, but like all good soldiers, she didn't shy away from her commander. "Look again. Go through everything again because what you told me cannot be true. Understand?"

"Yes, sir."

He narrowed his eyes at her. She didn't use his title, but he couldn't fault her on her respect. He'd let it go, even as it niggled at him. "And do not tell anyone what you have told me."

"Yes, sir."

He scrunched up his nose. "Dismissed."

She saluted and left him with Galen.

Galen…

She'd told him Galen had deleted the footage, his electronic signature over the whole thing, done while he couldn't verify where Galen had been. Not without taking his soul.

There had to be another explanation—someone had copied his codes or used his access while he wasn't watching. Galen would not do this, not unless he had no idea what he'd done. He was capable of it, certainly. He'd manufactured footage previously so that they could rendezvous unobserved, so he had the skills. But this…

No, Galen couldn't be responsible.

And yet the doubt was placed. Always the doubt. It ruined everything. He had to know the truth, but he couldn't be certain without waking Galen.

This was all about the gold. But if Galen wanted to kill him, he'd always had the weapon to do it. The gold knife had been in his possession until recently. He'd had more than enough opportunity to finish this if he so wished.

But why would he?

And yet…

The knife. Emrys wanted it. He needed to have it back by his side. He called in a soldier and commanded him to retrieve the blade. Galen had returned it to him, but Emrys had requested it be locked in a safe. If Galen wasn't going to wear it, no one would. But he cursed himself now for his imprudence. He should never have let it out of his sight, not even with Galen. Look at the jealousy it had inspired in the Tornshirts. Look at how he'd left himself exposed. If a secret faction operated in Providence, one that knew of his weakness, he needed to keep hold of it always.

He paced the room, anxious to do something, but he didn't want to have to hear more lies out of the mouths of traitors. He didn't want to feast on souls. What was he to do but wait?

"Excuse me, Immortal One."

Emrys stopped pacing and took his thumb away from his mouth, ripping a piece of nail off as he did and spitting it on the floor.

"What is it, Owen?"

"The Tornshirts have completed their search of Councilor Kira's quarters and her labs. They have found no gold."

"Are you sure?"

"Certain. If the councilor has it, then she has hidden it somewhere we do not know about."

"Fine. They can rest now. Have two Shadows keep watch. The rest can get some sleep. Yourself included." He waved Owen away.

"Thank you, Immortal One." The Tornshirt bowed and left.

It must have been a sign of his exhaustion that Owen did not argue. Or perhaps he had other plots to work and was eager to be at them.

He shook his head. He wouldn't allow paranoia to seize him. He couldn't assume everyone was against him, especially not Galen. That way lay madness and despair wrought of loneliness. He was trapped with these humans. He had to find a way that they could all live in harmony or else he'd forever be jumping at shadows.

He collapsed into the chair and felt every one of his five hundred years weigh on his body. When was the last time he'd slept? He couldn't remember. Not since returning to Providence. Not since adopting this ruse of being the all-seeing, all-knowing Emrys the Immortal, the eye that never slept. And exhausted as he was mentally, he did not feel like sleeping. He couldn't. Sleep had once been a blessed relief from his endless and empty existence. Now it was an impossibility.

Galen slept. He slept so Emrys didn't have to. At least

he wasn't awake to see what plots they embroiled him in and what blame they laid at his feet. Galen needed to wake. Soon. Then he could tell him what he wanted to do.

"Immortal One?" Trellain spoke softly, entering the hospital room.

"Yes, Trellain?"

He swallowed but forced himself into the pose of a soldier delivering his report. "The latest suspects have been rounded up. Thirty Defenders occupy the cells."

"That many?"

"Yes, sir. Their disappearance has been noted. The lower ranks are concerned about a purge and they think…" Trellain closed his mouth like he was trying to chew tough meat. "They think this is the work of the Tornshirts."

"Disavow them of that. You know this is not about them but about traitors in our midst." There were already enough conspiracies running through Providence.

"I do, Immortal One. It pains me to see my brethren corrupted like this, but I continue to hold to you. I hope you know that."

Emrys put his hand on Trellain's shoulder, feeling the knots like ball bearings in the muscle. "Yes, I do, Trellain. And thank you. I understand this must be hard on you, which is why I don't want you involved in the interrogations."

"If it's all right with you, I would prefer to participate."

"Why?"

Trellain shifted weight to his right foot then to the left. "Please, do not think me impertinent, Immortal One, or that I wish to question your methods or your right to treat us as you wish. But perhaps they will answer to me. They may yet be turned back to the path without such loss of life."

Emrys clasped his hands in front of his waist. "Does all this death bother you, Trellain?"

He looked down. "I would be lying if I said it didn't."

"And so, you think I should be merciful on these people who have caused the death of others through their refusal to accept the truth of my way and message?"

"Your touch may bring death, but it is merciful and more than they deserve. I am thinking of the effect on the rest of the Defenders and Security. They do not see what you see, and they do not understand what has happened. They think they are being persecuted."

"Then calm them, Trellain."

"I try, sir."

He sighed. "I will speak to them soon, but their fear suits me at the moment. Frightened people make mistakes, and I would like to catch them at it. This plot is still not worked through."

Trellain didn't reply.

Emrys breathed deep. "But I thank you for your advice, Trellain, and I will take it into account. I won't interrogate them tonight. You may join me tomorrow, though understand that I have final control over whether they live or die. And if they choose to lie to me, they will pay the price."

Although it wasn't a full pardon for his comrades, Trellain gave a small hopeful smile. "Thank you, Immortal One. Now, I have the Golden Knife with me as requested." Trellain held out the little metal box like an offering.

Emrys took it from him and lifted the lid. The knife glinted in the harsh light of the hospital room. Relief swept through Emrys like dawn breaking after the winter solstice. "Thank you, Trellain. I—"

But as his attention brushed over it, the relief turned to crystals and stabbed at his temples.

The shine on it was wrong. Not by much, subtle, true, but different enough to him. He narrowed his eyes at it then at Trellain. He tried to retain his grateful expression, but he felt it turn waxen and false. He closed the box. "Thank you. Get some rest."

Trellain bowed and left the room. Emrys turned his back on the door. He put the box on the bed, flipped the lid, and grabbed the blade's hilt. He picked it up. The weight felt the same, but the hilt didn't sit quite right in his palm.

And then there was the gold itself…

His knife was made of Welsh gold that was impossible to get now. It gave off a faint pinkish hue, but this wasn't delicate enough. It was as different as red paint to rose petals. Panic fluttered up his body.

It wasn't real. It wasn't his.

He flexed his left hand and wrapped it around the knife's blade, gritting his teeth in expectation of being burned, only to feel nothing but cold metal. Not a fleck of gold in the whole thing.

He pulled the knife free of his fist, slicing his skin open, and fought back a roar.

And blood dripped onto Galen's white sheets.

Emrys didn't know how long he stayed beside Galen's bed. Someone told him the time and left. Someone gave another report on what was going on. The surveillance officer returned to tell him that Galen's code was the only one associated with deleting the footage. She was dismissed back to her work. He didn't bother reiterating his order that none should know about this. The ones who'd done it already knew.

Just as they knew where the gold was, where the real knife was, and how exposed he was.

Trellain came, but Emrys dispatched him to deal with the interrogations himself while managing in Galen's place. He could have done with Micah around. He seemed to be the only other one that he could have trusted.

If he could trust anyone.

He wasn't even sure he could trust Galen. He still slept, looking no worse and no better. Had he swapped the knife? Had he ordered a replica made? It was not an easy feat to accomplish, but someone in the Factory would have done it. Is that what the explosion in the Factory had been? A way to cover their tracks, to silence whoever had made it and threatened to bring it to his attention.

His head felt full as too many thoughts squeezed into his skull and pushed against the bone. They mingled with the lives of the soldiers he'd taken, of Christos too, and of the countless others whose souls he'd imbibed in centuries past. At least Nimue wasn't in there. No matter how he tried to reach her, he couldn't find her. The connection had broken. Clara was gone too. He was alone.

The one bit of good news that reached him was that Laurence and the Scientists had confirmed the food was uncontaminated. The machines were running again. That was a relief.

"Emrys, I must speak with you." Elaina marched into the room with Owen hurrying behind her.

"The Immortal One is not to be disturbed."

"Fuck off, Owen," she said. "Emrys, are you aware of what's happened out there?"

Owen tried to bluster and intercede, but Emrys ordered him to stand down.

"Can you be more specific, Elaina?"

"I'm talking about the deaths."

"Which deaths?"

"You don't know, do you?" She turned to Owen and gave him a look that even a cockroach would have found demeaning. "There have been clashes between Tornshirts and the former rebels. Twelve people have been killed and another forty injured."

He surged to his feet. "What? Owen, did you know of this?"

"I didn't think it was worth bothering you with, Immortal One."

"I'm not surprised," Elaina said. "Considering only *one* of the casualties is a Tornshirt."

"I did consider telling the Immortal One about that, as losing one of the Faithful to that scum is a great tragedy, but our lives are as naught for the Immortal One."

Emrys advanced on Owen. "You are meant to be controlling your people. You are responsible."

Owen kept his gaze level, not looking at Emrys but also not looking away. "They were provoked."

"That is no excuse. You know my wishes. Everyone is to integrate with no distinction between believers and nonbelievers. This behavior only leads to more dissent."

"Then we should get rid of them all. Then there won't be any trouble." Owen's voice disclosed no emotion, not even hate. He considered the nonbelievers less than human.

"Emrys, please, how are we meant to survive when there's this kind of attitude coursing like sewage through the city?" Elaina flicked her hand at Owen.

The Tornshirt refused to look at her. "There wouldn't be any problem if the nonbelievers knew their place."

"What started this?" he asked.

Owen opened his mouth, but Elaina answered first. "Someone expressed concern about the executions."

"You say concern, but it was treason," Owen countered.

"We live in a free society—at least that's what you would have us believe, Emrys—so such discussion cannot be called treasonous."

Owen rounded on her. "It was deliberate incitement and to not respond would have been to invite a breakdown of our society."

She faced him and didn't back down. "On that, you and I agree, because the Tornshirts' over-reactions have resulted in the deaths of twelve people."

"They were justified in their response. They were defending the Immortal One and Providence."

Elaina sneered and ignored the zealot. "Emrys, this kind of bigotry and hatred cannot stand."

"I can't believe you're defending the nonbelievers," Owen said.

"I don't care what anyone believes." Elaina's voice soared like a heartbeat primed with adrenalin. "All I care about is ensuring Providence doesn't collapse around us, a mission that Emrys himself adheres to."

"You would presume to speak for an angel of the Divine?"

She snorted. Owen's eyes flared. He formed fists and made a move on the councilor.

Emrys grabbed his collar and wrangled him away from the councilor. "Remember yourself. Elaina is a member of the Five and she is acting in my interests—"

"*Her* interests more like. She wants to overthrow you."

Elaina laughed. "Perhaps you should put some people on Owen. Then he'd have real shadows to jump at."

The Tornshirt reared up to his full height, though he hardly packed enough muscle to be more than a birch. However, birch had made fine whips back in the day. "You forget that my heart is pure and devoted to the Immortal One, and I command people who know what true faith is. I don't take insults from the likes of you and your corrupt group. You should be grateful for your freedom considering Kira and Isaiah are under lockdown."

Elaina turned to Emrys. "Yes, that's another point. When will they be released?"

"When I am satisfied that they can be free to roam safely," Emrys said.

"I admit Isaiah is problematic, but what has Kira been accused of?"

"You don't need to worry yourself with that right now. You can function perfectly well without either of them around."

"You think so? Laurence is exhausted and has taken to his bed so that leaves me and I'm too busy overseeing people being patched up to respond to anything else. Where is the great agent of the Divine to reassure the population?"

"Point taken, Elaina. Owen, I want the people responsible for the murders—" Owen objected to the term, but Emrys continued, "I want them put in the cells. I will decide what to do with them later."

"It is already done, Immortal One."

"And that means *all* people responsible, not just the nonbelievers. Understand?"

"Yes, Immortal One."

Emrys glowered at Owen, but the strength of his displeasure could not melt the zealot's sour expression.

"And Owen, inform your followers that violence is not the solution to our problems. People may speak their minds, but anyone who raises a hand against another must accept the consequences, no matter their beliefs. That includes you."

His conscience pricked at him, but he shooed it away.

Owen bowed his head. "I apologize for my failures, Immortal One. Please forgive me."

"You should ask the councilor for that."

Owen regarded Elaina. His eyes cast down her body, the corner of his top lip peaked, and he left without uttering a word.

"Charming," she said. "His loyalty must make up for his manners."

"If you have a problem with his demeanor, you only have the Five to blame."

She blinked. "How so?"

"He was born in Providence. His growth was stunted because of your refusal to look for an alternative existence until I showed him a better path out of here. Perhaps if you had all worked harder at returning to the surface sooner, he may have had something to hope for."

She bunched the fingers of both hands together, so they formed a bow over which she inclined her head and tilted her condescension. "And now he has you. Lucky him. You cannot blame us for his behavior." She scrunched up her face.

"I can't blame you for what led to everyone being in here, but I can blame you for keeping them restrained and starved of hope for another life."

She burst apart the bow and opened her hands to carry her question. "And what good would it have done? No matter the divinity you claim to have, inspiration is no substitute for ability." She raised a doctor-knows-best finger. "And the fact is we do not have the knowledge nor the capacity to return to the surface with any meaningful success. Kira may have led you to believe that her Scientists have found ways to turn the Earth *green*," disdain blemished the word, "but the truth is they don't know what they're doing, and from what I've heard, it's hopeless anyway."

He riled against her superiority, whether born of profession or position. "Again, whose fault is that? Lifetimes of keeping a population downtrodden and demoralized and just plain dumb have led to this."

She coughed out a derisive laugh. "I couldn't agree more. Otherwise, what rational, intelligent person would believe that you—*you!*—are divine?"

He faced off to her, letting the tension drain from his muscles. He had the power. He had to remember that. "You have seen me and my abilities, Elaina. You'd do well to believe it."

"Ignorance may be bliss, but I'm a realist, and happiness was always alien and outdated."

"Are you refusing to work with me?" Was this the way it was going to be forever?

She breathed long and low, her throat tightening as she swallowed down her anger. "I do what's best for Providence, and for now, I entertain your fantasies of returning to the surface while doing my utmost to keep people from killing each other."

Her words bit into the back of his neck and injected their poison into his already heated blood.

"I find it rich that you—who served in a cabal with Isaiah and Christos—should lecture me on what is right for Providence, as if you do it out of altruism. You are as grasping as the rest of them and too terrified to reach for the surface, let alone the long-forgotten stars."

Her face hardened. "I have my own aims, yes, but they are more realistic than the fairy stories you spout. I'm fortunate that my plans for self-preservation align with keeping Providence underground until the situation improves."

"It will never improve, Elaina. We have reached a bottleneck. Providence is only so big, population can only grow so much, and knowledge kept in isolation withers. Providence is too limited a world for humanity to expand beyond what it already knows in here, and soon too much will be forgotten. Death will visit Providence if it stays underground."

"Better than walking into Death's open arms on the surface."

"I have more faith than you."

"I don't need faith when I have knowledge."

He smiled. "Then perhaps you can use that knowledge and wake Galen up."

"What?" She stuttered. "Wake him up? He needs to rest."

"I have seen his wounds. They look like they've healed to me."

"It's not the wound we're worried about. He has an infection that we're trying to manage. You've seen the sweat break out of his body? His temperature is higher than normal, and the doctors are concerned. It is better to keep him unconscious and treat him that way."

"Meanwhile Providence is falling down around us. Do it. Now."

She made to argue, but he cut across her.

"No, Elaina. This is what must happen. He needs to wake up, and he needs to wake up now. He is healthy enough, and if he starts to fail, I will intervene, but you will wake him up even if I have to go through every doctor in this fucking city to do it."

❁ 25 ❁

ELAINA STALLED THROUGH THE NIGHT. FIRST IT WAS because the doctors were busy patching up rebels and Tornshirts from their day of fighting. Reports continued to come to him of more battles being pitched while he was hiding by Galen's bedside. When he gave orders for her to focus on Galen first, she stalled again and refused to come.

He went to them instead. He marched into the hospital, grabbed three doctors and four nurses, and herded them into Galen's room with orders to wake him. They delayed, but when Elaina caught up to them, she was unable to do much else but again raise her concerns.

What would she know?

She left in a huff and the doctors got on with bringing Galen back to consciousness. A few injections, some monitoring, and Galen's face was screwing up in discomfort. They gave him painkillers, and his eyes fluttered open. His eyes swam with clouds.

Emrys turned to the medical staff. "Get out, all of you. You can check on him in an hour."

They hurried away. One of them paused to give

advice, but his glare shut their mouths and they left with the others. Only when everyone was gone did Emrys's heart slow its thudding.

Galen grinned a goofy, drug-addled grin that would have been adorable if not for it coming at the cost of life-saving surgery.

Breath exploded out of Emrys's mouth, and he couldn't fight the smile shining across his face. Pure relief rushed through him at seeing Galen awake and alive. Emotion rushed through his heart, but he cut himself on the need to ask Galen questions he should already know the answers to. His hand slipped into Galen's, and for that moment, he allowed himself to revel in his coarse touch.

"What's the matter? Did we lose?" Galen fought the drowsiness and winced through his discomfort.

"The rebels have been cleared out, but there's a lot more that's been going on since." He licked his dry lips. "And lots more that I need to attend to."

"I will help you." Galen tried to rise, but Emrys pushed him back onto the bed with barely any force.

"You're not ready for that. You need to rest, but I had to wake you."

Galen frowned. "Why? What's the matter?"

He didn't believe Galen would betray him. He wouldn't believe it.

"While you've been asleep, I've discovered who sabotaged the food supplies, which led to finding out who stole the resources from storage and where they took them. The problem is that I don't know who took them from there."

"And you think I might know? If I knew anything, I would tell you."

"I know." And then he said it again, much more quietly to himself.

"But you have doubts? About me?"

"No, I don't, but I have to ask you anyway. I don't believe you're involved, but there are things I need to ask."

Galen's lips thinned. "Go on."

"There's footage of the gold being taken to an empty room on level five, but everything after it's delivered has been wiped. I had an officer investigate, and your access codes are the only ones on it."

Galen crossed his arms over his chest. His thumb tapped against his bicep. "Is that all?"

"No. The Golden Knife. It's fake."

"What do you mean?"

"I mean, the knife I gave you was gold, but the knife Trellain pulled out of the vault is made from copper and brass."

The tapping on his bicep got faster. "Anything else?"

"No. No, that's all."

The tapping stopped. "So, these two events bring my loyalty into question?"

Emrys's chest felt like it was caving inwards. "I'm not questioning your loyalty. I'm asking for your help."

"You've a funny way of asking. I've put my heart and soul into ensuring your success, and you repay me with this suspicion?" He stopped, and his eyes widened in bad-humored disbelief. "And you put my life at risk by waking me up to ask me what you should already know the answer to?"

The cracking in Emrys's chest got worse, crushing bone and hollowing out his heart. "I did what I had to do." Desperation quavered in his voice. "Providence is crumbling around me, and I don't know who to trust. I have had thirty soldiers imprisoned for their part in these plots. The rebels are rioting again and fighting the Tornshirts. Meanwhile, your father was helping Warwick and the others, and I'm no closer to who poisoned me."

Galen remained resolute, the true leader in the room. "And you think that's a reason to turn on me? You think I've failed you?"

"No, I don't."

"It's either I've failed you or I'm betraying you. Which is it?"

"It's neither." He closed his eyes and breathed. How could he have let this doubt get to him? "I needed you here because without you around I lose my humanity. I lost my connection to this place, where I am an outsider and always will be."

"And that's my fault? That means I'm working against you?"

"No, I'm sorry. I shouldn't have had doubts."

Galen chewed his cheek and forced air loudly through his nose. "I committed treason for you, Emrys. I assumed responsibilities I never wanted because I believed in what you offered us. And yes, I had my doubts about what I could achieve, but I never, not for one second, doubted you. To know that you doubt me breaks my heart."

"I'm sorry, but I need your help. Why would anyone do this?"

Galen tightened his jaw. He looked straight up to the ceiling. "To undermine me. It shouldn't have been hard for someone on the inside to use my codes to do what they did. Get them to look harder and pinpoint where I was when the changes were made."

"I will."

"And as for the knife…it could have been changed at any time over the past month. I kept it on me, but someone could have switched it when I wasn't looking or when it was in the safe. I'll think if there were any moments that were more likely than others and let you know."

"Thank you."

"But if Providence is in as bad a situation as you make it sound, then there are other things you should be worrying about than finding out who stole your gold knife."

Galen didn't know the full reason, that for Emrys nothing was more important than ensuring Galen's safety. But that should be reason enough to save Providence from collapse.

"Agreed. Thank you. I should leave you to get some rest. There are two Tornshirts outside who are your body-guards and will relay anything to me that you need."

"Tornshirts? Where are my soldiers?"

"I can't trust them, Galen. The Defenders have been implicated deeply in the plot to remove me. Trellain is the only one I trust, but I need him for other missions. The Tornshirts have shown their fanaticism and loyalty."

"They will kill me."

"Owen's life will be forfeit if you are hurt, and sadly their support of him is much stronger than the soldiers' support of you."

"Great. Another failure."

"This is not your failure but mine. You will be safe."

"I don't share your confidence." He looked towards the door, lines deep across his forehead, but they eased as Trellain rushed in. Eased, but didn't disappear.

"Immortal One, I—" Trellain stopped at the sight of Galen awake. "You're awake. How are you feeling?" His greeting was a welcome moment of levity.

The two clasped hands.

"Alive. That's as good as it can be at the moment."

"I am glad. Security will be as well."

Galen barked a rueful laugh. "I am not sure of that from what I've been hearing."

"Seeing you will help. Are you able to come now?"

Emrys interrupted. "He's staying here until the doctors give him permission to leave."

"Understood. My apologies, Immortal One, but can I speak with you in private?"

"You can't say it in front of Galen?" Had they uncovered some other entrapment?

"Speak freely, Trellain," Galen said. "After what I've been accused of, there's little else that can shock me."

Trellain looked uncertain, but he pushed on. "Isaiah's escaped. His Shadows have been killed, and he's not in his room. I've checked the surveillance. Seven soldiers broke him out. All of them have disappeared."

His intestines twisted as if caught within two meaty fists. Every muscle, every sinew and synapse tightened to that knot in his stomach. The strain of it echoed in his voice. "Find them!"

"I'm trying, Immortal One, but resources are stretched since the interrogations began. The number of Defenders in Security's upper ranks has dwindled. I have about ten captains who I am certain remain loyal, as well as many soldiers beneath them, but there are gaps, and right now the city needs everyone it can spare to keep the peace."

"I'm coming with you." Galen tried to get out of bed, but he was too weak to go far.

"You're staying here," Emrys growled. "The Shadows will make sure of it."

"I am responsible for these failures, and I will help put them to rights."

"No, this is my responsibility." If only he knew how to fix it. "Trellain, let's go."

Galen swore after him, and the sound chipped against Emrys's soul while rage boiled his reason into vapors. Isaiah had been freed. Rebels and soldiers filled the cells. The Tornshirts ran rampant. But the worst of all was how he'd allowed paranoia to infect his relationship with Galen and weaken their bond—a bond that had never been strong enough, not when it had been built on a lie.

And Galen had almost died because of it. Would the truth even be able to heal him?

Could it heal them?

He promised himself that if he could save the city, he would tell Galen the truth and let him decide his fate.

EMRYS ORDERED TRELLAIN BACK TO COMMAND TO coordinate a search for Isaiah while also ensuring the city didn't fall apart. The dark bags under Trellain's eyes were an indication of the pressure he was forced to bear but being the only one Emrys could trust—or he hoped he could trust—it was a trial he had to endure.

Meanwhile, one of the traitors locked in the cells would know something about Isaiah's plans. He hadn't escaped without assistance. Emrys would flush the plot out of someone's soul. And the euphoria of a soul would give some respite from the sticky feeling of guilt from accusing Galen and the oily slick of failure.

Trellain had not lied. The cells were crammed with people and more were being added as he entered. Each one he passed was crowded with at least ten people, if not more. His steps slowed as they looked at him, watched him, most faces impassive, a few outright hostile. Two of the cells were filled with Tornshirts who begged and pleaded to be let out, but the rest, easily fifteen cells were filled with others. Security had been harsh on the rebels.

He pushed past. He'd deal with them later. He had to find Isaiah, because to know he was loose in the city with an armed guard made the hairs on the back of his neck stand on end. Who were those soldiers? How many other traitors did he command without Emrys knowing?

He'd know soon.

While the rebels and Tornshirts were jammed into cells, the traitors whose names he'd read in the souls he'd already taken were kept isolated. He stopped at the glass of one of them, and the soldier stood to attention and saluted. He barely recognized the face and what part he had to play in the plot. He didn't even know his name.

Which was how it used to be for much of Emrys's life. He'd take the soul and learn that after. If he truly were merciful, he'd give them time and ask his questions and hope for the right answers. Trellain had interrogated ten of the twenty-five, all to no avail. He picked up where Trellain left off. Unfortunately for these soldiers, he did not have time for a drawn-out interrogation. They would have mercy but would not avoid their death sentence.

He took a deep breath, but it couldn't quell his simmering anger. He should have killed Isaiah when he had the chance. These people were going to die because of that bastard.

He opened the door and entered. He walked straight up to the soldier, took hold of his hand and, once bare skin touched bare skin, took his soul. The soldier fell to his knees. Emrys released his grip and sat on the bed. He watched him die while filtering through his memories.

The soldier was involved to the point of removing the resources, but as for his connection with Isaiah, it was loose at best. Beyond witnessing a few weeks of the soldier's life, Emrys lost interest, sucked in the rest as he was leaving, and continued to the next.

The rush was faint beneath the grim melancholy that had encased his heart. He was on a mission and could not let even this familiar joy distract him.

He opened the next cell. Took the soul. Found nothing. The soldier was innocent of any true plot. Emrys forced himself to keep going. Innocence or guilt, it didn't matter. Not in this. He had to convince himself of that.

The next one revealed they had been the one to delete the footage of the gold being collected. They'd used Galen's security codes. A close friend, a coworker who'd had enough of his own organizational power to do it. Emrys watched as he had watched. No one came to collect the gold. Not through that corridor anyway. It had all been a misdirection. There was nothing to see, but the orders had come through to delete it anyway.

He'd doubted Galen for nothing.

On to the next and the next. None of them revealed who'd switched the golden knife but the one after that, a soldier named Mark, was ready for him and cowered in the corner of the room. He sank to the ground as the door opened and put his arm out as if that could protect him.

"Please, Immortal One. I'll tell you everything you want to know. I promise, I will reveal it all. I don't want to die. I didn't do anything. I wasn't part of any plot. Please, Immortal One, please."

His tears and sobbing struck Emrys, but only a few drops splashed the hardness of his heart. The rush of souls worked its magic, made him hunger for more, even if it didn't lighten his mood. He took Mark's hand and took his soul. In swept Mark's memories…

And Emrys saw what he saw, was witness as he was witness to the conversation between Isaiah and Kira.

Gold is the only thing that can kill him.

You've told me that, Kira, but still, he's alive. You mustn't have used enough.

I used plenty. We now know his true weakness.

Little good it has done us.

Kira looked at Mark. *Send him away.*

And Mark was dismissed.

Emrys sucked in the last of Mark's soul in a violent inhale, and his throat reverberated with the need to roar. He knew Kira had been up to something, but he never would have thought those two would work together. She had known about the gold, and she would pay dearly for that knowledge.

He marched from the cell and left the prison. Once out in the rest of Providence, the din of shouting and fighting hit and aggravated him like sand on sunburn.

Owen attached himself to Emrys and informed him that while Emrys had been in the cells, three of his Tornshirts had been killed. He demanded to know what retribution there would be.

He grabbed Owen by the shirtfront and slammed him against the wall. "Listen to me. There is more going on here than you realize, and the deaths of a couple of fanatics is a small price to pay for ensuring the city survives."

"But Immortal One—"

"I gave orders for the Tornshirts to stand down, and yet they continue to stir trouble. The cells are filling with rebels because of your refusal to act."

"Forgive me, Immortal One, but the soldiers are the ones doing the arresting, and the rebels are the ones doing the provoking."

"I don't want excuses. Make them stand down. Tell them to sit in their rooms if need be, but I won't have this insolence." He dropped Owen to the floor and marched away to interrogate Kira.

He reached her room and was relieved to find that the Tornshirts were standing guard and had not been murdered in any rescue attempt. Perhaps her alliance with Isaiah only extended so far. They stood aside to let him in.

Kira was seated at the table as if expecting him. She didn't stand, and he didn't sit. He wasn't going to be there long enough to get comfortable.

"How long have you been working with Isaiah?"

"What do you mean?"

"Don't play dumb, it doesn't suit you. I know you collaborated with that odious reptile, and I want to know how long it's been going on. You can either tell me, or I can suck it out of your soul. Your choice."

But rather than quail at the threat, her eyes lit up. "How did you find out?"

"One of Isaiah's traitors witnessed your conversation."

"Which one?"

"Mark."

"Not which soldier, which conversation?"

His fingertips itched, a feeling that spread up his arms and across his chest. How had he become the one being interrogated? "Does it matter? If there was one, there are bound to be others."

"It matters very much which conversation. Was it about gold?"

He kept his mouth shut.

The light in her eyes reached her lips but she remained poised and posed in her chair. "It seems that you're obsessed with this. It's good to know that my theories were correct."

"And which theories are they?"

"That gold is your weakness—and I don't mean in the way it has been for humanity. I mean gold is your real weakness, like elemental fluorine is to carbon lifeforms."

The prickling sensation spread, pumped with adrenaline and the drive to stop her speaking his secrets. "And what of it? You haven't been successful in wielding it as a weapon. You might think you have found a way to destroy me, but you haven't succeeded in anything other than revealing your own duplicitousness."

"Oh, Emrys, it wasn't to kill you. Not at first anyway. I wanted to confirm my theory about what you really are."

"Which is?"

"A Darisami."

All that spiky fear sharpened and pierced his heart at hearing that word on her lips. Very few humans had ever uttered it and lived to repeat it. "I don't know what that is. I am an angel." He didn't sound convincing, but it was hard to hear from the blood filling his ears.

She laughed and her face became more animated than he'd ever seen it, like he'd found the one subject that truly engaged her. "You're much more interesting than an angel, but by all means pretend you aren't a Darisami to your own detriment."

Deflect. Deflect. Deflect. "What the hell is a Darisami?"

"An immortal soul-eater, as well you know. You glow under moonlight, you can change your appearance, you take lives with a touch, and you are susceptible to gold. I've done my research. There were a few scant records in our archives, fairy stories mostly, but myth often masks truth. I was surprised nothing showed up in your blood samples, which was a shame, so I experimented on you."

"Hence the gold dust in the decontamination chamber. You planted it on Owen."

"I did. I knew it wouldn't be long before you suspected it came from me. I admit I could have done it with more subtlety, got someone else to do it, much as we went through that ridiculous charade to have the stolen gold delivered to level five. There's a secret entrance to that room, by the way. That's how I got it out of there without you knowing, but once I had it, I *wanted* you to turn your suspicions to me."

No demure denial. She claimed her crime. That made it easier to convict. But why?

"You must realize I'm going to kill you for what you did, for what you know."

"Perhaps. But I want to make a deal."

He snorted. "And what would this deal entail?"

"Turn me into a Darisami."

He laughed hard, the sound breaking through the lock that had constricted his throat. "Why would I do that?"

"Because of what I know. Because of the help I can give you."

He smiled the smile of a benevolent and all-powerful being. "Kira, the soul always reveals the truth. Yours will be no different. I can at least promise you it will be painless, which is more than you deserve. Perhaps I should allow Owen some time with you first."

"But having another around like yourself will make your control of the city easier."

"That has not been my experience in the past."

His denials and threats didn't faze her. Her dark eyes twinkled like the ever-expanding universe. "Ahhh… Endurance. So, you were there, after all."

He nodded.

"If I am the same as you, we can do away with the council and rule together."

He narrowed his eyes. "Why? Why would you want this?"

"Who wouldn't want this? The chance to live forever and solve all the problems that we face. We can finally see the future you and I both dream of." She stood as if the fantasy pulled her up.

"You have no idea what it's like being this."

"If you think the killing will sicken me, you'd be wrong. Besides, that is not for you to decide whether I think I can cope or not. I know I can. Will you make me into a Darisami?"

"As if I would saddle myself with you, a manipulative sociopath who would think nothing of turning on me when it suits her."

"I know where Isaiah is."

He shrugged. "I'll take that information from you without creating another one like me."

"You won't kill me, Emrys."

"Why not?"

Her body stayed still, a little too still, a little rigid. Her fingers retracted slightly, ready to reveal their claws. "Because if I die, the Scientists have strict orders to release a gas throughout the city, a gas laced with gold. It might not kill you, but it will incapacitate you and leave you weakened. You didn't wake for two days last time; who knows how long you'll sleep for this time? And anything can happen while you're asleep."

The prickling and itching returned. "You're bluffing."

"That's not a risk you want to take. Turn me into a Darisami, and I'll tell you where Isaiah is. Better yet, I'll help you stop him and decontaminate the gas."

He approached her but she didn't quail. "I could kill you and it'd be hours before anyone knows what's happened to you."

She pulled down the collar of her robes to reveal a small heart monitor attached to her chest. "The moment it stops, they'll know and release the gas. It'll circulate through the ventilation systems endlessly. Providence will be poisoned, and so will you." She let go of her collar. "Do it, Emrys. Turn me into a Darisami, and we'll rule together. Without me, all is lost."

"I don't make deals with terrorists." He turned to leave.

"Stop, Emrys." She grabbed the heart monitor through her clothes. "You will make a deal with me. I may not be dead, but if the monitor stops, the results will be the same."

He held up both hands. He believed her threat that she had the city wired ready to release gold into the ventilation. "All right, Kira. Go easy." He took a step closer. "You don't know what you're asking me to do."

"I do. I will live forever, and all the answers of the universe will be mine."

"I've been alive for five hundred years, and I barely have any."

She tutted. "That doesn't surprise me. You've allowed yourself to become distracted by Galen. Fancy wasting immortality on so-called love and affection. What good has that done you?"

"You think you can do better with endless days ahead of you and the blood of thousands on your hands?"

"Without question."

"Then who am I to say otherwise. I will make you a Darisami."

She smiled and ambition blazed in her eyes. She relaxed her fist, and in that millisecond, he punched her in the face. She slammed into the wall and sank to the floor unconscious. He grabbed her wrists and dragged her across the room. He kicked and hollered for the Tornshirts. They stared aghast at what had happened, but he shouted them out of their stupor.

"Get some rope or handcuffs or anything and tie her up. There's a heart monitor attached to her. Whatever you do, it cannot be stopped. And mention this to no one. Do you understand? Absolutely no one."

He left the Tornshirts inside the room with her. What a

mess. Did Isaiah know Kira had fit the gold to the ventilation? A hunch told him that she wouldn't want to reveal that in case she succeeded in convincing Emrys to turn her, but that didn't mean he hadn't worked it out on his own.

And what of Laurence and Elaina? What did they know?

He hurried back to Galen to discuss what had happened, but when he raced down the corridor to Galen's room, the bodies of his Tornshirt-Shadows lay out the front, bullet holes in their chests and blood on the floor. His heart kicked up faster than his feet, and he ran into Galen's room.

The empty bed, the disheveled sheets, the disconnected drip dribbling on the floor, the cold stab of dread…

Galen was gone.

❧ 26 ❧

Trellain and Emrys watched the soldiers on the screen approach Galen's quarters, four of them dressed as Tornshirts but unable to hide their rigid back and stance. The murders happened in plain view, a few gunshots, and a short while later Galen was being carried out of the room. Unconscious but breathing.

The time stamp lined up with Emrys's conversation with Kira. It had all been coordinated, and without a doubt there were soldiers with him in the command center who had helped.

"Show me where they took him," he ordered the officer controlling the footage.

"We don't know."

"Why not?"

"After they went through this door, it all goes dark. There aren't any security cameras in those wings because of…well, security."

"And you can't find Isaiah either?"

"He's gone into the same warren where they took Galen."

"Then at least you have some idea of where they are. Start searching."

"We're pulling up all access points and codes entered, but we think Isaiah must have another set, a superset that allows him to move about without his movements being recorded. We're going through them one by one, each of the doors, because even if the code isn't recorded then—"

"I don't care how it's done. I just need to know where Galen is."

"Yes, sir."

Emrys stared at the bank of screens. Some showed the footage of what had transpired, but the rest showed the citizens of Providence and the growing unrest. He caught the occasional grimace, furtive look, the shying away, or an outright brawl. Soldiers were dispatched. More people were dragged to the cells. The rebels had only been out a few days, but for all his hopes that they could integrate now that their leaders were dead, they hadn't wanted to.

His own followers hadn't made it easy. They were too susceptible to insult. Their faith vulnerable to criticism and quick to anger. Though he hadn't chosen them, most of the soldiers had discipline, but even they weren't immune to a flash of passion and a willingness to fight for a cause they believed in.

Or to kill those who didn't.

The more he looked at the screens—hopeful yet knowing it was impossible that Galen would appear in one of them—the more dissent he saw. His forces were stretched across the ten levels as they tried to settle peace throughout the city. Resistance and arguments started here and there—spot-fires that needed to be extinguished in case they exploded into an inferno.

Providence was burning.

And they had nowhere else to go.

It was clear that this discord was his fault, and the chances of getting it under control were slim. He needed to make sure Galen was all right, and then…

And then?

He couldn't think too far ahead because all he saw was a future where he and Galen couldn't be together—not if they were both to survive.

And Galen must survive.

"I want every entrance and exit to that warren blocked off and guarded. Deactivate the doors once I'm on the other side."

"You can't go in there, Immortal One," Trellain said.

"That's exactly what I'm going to do. I'm going door-to-door to find Galen."

"What about the rebels? And the Tornshirts? They're still causing trouble."

"They've had their chance. Drag them back to the cells."

"I'm not sure it's enough."

"Then do your best, Trellain. Saving Providence is all that matters now."

"Shouldn't I come with you?"

"I need you here. Fix me up with a radio, and we'll stay in contact."

Trellain ordered soldiers to fit him out, and they checked the channel was clear and working. He was forced into bulletproof armor and a helmet. They pressed two guns into his hands. He could kill quicker and more surely with the harvest symbol, but he didn't want to get closer than he had to, and the rush had a tendency to distract him from his mission.

His mission: save Galen, save Providence.

In that order.

He was escorted to the entry point that Isaiah had used

while sifting through the memories he'd gleaned for any hint of Isaiah's plan. Some knowledge of the twists and turns in that warren came to him but not anything else of use.

Emrys touched his hand to the sensor, and the door opened. He hurried in, leaving his followers behind, and the door shut behind him.

"All other entrances and exits out of there have been blocked." Trellain's voice squawked in Emrys's ear. "No one's getting in or out except through the main gate to the prison cells."

"How many confrontations are going on out there?"

Trellain paused. "Eight. No, nine. One more's just started."

"Get them under control."

"Yes, Immortal One." Trellain signed off.

The corridors were a nondescript gauntlet of doors that hid uncounted surprises. His muscles tensed as indecision sought to bind him in place. What secrets and traps had Isaiah set for him, and for how long would he have to search? Did Isaiah know of Kira's plans to poison him? Did he know exactly what Emrys was? He felt she would have kept a lot of that knowledge to herself, but Isaiah knew gold was a weakness. How would he twist it to his advantage?

Emrys proceeded down the corridors, opening doors and searching empty rooms. The path Isaiah had laid out provided little insight into his ultimate aim, but Emrys could guess.

Use Galen as a bargaining chip, a hostage he could trade in exchange for...

For what?

His own banishment? His power? His death?

Whatever Isaiah thought he could bargain with would

be as nothing once Emrys got Galen back. Isaiah would die. That would be his end.

Storerooms and offices soon gave way to munitions chambers and apartment quarters with their beds unmade and the smell of rot and must in them. Had they been built in the hope of a greater population, a place to grow into, or had they once been filled but Providence's numbers had fallen? He couldn't dwell. Galen wasn't in any of them.

He turned down a corridor, searched the rooms, reached a dead end, turned back and— The first volley of bullets hit him in the chest, and another clipped him on the arm and in the head. He took the hit and resisted, but the force of them floored him. He returned fire, but the soldiers were well protected. He would have to fight at close quarters.

He reared up, threw aside his weapon, and charged them with the symbol leading his advance. Bullets flew at him. He dodged some, not others, as he aimed for the nearest soldier, realizing that they were covered from head to toe.

No exposed skin.

The bullets kept coming.

Five, six, seven soldiers standing in his way, retreating, forming a wall of gunfire, but he'd been through this before and he was stronger than before, and he was angrier than before. The souls of all those soldiers and rebels in him fired up with his rage over losing Galen. And if he couldn't take their souls, he'd take their lives.

He barreled into the soldiers in the center and knocked them to the ground. Bullets pumped into his shoulders, kidneys, head. He flew back, grabbed the nearest one, swung them into their comrades, knocked them down, wrestled a gun as bullets tore off more of him, and turned the gun on the soldiers, finding the softest, weakest parts of their armor, and firing.

One down. Another, another, the ricochet of bullets, the smell of gunfire scorching his nostrils, his blood mingling with theirs. Four left alive.

Another shot.

Three.

They retreated, guns wild, but he staggered towards them. He needed one soul. He grabbed the gun, shot out the soldier's knees, mowed them down like a thresher, and in their pain and torment, in their screams and grunts and despair, he shuffled closer to them, shot out their arms, let them bleed in their helplessness.

One by one he pulled off their helmets, the symbol brilliant in his mind and desperate for nourishment. He swept his hand across their forehead like a benediction, like a blessing, like the Holy Spirit breaching their bodies, and he snatched their souls.

He slumped with his back against the wall and slid to the ground as the soldiers' life force slipped into his body and worked their magic, pushing out the bullets that had rent holes, healing the wounds that had wept blood.

Isaiah was waiting for him. That's what he learned. And he knew where and how many were with him in a nearby room. A room where Galen was tied to a chair.

Emrys let his head droop, taking some of the pleasure of harvesting to buttress his heart's strength yet knowing more death lay ahead. More treachery, more risk of losing everything. He listened for the sound of footsteps, but the only noise was Trellain's plea for answers.

Emrys reassured him. "There was an ambush. I'm all right. Seven soldiers are dead."

"I'll send help. You shouldn't do this alone."

"No. They won't stand a chance down here. Whatever

Isaiah has planned, he has the upper hand. He knows this place better than us. And considering the numbers that Isaiah has loyal to him, I don't think there are many we can trust. Get yourself to safety. That's an order."

"I am safe, Immortal One. I won't leave you. We are having some success out here. More fights have broken out, but they don't put up much resistance once we show up."

"At least they have the sense to act for their own self-preservation. I'm going on."

"Be careful."

Emrys closed the channel, picked up one of the unbroken helmets, and replaced his. He stripped a soldier bigger than him of his bulletproof vest and put it over his own. He'd been shot in the chest enough times for several lifetimes. He grabbed a couple of guns, strapped them to his back, and continued his search for Galen.

He took comfort in the fact that he was drawing closer to Isaiah and had some idea of what he would find. The corridors and rooms he'd searched were empty and, barring the presence of any secret passageways, he could rest assured that he was advancing in the right direction.

Right into a trap.

Anyone within a large radius would have heard the gun battle. His heart braced every time he opened a door or turned a corner, the tension ratcheting up his spine, locking out his shoulders and tensing his neck. He hated breathing through the helmet, the claustrophobic box and darkened visor a hindrance to wide vision. He turned quickly, sharply, his heart jumping and fibrillating from fear and the feast.

He hurried from door to door, corridor after corridor, expecting enemies at every bend, but they were empty. He reached the exits and entrances that remained locked, backtracking when he had to before going deeper into the warren.

He passed into an area with long corridors of blank walls and fewer doorways, until he reached one that ended in a single door.

One he recognized from the soldiers' souls.

He armed the gun, rested his finger next to the trigger, and proceeded. He pressed his hand to the sensor and hid behind the door jamb as it opened. He peered around the frame as a volley of shots whizzed past him. They missed but only just.

Under the cover of fire, he stole small glimpses and pieced together a rough picture of thirty soldiers, armed, donning protective armor, in formation with their weapons trained on him. In the middle of their formation—

Galen.

Bullets hit too close to Emrys's face, and he pitched back.

He looked again quickly, his hand clenched on the gun.

Galen was tied to a chair, muzzled, unprotected, and in the line of fire. Emrys would have to take care.

The bullets stopped.

"Throw down your weapon, Emrys." Isaiah's voice boomed out of the room.

Where was the bastard? Was he one of the armor-clad soldiers or had he ferreted himself away behind some protective wall?

Emrys opened his helmet's visor to make his voice easier to hear. "Free Galen, and I'll consider leniency for you and your soldiers."

"You have no power here any longer. Come out or Galen dies."

"You wouldn't shoot your own son."

A single gunshot fired, and Galen groaned against his

gag. Emrys's heart started from the bang and almost pitched him into battle. He ducked a look: one shot to Galen's leg, blood on the floor.

A bullet hit Emrys's helmet, the force and the surprise knocking him to the ground, as another embedded in his shoulder, hit his chest, his hip, his leg, as he slid across to the other side of the door to get out of the way. He didn't have enough protection to stop the level of firepower Isaiah commanded, but he had enough strength to not succumb. Even if it didn't kill him outright, that many people firing that many bullets would pump more holes into him than a mosquito net before he reached Isaiah.

But he didn't need to take them all out at once, just one by one, with bullets or with the symbol…if he could get close.

"Lose your weapons, Emrys, or the next bullet takes out his other leg."

And he'd do it. Or worse.

Emrys took off the guns from around his shoulders and threw them into the room.

"Now your helmet and armor."

He complied. Isaiah was not doing this to negotiate. He didn't want Emrys to reach Galen. He wanted an easier target. But Emrys could move fast enough to make that difficult. He'd run across the country in less than a month. He could move fast when he needed to.

And he'd never needed to more than at that moment.

He threw the armor into the room. "Let Galen go."

"Not until you're under arrest."

Or dead.

"I'm coming out."

The clink and clatter of weapons being raised and armed followed. He put his hands behind his head, took a few deep breaths as adrenaline pumped through his system, and stepped out to face thirty guns and murderous traitors who, once their bullets ran out, would have seconds left to live. He had to comfort himself with that.

He walked slowly forward, aligned with Galen tied to his chair. His breathing was labored. Isaiah stood behind his son in full armor, the visor on his helmet open so he could speak, a gun pointed to the back of Galen's head.

"Stop there."

He stopped. "Let Galen go."

"Not yet."

Sweat dripped down Emrys's back. His eyes darted from soldier to Galen to soldier to Isaiah to soldier to soldier to soldier. Waiting, anticipating the moment when the order would be given, and the bullets would enter his body and make it dance. Exposed, unwilling to submit to such a stream of firepower, he struggled to see a way out. Galen would die if he attacked. Galen would die if Emrys didn't die first.

Galen's eyes pleaded with him to retreat, but there was no chance of that. The only thing…

His lips twitched, but he resisted the smile. It may have been madness, but the gamble was the only thing he had left. Isaiah wouldn't kill Galen. He'd shot him to suggest it was a possibility, but he wouldn't kill him. Because if he did, nothing would stop Emrys from exacting revenge.

He just needed to wait for the right moment.

"You won't get away with this, Isaiah. The citizens won't accept it."

"They'll accept whatever I tell them to accept. Your insurrection has gone on far too long. It's time Providence went back to the way it was."

"That'll never happen."

"You're right. It'll be better. With Christos gone and all the traitors flushed, we'll live in peace."

"You'll never have peace. Not with what you've done."

"Killing you will give me all the peace I'll ever need." Isaiah raised his handgun, pointed it at Emrys's chest and fired, but Emrys dove out of the way of the bullet.

"Kill him!" Isaiah ordered.

Emrys rolled, but with nothing to hide behind the bullets caught him, the rapid fire of machine guns and rifles lodged into his body and tore holes clean through him. He gritted his teeth against the searing pain and charged the nearest soldier, grabbed the soldier's head with both hands and snapped his neck. No time to suck out his soul, he used the corpse as a shield, blocking the worst of the barrage.

The soldiers tried to corner him, circling around so his back would be up against the wall and they could be his firing squad, but he kept moving, limping along with his leg mangled from the bullets and the magic in his body trying to make it right.

He threw the corpse at a row of soldiers, knocking three to the ground, but exposing himself to fire. He launched at the nearest soldier, grabbed his gun, pulled him close, and groped for the unprotected part around the soldier's throat. He crushed his windpipe as he held him tight.

The bullets mostly stopped, but he didn't, hugging the soldier and searching for a seam he could pry apart to touch his skin. The harvest symbol blazed, hungry, demanding, angry, and in his rifling through layers, searching for the spot where shirt tucked into trousers, his hand scurried in and brushed bare flesh.

The symbol released. The soul his.

He grabbed the gun from the dying man, let him drop, and fired. His assault was met with more bullets, but the soul did its best to heal as he mowed them down. Their armor only protected them so far, and they didn't have his healing ability.

Emrys sprayed them with bullets, watching them run, watching them fall, a giggle erupting out of his throat at the pathetic nature of it all, at the insanity. Bullets lodged in his face, his neck, his chest. They punctured him at every turn, but for every bullet that hit him he retaliated with his own.

And not everyone got back up.

He pursued a soldier who had fallen to the ground, his hand held up trying to stop him, but Emrys kicked his helmet, dazzling him before pulling it off. He wiped the blood out of his eyes and slipped the stolen helmet over his head. He swiped his hand across the soldier's forehead, anointing him with blood and taking his soul.

It rushed into him, recharging his health and closing a few of the bullet holes as they were replaced with more. He took his victim's gun and turned on the wall of ten soldiers. They'd formed a line in front of Isaiah and, by virtue of their positioning, Galen as well. He'd have to be careful.

The bullets kept coming. He couldn't stand still. Limping and wounded, their bullets didn't fire as rapidly, and one soldier did not fire at all. His weapon was empty and shaking.

Emrys charged him, a vision in viscera, a monster dragged out of the deep, and the soldier flailed. Emrys tackled him, wielded him as a shield, got to his soul before he died, and threw him at the next soldier down the line.

He advanced again, took that next one's soul, forcing the soldiers to fan out to get any hope of attacking him. He took the next and the next, and his body healed now that it was free of fire, free to mend.

Out of the corner of his eye, he saw one fled from the room, leaving three soldiers, Isaiah, and Galen behind.

The soldiers were the least important in all this, their weapons perhaps loaded, but irrelevant. He could endure whatever they launched at him.

He held onto a corpse, his helmet dented but offering protection. The three remaining soldiers attacked, forming a pincer as they fired and pushed him backward, the body he held only stopping so many bullets. They released round after round. They had nothing left to lose and everything to gain if he fell.

But he wouldn't fall.

And then the bullets ran out.

He threw the corpse at two of the soldiers, knocking them down, and swiped down to uncover a bare patch of skin. He took a soul.

A bullet from Isaiah narrowly missed his shoulder, its path stinging as it grazed over flesh.

He took another soul.

Isaiah fired another bullet.

Emrys ducked, and it missed.

The two downed soldiers died. The third dropped his weapon and ran, but Emrys chased him, knocked him down, took his soul.

Another bullet from Isaiah and another, a bad shot, a graze that burned against his skin.

He picked up the body, ripped off his vest, and put it on as a bullet found its mark in the armor and thudded into him but didn't break the surface.

Another bullet to his helmet, cracking it further, but it didn't pierce.

Isaiah was next.

"Stay there, Emrys." Isaiah fired again, but he dodged it, healed, healthy, strong and fast. A single bullet at a time would not matter to him. It could go straight through him, and its path would heal as soon as it left his body. He stalked Isaiah, the animal tracking the hunter, primal versus human.

Isaiah wavered on his feet, sweat making his face shine, his fist uneasy on the gun's handle as he pointed it Emrys's way and fired another round.

He weaved, and it hit his chest plate. He kept coming, closer and closer. Isaiah was his.

Isaiah turned the gun on Galen, shot him through the neck, and ran.

Emrys's heart launched into his throat and forced him to Galen's side. The blood spouted out of the wound, Galen's eyes flared wide and struggled to focus. Emrys clapped his hand over the holes where the bullet sailed clean through, but even with the pressure, his hands turned red and slick with Galen's blood.

"Nonononononononononono."

He couldn't lose him. He couldn't let this happen. He couldn't watch Galen's life end. Without him what hope was there for an eternity? He would empty Providence of its souls if Galen died.

But Galen didn't have to.

Two symbols lit inside his head, and with eyes open and fixed on Galen's lolling face, he whispered a prayer of forgiveness for what he was about to do. He released the symbols of transfiguration.

They fired down Emrys's arm and into Galen. He jerked as they touched his soul, and Emrys tensed. He forced himself to witness the magic take place in the blind hope that it wasn't already too late. His own soul remembered the destruction those symbols wrought and prayed that Galen had enough strength to withstand the decimation.

Galen's head pitched back, the tendons in his neck straining and bulging, his body shaking as the symbols fought over his soul. Emrys braced, maintained strong contact as Galen's soul flew into his body with the force of a hurricane and railed against him, pouring itself into and through Emrys's soul, snatching a piece of it, a memory of it, the magic of it, and slammed back into Galen. It kick-started his heart, and Galen gulped large lungfuls of breath. His green eyes opened, shining with the light of his immortal soul. Emrys didn't let go until he felt the bullet wounds in Galen's neck knit shut.

Galen blinked at him, shaking from the shock.

Alive.

Immortal.

Emrys smiled, relieved, breathing heavily, his soul rattled from its own ordeal. But he had no time to delay. The process wasn't complete.

Galen's face screwed shut and he hunched over as well as he could. He screamed as the magic went about its terrible work, but Emrys could do nothing to ease that pain. Galen was being ripped out of natural order. Made powerful, made invincible, made immortal.

He waited until Galen's howling died down and he sagged in his chair, panting, sweating, miserable, and afraid. Galen had one last thing to do, and Emrys would have to help him.

Isaiah had vanished, taking his soul with him, but a bloody handprint smeared on the wall behind Emrys lead out the way he'd entered.

"Stay here."

"But—"

Emrys ran out of the room and into the corridor at full pelt. He followed the trail of blood through the warren and into a dead-end room where the soldier had hidden himself. Weapon gone, helmet gone, courage gone, he screamed and put his hands up to ward Emrys off, but he didn't have any patience left for these theatrics. He reached out, grabbed the soldier's hand, broke his wrist in his crushing grip, and dragged him back to Galen.

Galen had broken out of the cuffs and straps that had kept him bound. He probed for the bullet wounds that should be in his neck, while his eyes examined the symbols that would be swirling through his head. They would be sorting themselves into the right order and burning into his muscle memory.

The soldier babbled for his freedom, that he was sorry, that he didn't want to die. Emrys punched him in the face and knocked him unconscious.

"What did you do to me?" Something wild, something desperate, something hungry stalked Galen's eyes.

"I saved you from death."

"But…but this is different. This is…I'm different." His fists opened and closed, grasping for an explanation. "I don't understand. What have you done to me?"

Emrys took a deep breath. *I did what I had to do.* "I made you like me."

"What? No one's like you. You…you're an angel." But even as he said it, the conviction didn't stick. Doubt shuttered across his face. His hands stopped their grasping.

This was it. The moment when the lies could be untold. A moment that would have to be rushed. "I'm not an angel, Galen. I'm a soul-eater, a Darisami, and the only way I could save your life was to make you one as well."

"But…but what does…" He looked at the soldier in Emrys's fist. "Why have you brought him here?"

"You need to feed."

Galen's mouth gaped. "What? Feed? I'm not…"

"You need to feed for the magic to take full effect. It needs to be consummated with a human soul."

"I don't want to… I can't…"

"You can. And I know how much you hunger for it." He let the soldier crash to the floor and took Galen's face in his hands and forced him to look into his eyes, forced him to confront the reality of what was happening. A Darisami that didn't feed was a dead Darisami. "There's a symbol burning in your mind, and it needs to be used. There's a hunger in your soul that needs to be sated. And it has to be now."

"You want me to kill him?"

"Yes. I did this to save your life because I couldn't bear a world that doesn't have you in it. I couldn't lose you because of my own actions and my own lies. Now do it, Galen, because this bit is up to you." He picked up the unconscious soldier. "Put your hand to his skin and let the symbol go."

"I don't want to." Disgust, horror, and despair wrestled in his brow, his eyes, his mouth, his breath.

"You do! You know you do, but you think you shouldn't. And believe me, we will talk about this and I will help you, but you need to do what I say. Put your hand on his forehead and let the symbol go."

Galen hesitated. He looked around.

"Do it!"

Galen wouldn't, so Emrys grabbed his hand and pressed it to the soldier's forehead.

"LET IT GO!"

Galen resisted, but the harvest symbol was too strong, and the need was too great, and Galen was too tired. The tension broke. The symbol released. The soldier's body seized in his grip and relaxed as the soul was swiftly taken. Emrys let the corpse drop.

Galen stumbled back, whirled, and collapsed to the floor on all fours. He heaved as the soul's breath coursed through his body and the final piece of magic damned his fate.

Then he shrank into a ball and wept.

Emrys remembered that part, the soul-breaking, heart-wrenching destruction that taking his first soul delivered. The way it cut through his psyche, welling up in little hits of agony that sang and scorched. The awful realization that he'd taken a life with nothing more than a touch before the ecstasy of it, the beauty that rose up through the mire, through the muck and mud, to burst with bliss.

Nothing in the world compared to harvesting a soul.

And he'd subjected Galen to it for an eternity.

He tried to justify it to himself. He'd saved Galen's life. There would be no more lies between them. They could love each other with a truth that would transcend time. But guilt stoppered his veins. He'd given Galen not a gift, but a curse.

"Galen, we need to get out of here."

Isaiah was still on the loose, and Emrys had to return to the control center to check that he retained control of Providence. Around him was a bloodbath, thirty corpses shot to pieces, and in among the field were the two of them, unharmed, unscathed, and unhappy.

"What have you done to me?" He reared back from Emrys.

"I saved your life, but that won't mean much if we don't get out of here." He grabbed him under the arm and hoisted him up.

Galen shrugged him off and looked around at the massacre. "You're a monster."

White heat flared hot enough to melt rhodium, but it burned itself out as quick as it had come. "I tried to tell you. I tried to make you see what I really was but——"

"You didn't try hard enough. You let me believe it all. You let me believe… How could I have been so stupid?"

"Galen, I promise we will get through this. I will explain everything, but we need to get out of here before Providence collapses."

He took Galen's hand, and while his lover was lost in his thoughts and in the sight of gore and blood and death, he allowed himself to be led across the room. They picked their way through the bodies. A glint of light caught his eye by the back wall.

Curiosity and dread increased the closer Emrys got. He let Galen's hand go and crouched to examine a discharged bullet. With bare hands, he picked it up and held it in his palm. It stung his skin. He turned it around, ignoring the hiss of it in his nerve endings.

Isaiah has gold bullets…

Shot in the head and lodged in his brain, it would have been the end of him. He plucked the two embedded shells from his vest. He collected and compared other spent shells and bullets that hadn't found their mark, but they were ordinary. He raced around the room in search of more and found four shells, all gold. Isaiah had been the only one to have them.

Which meant they only had a limited supply.

He pocketed the shells. Isaiah had to be found.

He returned to Galen and opened his mouth to speak, but the shrill cry of sirens overwhelmed what he'd been about to say. Lights flashed, dousing them in red.

"What does that mean?"

"Providence is under attack."

He picked up the radio where he'd left it and called for Trellain but received no answer. Had he been killed? Was he part of the subterfuge all along?

"Galen, we need to fix this."

"How can we fix it? We *broke* this. *I* broke this. My own stupidity led me to believe you were something special and could save us all." He dropped his face into his hands and shook his head. "And I swallowed it all. Every miracle. Every lie."

"Yes, I lied to you about what I was. I let you believe what you wanted to believe because the truth was much worse, but the one thing that was not a lie, the one thing that was a blazing truth throughout all this, is how much I want to protect you. What I did to you is unforgivable and selfish, but I did it because I can't bear to lose you. I've lost people before, my wife, my daughter, and if I had my time again, I would save them as I saved you. I realize what I've done to you is a curse, but it was done with love."

"You don't know what that word means. Love demands honesty, and you're incapable of it. You've ruined me, and you've destroyed Providence."

He wanted to take Galen's hand but refrained. Galen would only withdraw. He could handle the sting of the gold bullets but not the sting of Galen's rejection. "Then help me make this right. Help me save Providence, and after that, we can save each other."

Galen's green eyes hardened to rough-cut emeralds. "You don't want to save Providence. You just want their souls."

"That was part of it, but not the only reason. I was trying to help them. I was putting them on a path out of this place, a path that you all needed and some of you hoped for."

Galen beat his chest. "But that should have been our choice, not yours, and not built on these lies. You've doomed Providence."

"We can argue about this for the rest of time, but we

need to stop Isaiah. Too many people have died. We need calm. We need to make this right."

"I can't. I want nothing to do with you."

Galen's words sucker-punched him in the solar plexus. Winded, wounded. Only self-righteous anger kept him fighting. "So, you'll just stay here? You believed it as much as everyone else, you wanted me to be an angel. You wanted something to hope for. You wanted a savior. I tried to tell you, I begged you not to fall for it, but you wouldn't listen."

"I thought I'd found something true."

"Then you should have questioned it instead of following in blind faith. You should have *listened to me.*"

"I will have to live with what I've done for the rest of my life, but you're on your own."

His anger drained. The wounds remained. "Galen, I need you."

"But I don't need you." He sat down with his back against the wall, staring at the destruction, the siren and flashing lights washing over them. No matter how much he begged, Galen wouldn't move. The shock had crushed him into inaction.

The screen on the wall near Galen's head turned on, showing Isaiah in the Temple. Red-faced and breathing heavily, as if he'd run all the way, but whole and quivering with righteous vengeance.

"It's over, Emrys. All the rebels that had been taken to the prison cells, all of the followers that have rejected you, are sweeping back into the city to reclaim it."

Emrys swore. No wonder they'd been so eager to be marched off. What better place to build an army than in the midst of an armory?

"The citizens have grown tired of your mismanage-ment, your lies, and your empty promises. The Tornshirts and Defenders are being hunted down. Their blood will be on your hands. Your rule is over, but there is one thing you can do for Providence." His eyes flared. "Tell everyone the truth so this ridiculous charade will be over. Come to the Temple now and confess. And if you don't, their deaths will be your fault."

He stood aside and revealed Tornshirts whose names he didn't know, Defenders with black eyes and grim determination on their faces, and Owen, Trellain, and Juliet.

Could he leave them all to die? What was his one long life in exchange for all theirs? He looked at Galen. If he could bargain his safety, a reprieve from execution, then surely it would be worth it. And he could save Trellain and Juliet at the same time.

But did he trust Isaiah enough?

"You have ten minutes," Isaiah said.

The screen went black.

"Galen, I need to go. I'll make this right."

"How? There's nothing that you can do now that will make any of this better. Look what you've done to me."

"I am sorry, but there is nothing I wouldn't do to ensure you live. Nothing."

He wanted to wait with Galen in the hope of seeing some glimmer of forgiveness, but it was all too soon, and he didn't have time. The sirens got into him and wouldn't let him delay. But first, he had to protect Galen one last time.

He ran to a nearby storeroom and retrieved two gas masks. If Isaiah was loose and in control, was Kira already free and implementing her little trick with the gas?

He crouched in front of Galen. "I'm going to Isaiah. I need to atone for what I've done and do my best to salvage what I can, and that means making sure you have a place to live and thrive. Put this on." He held out the mask.

"Why?"

"Because there are only two things that can kill us. The first is starvation. If you don't feed on a soul once every thirty days, you will die. The second is gold. It needs to damage your brain." He showed Galen the gold bullets, the shells burning into his palm. "Isaiah has these so don't let him shoot you. But there's something else they're planning. Kira intends to gas me with gold in the ventilation. It won't kill you, but it will incapacitate you. Remember that."

Galen refused to take the mask.

"Please, Galen."

"I want nothing from you."

Emrys put it on the floor beside him. He wasn't able to do more. "I'm going to make this right, but please do everything you can to stay alive. Please, do that for me."

He wanted to kiss Galen and tell him he'd see him soon, but Galen wouldn't look at him. Galen was safe, but Emrys still had Providence to save.

❧ 27 ❧

EMRYS EMERGED INTO CHAOS REMINISCENT OF Endurance's final days. Sirens blared and war cries reigned. The Five didn't have as much control as Isaiah suggested they had, but it would only be a matter of time before they flexed their power and broke the dwindling resistance.

Emrys sprinted across a raceway and into the Tower. He knew he was heading into a trap. He knew he should have stayed with Galen. But he knew he couldn't let any more people die in his name.

The corridor leading to the Temple was empty and quiet except for the sound of his heart thudding inside his chest. He paused outside the doors, hoping his breathing would be enough to calm him but each thud-thud thud-thud thud-thud was the drumbeat accompanying an execution. He waited, but it kept drumming, and time kept passing.

He would do whatever he had to do to ensure Galen remained safe.

That was all.

That was everything.

He unkinked his spine and opened the door.

Defenders and Tornshirts knelt on the floor with their hands behind their heads. Soldiers stood behind them with guns armed. Where the people would sit to hear his sermons, their hearts and minds trained on him, now stood soldiers, armored and armed.

Emrys stepped into the center.

"Lose the gas mask," Isaiah said.

He swiveled to the four councilors standing in their usual position.

The doors closed behind him, but he didn't take off the mask.

A soldier shot a Tornshirt in the head.

"The mask. I won't ask again."

He lifted it off his head and dropped it on the floor. How many soldiers had gold bullets? How much gas was ready to pump into the room?

"Your reign of terror is over," Isaiah said.

Looking around the room, his supporters were in the minority.

"So yours can resume?" Emrys said. "Did you tell them you shot your son?"

Laurence and Elaina looked at the councilor, but he ignored them. The jaw in his muscle tensed. "A price that had to be paid."

"Lucky for you, he's alive. Your aim isn't as good as you think it is."

Better to have them believe Galen was human. The councilors may yet discover the truth, but any chance of keeping Galen among the masses—among the food—was worth taking.

"Apparently so. If it was, you'd be dead."

"Unlike you, my aim is much surer and my touch much deadlier, but I have come to negotiate."

Isaiah laughed. The other councilors did not, nor did the soldiers, and the sound was a raven's caw. "You have nothing we want."

"That's clearly not true or else you wouldn't need the hostages. I want to bargain for their freedom."

"They are traitors. *We* will decide who goes free."

"We? I see you all standing here, but are you working together? I find that hard to believe of you, Laurence."

Something that could have been shame flickered in the councilor's eyes. Whatever it was, it made it hard for him to look at Emrys. "You have not delivered what you promised, and I have no faith you ever will."

"You have broken Providence." Elaina's voice was stronger than Laurence's, but for all the power within it, she couldn't keep it steady. "We are afraid it may be beyond repair. Your presence harms us. It's time we took back our city."

"And you all agree?"

"We do." Kira was as impassive as ever.

"That's a first. Your squabbling is what made this so easy and why the citizens were so quick to turn to me. I gave them hope. I gave them a new way."

"You led them into destruction," Isaiah said. "And from what we have seen, it looks as if that was your intention all along."

"Everything I did was to help you and save humanity."

"By forcing us to go beyond the city's safety," Isaiah said.

"You needed that push or else you would have stayed inside forever, your world shrinking until you even forgot there existed an outside worth reclaiming. Your systems would fail, your society collapse, and your people perish. You needed me, and you need me still."

"You're wrong. The only thing we need is for you to tell the citizens that you are a false god, that you have no power, that you used tricks to deceive them. You will tell the citizens to return their loyalties to the Five."

Emrys wet his lips before they cracked. "They'd say you threatened me so you can shore up your own power. What about the witnesses here? They will know the truth."

"Everyone will be given a choice. They can stay and submit to the will of the Five, or they can leave with you."

Emrys's heart sputtered and tripped. "Leave? With me?"

"If they want to believe you can make all things right, then they can follow you out of Providence."

He gaped at the councilors, unable to hold his composure. He couldn't take them with him. They'd die within days. "But why would you do that?"

"You would prefer them to die with you, here and now?" Isaiah smirked. "Tell them the truth and most will stay. Or you can give them false hope for a world beyond Providence, and they can be your chosen people for as long as it takes them to die of thirst."

Emrys took his time, looking from one councilor to another as he hunted for some hint at their real game. But they appeared resolute. Even Laurence, crestfallen and broken, showed no slyness. It couldn't be that clear and easy. "Is this a bluff?"

"No bluff," Isaiah said. "We want Providence to survive, but we must separate those who want to stay from those who want to go."

"That's...reasonable of you. You'll let us leave? No tricks? No bullet in the back?"

Isaiah narrowed his eyes. The bastard had been

thinking it, but perhaps his fellow councilors had demanded he show restraint. "They can leave."

"What about food and water?"

Isaiah ground his teeth. "They can take what they can carry."

"I don't trust you."

"The feeling is mutual."

"But this is what we have agreed upon. All of us," Elaina said.

Isaiah looked as if he'd swallowed radioactive waste, but consensus appeared to have won the day. Security could not run Providence alone. The Workers and the Scientists still had their agendas. Who knew what Service or Health wanted? Could he trust them? The guns pointing at him would suggest otherwise, but perhaps this was how he could avoid bloodshed.

"You're wasting time," Isaiah said. "The small number of followers you still have needs to be brought to heel. Declare yourself a fake, and those who want to follow you into exile may leave. You have our word on that."

"And if I refuse?"

"You and your followers will be executed."

His gaze widened to its edges, and he took in all the people he could see. If he didn't comply, every one of his supporters in this room and throughout the city would die. And that included Galen.

It was time to give it all up. He couldn't control an entire city that sat so uneasily under his authority. The tide had not just turned on his popularity but sucked it out to sea.

He rolled back his shoulders. He would have honor even in defeat. "I'll tell the citizens I give up my position and that they must follow you."

"You'll tell them you're not real," Isaiah said, "and that you've been lying to them."

"I want a guarantee that if they stay, they'll be given amnesty. Galen, too."

"If they turn from you and give up their battles, they'll be safe, but if they remain and continue to fight, we will have no choice but to respond in kind. Otherwise, they have an hour to get out of Providence. That's the best we can offer. Will you accept?"

No matter how generous the Five were being, he had to convince the people to stay behind. He couldn't protect them on the surface. And he hadn't given Galen eternal life only for it to be over so quickly.

"I will."

"Good. If there's even a hint of you trying to double-cross us, we will execute you on camera. You know we have the means of doing it. Do you understand?"

He nodded.

Two soldiers covered head-to-toe in armor brought in the camera and trained the lens on him. He must have looked a sight, his shredded clothes, his gore-stained skin.

"You don't want me looking my best?"

"We want them to see you for the monster you are."

He prepared himself, widened his stance, lifted his head. The light turned on. He took a deep breath.

"Citizens of Providence, I am speaking to you…"

He swallowed.

Could he really give it all up? Could he make them believe once more that he was not to be believed?

"I am calling for peace. The time for fighting is over and…and I am…"

Isaiah shifted in the corner of his vision. The other three councilors loomed in judgement.

"I ask all my followers to lay down your arms." He

swallowed and tried to return the saliva to his mouth. "I am not divine. The miracles you saw were not real, but tricks designed to fool you. I believed that what I was doing was the right thing, and I believe that Providence's future does lie on the surface, but I do not know that with any fact or divine knowledge. The work required does not come from some divinity but from the hard toil of working together for a common goal. Your future does not belong with me."

The words came easier, drawn from the well of his own abject horror at his existence.

"For my crimes, I am willingly banished from Providence. I accept that fate absolutely. I do not belong here, and if I had my time again, I would not visit upon you the destruction that I have wrought with my lies. I apologize for the trouble I have caused, for the lives I have taken, for the faith I have destroyed. I wish I could take it all back. I wish I had the power to do so. I wish I had any power of any kind. But I am an ordinary man who conned you.

"I beg all who believed in me to accept the authority of the Five and throw yourself on their mercy. If you submit to them, you will be forgiven. Do this to save yourselves and do this for the good of Providence."

"Tell them," Isaiah said.

He cracked his neck. "The Five permit any who wish to leave Providence the chance to do so. You have one hour to collect only what you can carry and meet me at the city's exit. But I beg you not to. You must stay within the city. I cannot protect you on the outside. I cannot provide food or water. I cannot guarantee your survival. If you remain, I believe that one day you will have the freedom to walk on the surface of the Earth, but that day will come thanks to the Five. No matter what happens, Providence is your home, and one I can no longer remain within. I am sorry. Goodbye."

The feed cut. The camera pulled away.

"Is that good enough?" He eyed the guns that remained trained on him. It wouldn't take much for them to double-cross him now that he'd said his piece.

"It'll do." Isaiah signaled the soldiers and they moved to surround him. "Get him out of here."

He kept his hands high, so they'd have no cause to attack. His former followers stared after him, aghast at the lies he'd spread, at the trust he'd broken. But it had to be that way. They had to stay behind.

Everyone had to stay behind.

Including Galen.

He was marched out of the Temple. He glanced at the plant on its pedestal. It had grown since the last time he'd seen it. More leaves sprouted from its branches. At least he would leave behind something good.

Behind him, his followers shouted their curses—at him, at the soldiers, at the Five—but they were beaten back, the sound of rifle butts hitting skulls punctuating his retreat. The doors closed, and Emrys was spared from having to hear it any longer but not spared the acid touch of guilt burning a path through the chambers of his heart.

He was taken to his quarters. He stripped beneath the glare of guns and was permitted to dress in clothes more fitting for his exile. Boots, trousers, long-sleeved shirt and tunic with a deep cowl, and gloves.

He looked around the room as best he could with the soldiers standing in the way, but he didn't want to take anything. No trinket that could represent his time as the Angel of Providence. His gold knife was gone, likely melted down to make bullets. All he would be taking with him were his memories. Not even a proper goodbye with Galen.

It was right that Galen should stay and pretend as best he could to be human. The lack of bullet wounds would be hard to explain, but perhaps he could spin some lie about being healed by Emrys. Isaiah might know the truth, that the bullet was deadly, but perhaps he would be grateful that he had not killed his son. And perhaps one day, Galen would suck that vile, manipulative, conniving soul out of his father's ageing body.

"Let's go," he said to the soldiers.

They moved to allow him through, eerily silent like killer robots who had not been programmed to speak. What if one of them decided to take revenge? What if one of them had been given orders to take him down? What if there was more than one?

They escorted him out of the Tower and across the raceway. The sirens had stopped their screaming, the people had stopped their shouting, and Providence had stopped its sinking. At least he could be proud of saving some lives, but how many lives would he have to save to absolve him for the souls he'd taken with this charade?

The soldiers crammed into the elevator with him, gun barrels pointed at him in their center like petals on a flower. All one of them had to do was pull the trigger, and all of this would be over. He didn't even try to deny that a part of him wanted it over. What life would he have to look forward to once the heavy gates of Providence closed behind him? Where would he go? Would Endurance provide food and shelter? Would he have to search elsewhere? Would he even bother?

The elevator stopped on the top level and the doors opened. He was marched out to face another unit of soldiers. They also protected Isaiah, Kira, Elaina, and

Laurence who'd come to watch him leave. There were no other people. No Galen.

"Open the gates now. I am ready to leave."

"It's not yet time. We must be fair," Isaiah said.

"Why start now?"

But before Isaiah could answer, even if he intended to, attention turned elsewhere. Emrys followed their gaze across the way to another elevator as its doors opened and out stepped Owen and Leya.

Emrys spun back to Isaiah. "You can't let them leave."

Isaiah smirked. "They have made their choice."

Emrys walked over to the two Tornshirts carrying lumpy sacks made of bedsheets. "What are you doing?"

"We are coming with you," Owen said.

"Didn't you hear what I said? Didn't you see it all? Haven't you learned anything?" If he spoke fast enough and loud enough, he might awaken their common sense.

The fanaticism had gone from their eyes, replaced with a steely disdain that hadn't been there before. "We heard. But we're not the only ones who can't stay here."

Emrys's heart sank into his stomach, a heavy weight that dragged both heart and stomach down to the floor and down through the ten levels of Providence. "You can't come. You won't survive out there."

"We've brought bottles filled with water. We've brought whatever food we could carry. We know it might be suicide—"

"Might? It is!"

"But better to risk it than stay behind where we will certainly be killed."

"The Five have given you their word."

Owen's lips flicked up. "Now who's the gullible one? We are leaving with you. That is our choice."

"And if you die out there? Will I be responsible for that too?"

Owen's eyes hardened. "Yes. You chose this path for us. You gave us hope, and you abused us with it."

"Then all the better the reason to stay away from me. I am sorry for what I have done to you, but I cannot save you. Stay. Please, I beg you."

"It's too late for us."

Owen and Leya pushed past him and walked towards the tunnel. They ignored the soldiers and their sniggering. Laurence and Elaina had the decency to look concerned, but Kira remained neutral, and Isaiah looked gleeful.

Trellain and Petra, another of the Defenders, appeared next and ignored Emrys's pleas for them to stay behind. They didn't listen to his apologies, but the pain was clear on their faces as they shuffled past him for the tunnel. They were searched for weapons—didn't have any—and sat as far from Owen and Leya as possible. That was going to be fun to manage.

More Tornshirts, more Defenders, more citizens appeared. Not many, a trickle of the most deluded and the ones with the most to lose deciding to take their chances in the Great Beyond. He didn't bother trying to convince them. A weariness settled over him as he leaned against the railing and peered down, down, down to the bottom of Providence. The deadline approached, and he gave thanks that only thirty showed up.

Maybe he had a chance at keeping them alive. His strength wouldn't flag, so he could dig through the earth for water. He could hunt—if anything living still roamed. But he'd want to find them somewhere safe before his thirty days were up.

How would it feel to harvest from them? Harvest one by one until only one remained, one sad sorry remnant of humanity that he would take to satisfy his hunger. The thought was too horrific.

He watched for Galen, a whisper of hope fluttering through him that he would come to say goodbye, let Emrys apologize again, but that seemed too far a stretch. Emrys had cursed Galen to be a soul-eater, an unclean thing, a monster, a horror that would live within Providence for as long as it took for them to figure out what he was and destroy him.

They had gold bullets. They had gold gas. But Galen was smart. He could survive. He'd done it before. It was only when Emrys was around that Galen's life was in danger.

"It's time to go," Isaiah shouted, a spring in his voice.

Emrys lingered on the last sight he'd have of Providence, then turned to the tunnel, but the elevator opened, and his heart seized, tricked into anticipating Galen.

It was Juliet.

No! "What are you doing here?"

"I'm coming with you." Her eyes met his, her expression on the quiet side of defiant.

"You're the last person I'd expect to follow me. You must know it's suicide."

"There's no future here. I know you're not divine, but you are special, and I'll die here if I don't go with you. The Five won't let us out again and…and that thought crushes me until I can't breathe." For a second, her shoulders bowed, but she flicked back her hair and grabbed his gaze. "I'd rather die outside than in here. I hate that I can't stay, but this will be my only chance. Just promise me that if it all goes to shit out there, you'll give me a quick death. That's the one thing I know you can deliver."

Of everyone, he expected her to be the most furious, the most contemptuous, the most dismissive. But her voice was steady, her face relaxed except for a slight pinch at the corners of her eyes. If this were any of the others, he'd have said that she was delusional, that her ordeal had broken her, that she saw a different reality. But this was Juliet—practical, steadfast, reasoned. As much as he wanted her to remain, her declaration for this death-march fortified him.

He smiled a soft smile, a grateful smile, a hopeful smile. "I promise."

She nodded, hefted her pack, and joined the others. Seeing her had raised his spirits a little, but they were quickly exorcised as the full weight of what they were about to do swept through him.

They were going outside.

And they were going to die.

He cast one last look around Providence, hopeful to see Galen, hopeful to not. He turned back to the tunnel, to the armed guard waiting for him to leave, to the dignitaries ready to farewell him out of Providence's cornucopia. Emrys and thirty-one humans began their exile.

❧ 28 ☙

THE GATES TO PROVIDENCE GROUND CLOSED BEHIND THEM. It was done. Night had fallen over the wasteland. A gentle breeze blew across the remains of the scientists' experiments and infertile fields. Emrys hid his face deep in his hood, away from the exposing light of the waxing gibbous moon. He checked his gloves were in place. The exiles would see him glow soon enough, but he didn't know what he'd say to explain it. The truth? Then he'd watch them flee into certain death.

All but six of the exiles had been to the surface. Emrys was glad he couldn't see their faces. Their pitiful moans were enough to dissolve his heart. He heard more than one sniff back their tears, and two seemed unwilling to leave the shadow of Providence's gates.

"Where to now?" Juliet said.

As if he had any idea.

As if he had any plan.

As if he had any right to tell them what to do.

He considered their options, none of which were

encouraging. They could camp where they were for the night or seek the shelter of the ruined city. Would Providence allow them to stay there or would soldiers force them on? Moving at night brought one set of dangers, while moving by day increased their risk of dehydrating from the heat of the sun. And where would they go to? The arks he and Nimue had explored on their journey to Providence had been uninhabitable. Where else did that leave them?

"Well?" she said.

He was lost in the churn of choices, each one with myriad consequences he couldn't untangle. Responsibility for ten thousand paled in comparison to responsibility for thirty-one. Before he only needed to consider the collective; now he would see first-hand the effect on every individual.

Or he could run away and be done with them. What good had he ever done? What hope could he ever bring?

"I think we should stay here for the night," Trellain said.

"Oh, yeah? Right where they can come shoot us," Owen said.

"Then what do you suggest, you little shit?"

Owen responded by shoving his hands into Trellain's chest and knocking the former soldier back. "Fuck you, Trellain. If you hadn't been so fucking stupid, none of us would be in this mess."

"You're blaming me for this? You started a cult too, for fuck's sake. Your little maniacs ruined everything." Trellain threw a punch, and it collided with Owen's jaw, knocking him down.

Leya rushed Trellain, another soldier rushed her, Owen got back to his feet, and more exiles piled on until the scrum grew. Emrys and Juliet stayed back with a couple of others and watched as Tornshirts and Defenders beat each other up and vented their frustration.

"You have to do something," Juliet said.

He did. He knew he did. And he could take whatever they threw at them.

"Enough!" He entered the fray and pulled people off each other and sent them skidding into the dirt. He reached the middle of the pack and wrestled Trellain and Owen apart. They tried to keep fighting, but they were no match for Emrys's strength. "If you want to hit someone, hit me. I deserve it. I can take it. Any and all of you, if you feel the despair or the anger welling up inside you, come find me, and I'll let you beat me until you're exhausted. But right now, we need to settle on a plan."

Owen and Trellain stopped trying to kill each other. Emrys let them go, the two men sneered at each other but stayed apart. They righted their clothes and returned to their factions. As far as Emrys could make out, there were three—the former Defenders, the former Tornshirts, and a small group of former citizens who had no prior allegiances one way or another. He counted Juliet among them.

Now that they were calm, they could work on a plan together.

"We can stay here for the night and work things out or we can keep walking. Prosperity is probably two weeks' walk from here. I say we set a course for there."

"Prosperity went dark some years back," Trellain said.

"Did anyone investigate to make sure it was abandoned?"

"No, of course not."

"Endurance cut itself off from the other arks, so it's not

unreasonable that Prosperity did the same. None of the arks to the west that I explored supported life. I vote we make a break for Prosperity in the morning when we can see where we're going. Does everyone agree?"

Hands raised like shoots pushing through the soil, slow but determined. He had consensus.

"I still think we should move now," Owen said.

"Good idea." Trellain hefted his pack onto his shoulder. "You start walking. We'll catch up."

Emrys put his hand on Owen's shoulder but he shrugged it off. "I know you're anxious to get away from Providence, but it's safer to walk during the day."

"As if you give a fuck about our safety." Owen walked towards the city and shelter. "Let's go."

They walked for half an hour and settled on an abandoned store where they could rest. He wanted the exiles up with the sun so they could make the most of the cooler morning. If they slept now, they'd be refreshed for their journey. Though he wondered who would sleep, who would find respite in unconsciousness while the night lay thick around them and uncertainty crept in the shadows to steal the last of their delusions.

They cleared the rubble on the cracked but otherwise smooth floor. The roof was intact even if the windows had all been blown out. He helped them where he could, getting them as comfortable as possible. He couldn't see all their faces, but he knew from the way they turned from him, from the way they stole back their hands for fear of touching him, that they did not trust him as much as they once had. Whatever they'd pieced together, whatever they understood from what the councilors had said or what he'd delivered over his message, they didn't know what to make of him but knew that he was the cause of all their troubles.

And yet they chose to follow him.

Only one of them cried, that sole pitiful sound, whereas the others met him with grim determination. Were they the adventurers? Were they the ones with fire in their souls and a yearning to breathe free? Could he read any hope in their faces? And how soon would it be before it sputtered and died?

"If you don't stop that sniveling, I'll beat you to death," a harsh voice fired out of the gloom. The crying stopped. How long would that exile last?

Emrys left them to get what sleep they could and sat at the doorway alone.

What was Galen doing now? Had he escaped the Five's purge? Was he cursing Emrys's name? Would he survive in Providence longer than thirty days?

Emrys should have tried to talk to him one last time, but what would he have said? Nothing could have made it right. If he'd somehow managed to convince Galen to come with him, the chances of finding souls to harvest were slim.

Perhaps Endurance had some and they could have stayed there, but for how long? And what kind of life would that have been for Galen?

And staying in Providence… If Isaiah found out Galen was a Darisami, would he let his son live? Would he try to take Galen's power for himself? Would Kira? What mess had he left Galen to sort out?

Damned if he did, damned if he didn't.

Damned if he didn't, damned if he did.

Round and round the thoughts went like a wheel crushing his heart, a torture to break him. One without end. Because he would never see the inside of Providence again, never see Galen again, and never know the truth about what happened to him.

He stared into the darkness as the night grew old and cold and the sounds of the exiles' sleeping rose at his back. The darkness provided a blank canvas on which he could project the various scenarios of what would happen to Galen. He tried to turn his mind to some sort of plan for the exiles, but he kept getting pulled back to Galen. And not just the worries over his future, but the memories that he had, resurrecting the far too few nights they'd spent together, the far too few times they'd made love, but also the times they'd shared a look, a touch, a vision of the future.

If he hadn't been staring into the darkness, he wouldn't have seen the shadows move down the street.

He blinked out of the thoughts and focused. There were no trees with their branches blowing in the breeze. There were no curtains left to flutter or animals left to scurry. The only thing that could produce a moving shadow out there was—

The shadows moved again, vaguely human shaped. More than one, more than two.

Molten lead sluiced through his veins and hardened in his muscles. He sharpened his hearing and heard the faintest sound of boots on asphalt and grit. Soldiers' boots.

They're coming for us.

Lightning crackled in his chest, igniting adrenaline and blinding his vision with a flash. Those fucking double-crossing, lying murderous bastards. He should have killed the council when he had the chance. But he couldn't dwell on regrets. He had to assume that the soldiers came armed with gold bullets as well as the ordinary kind that could slaughter thirty-one unarmed exiles. He had to protect them himself and hope he didn't get killed in the process.

He rolled over and slunk close to the ground, keeping watch on the shadows as they approached, as they became more defined, as the sounds of their approach grew louder. Could they have grenades? One or two lobbed into the structure would be enough to kill a good number, then they could pick off the rest.

Once they'd taken him down.

He crept along the ground to get out of the doorway and behind the building. He peered back and tried to count the number of soldiers but a noise behind him caught his attention. More boots. More soldiers. They were being surrounded. How could he defend everyone when he had no idea how many there were? One lobbed grenade, a detonated bomb, and it would all descend into chaos.

He had to be quick.

He had to be merciless.

He had to be fearless.

Any one of them could shoot him with a golden bullet. And that would be his ticket to the afterlife. But he wasn't ready to go yet. Not until he'd given these thirty-one people a fighting chance.

He sprinted towards the nearest sound, faster than any human could run. Their march was getting nearer, their attack imminent. He shot out of the shadows to barrel into two soldiers, catching them unawares. One swore, one fired, the gun loud in the silence. Too loud, too close, but it missed him.

He drove his fist into one's chest, knocked them down, and fought with the other. He grabbed their gun, grabbed their throat, broke their neck, then broke the silence again as he ripped the gun from their dead hand and turned to the soldier lying the ground and fired. A spray of bullets put an end to struggles as they tore into his arms and legs.

It was enough to keep them down. He couldn't waste time trying to take life and soul. The noise they'd made was enough to make everyone hurry to their positions. The exiles would be awake. His heart rattled loud enough to stir them.

He grabbed the guns and ran back to the shelter, shouting for Trellain and the soldiers to wake up. He passed them the guns, told them to defend themselves, and ran back out into the night.

He ran far, tracking the sounds as best he could as they slowed and crept in much more quietly than before, now that they knew he was alerted. A pop of gunfire came from the direction of the shelter, and the response followed swiftly, cutting the attack short.

He bowled into three soldiers and fought them in close combat, drawing them towards him, and taking them out one-by-one until only one remained standing. The soldier raised their gun and pointed it at Emrys, but Emrys acted fast, ducking and charging into the soldier's middle, the gun flying from their hand. The soldier tried to fight him off but Emrys was too strong. He grabbed their head, twisted, and broke their neck. The soldier's flailing stopped.

Emrys grabbed the guns and raced back to the shelter. Gunfire followed him as he crossed the street, but he was too fast. He delivered the weapons and flew out, gunfire tracking him again.

He raced into the night, raced into more soldiers, took them down, took their weapons, took his chances. Bullets whistled by him as he whistled by the soldiers. He killed them, quickly, mercilessly, then drove on.

He scoured the ruins for any signs of soldiers, but he had no way of knowing if he'd got them all, or if they'd merely hunkered down for a long siege. He collected all the weapons and the armor he could, dumping it with the exiles. Would it be enough? Isaiah could keep sending soldiers until he'd succeeded. He could think of only one way to ensure no more came out. He had no doubt that this was Isaiah's plan, the look in his face as he'd given him his word…

Emrys should never have trusted him.

But if this was Isaiah's plan, it was unlikely to be done with the blessing of the rest of the Five. Otherwise, why let any of them leave? Why wait until they'd left Providence when they could have slaughtered them in the tunnel with nowhere to escape?

No, this was Isaiah's plan, which meant it was being done in secret through the back entrance. Emrys would destroy it to give them time to get away.

He searched the dead soldiers' packs and bodies and collected their grenades. One of them had a pack filled with mines. That would do. More than enough to slow their pursuers. He gave Trellain his word he would come back and that he was to do everything he could to protect the exiles. And then ran into the city.

He'd gone about halfway when he found the bodies. Soldiers' corpses were scattered beside the street, one close to him, then two, then five, then twelve as they died in a huddle. Killed by bullets, killed by hand, but not killed by him. Who had done this?

He searched, not yet daring to hope who it might be. He checked the bodies, lifting off their helmets to make sure Galen hadn't died among them. He had no way of knowing Galen had killed them. It could have been one of his former followers buried in among them. It could have been anyone, but only one person he wanted it to be.

He kept going. Isaiah might have sent another unit. His eye caught on a light high above and far away, a glinting glowing body in one of the skyscrapers, shining in the light of the moon. Could it be Galen?

He raced towards the light, running as fast as he could. He pulled back his hood so the moon could show Galen his approach. He kept his focus on one thing only.

Galen. Galen. Galen.

He'd come after all.

But first, he had to destroy the warehouse.

He lost sight of Galen's light as he raced through the narrowing streets onto the road where the warehouse stood. He pulled up short. Corpses lay in the entrance. Another unit of twenty or so that had been brought to—

A gunshot sounded inside the warehouse. Someone groaned.

Emrys poked his head through the door. One lone figure stood among the corpses. The warehouse was dark, but he recognized that shadowy form.

"Galen?"

He spun. "Emrys? What are you doing here?"

"Me? What are you doing here?"

"Trying to buy you some time. What's happened to the exiles?"

"They're safe."

"I killed another unit—did you see them?—then I came back to blow up the elevator and got stuck dealing with this lot."

"Are you all right?"

Galen was breathing fast. "I'm fine." Very fast.

Emrys approached with care, trying not to startle Galen. "What are you doing here, Galen? You should be in Providence."

"How could I stay after what you did to me?" Galen's accusation skewered the tender meat of Emrys's heart. "I had no choice but to leave. I would have come with you out the front entrance, but as I was sneaking out, I got wind of Isaiah's double-cross, so I embedded myself in a unit."

Emrys felt a hundred times an idiot for trusting Isaiah. He should have been on guard. He'd almost gotten everyone killed.

Again.

But Galen had saved them.

Again.

"Did you feed on any of them?"

Galen's head shot up, eyes assuming guilt for a crime he wanted to commit. "No. There wasn't time. They were too protected. And I didn't know if I could stop. This need to feed, the rush of it… I hate it, but I want it."

"It gets easier to manage. No matter how often you do it, it always promises euphoria, but you can avoid becoming overwhelmed. It just takes time."

"Time we might not have if we don't find another ark to take us in, right?"

"It's not too late for you, Galen. You can go back. Isaiah might spare you."

"I can't. Even being Isaiah's son wouldn't save me from execution, and one less figurehead to follow would make things easier to get back to normal." Galen's lips twisted, and he scraped his fingers through his hair. "What have we done?"

"We tried to give them a future."

He snorted. "And failed."

"I'm sorry, Galen. For everything that I did to you, for changing your life so much, for making this so hard."

Galen paused, and he became a screen upon which myriad questions swam past. Emrys's gut shrank as Galen took his time choosing one. "Why didn't you let me die?"

"Because I decided it wasn't your time. I thought that

if I could give you immortality, you could do more with it than I did. I wanted you to have Providence because I believed in you and your abilities and your goodness."

"Is that the only reason?"

Emrys chewed his bottom lip. Why did he hold back when he had no more reason to? He broadened his chest. "I couldn't bear to lose you, and I was selfish. If I'd had more time, if your life hadn't hung in the balance, I would have asked permission, but we didn't have that, so I decided for you. I'm sorry for cursing you, but I'm not sorry for saving you."

"Part of me wishes I had died believing you were an angel. Now that I know the truth, it's so much worse than I imagined. It's worse than before you came, knowing you—that *we*—exist. How am I meant to live like this?" The strain shrank Galen's voice.

"It's no different from being human. Everyone has to control the worst of themselves so they can live. It gets easier, but it never goes away. And like most humans, you didn't want to die. That's why you're here. You could have stayed and tried something and probably died for it, but you wanted to live."

"I wanted it to end." Galen's voice dipped to a whisper as sorrow bowed his head.

Emrys shuffled forward, eager to hold him. "But you fought against that urge. That's what matters. That choice. And it's the same choice you'll exercise when you feed. We have an incredible and terrible power, but it's a power every human shares. The ability to take life, to inflict our will on others simply because we want to. Isaiah has it—he has it in spades—but he can't cope with another having more power than him."

"He does it to survive."

"And so do we." The gap between him and Galen was

only a few feet, but it felt uncrossable, a great divide over a thousand-foot drop chasm. "I'm sorry for lying to you. I'm sorry for making you the same as me and for doing it without your approval. I understand if you can't forgive me, if you can't love me anymore…but if you'll have me, I'll do my best to help you not only survive but live."

"I don't know, Emrys. It's…it's going to take time. I'm not used to this, feeling this way, having this power. I thought I could cope with loving an angel, but this…what you are, what I am…I don't know."

"If you could give me some hope, some promise that you'll stay with me until you've learned all you can—for your own sake—that's all I ask. Because if you won't fight for your own survival, I can't fight for mine."

Galen looked at him, scant light catching his eyes, but they shone with a familiar intensity. "As much as I hate what you have made me into, I want to live."

Emrys's wounded heart lifted. "Then I promise I will keep you safe."

He wanted to hug him, but Galen hugged himself instead and looked down at the corpses at his feet and shuddered. "I guess we should go."

"We're doing the right thing, aren't we? Blowing up the elevator?"

He shrugged. "Isaiah has forced our hand. Let him explain why it's been destroyed. It'll buy us time so we can put some distance between us and Providence."

But before they destroyed it, they pulled the corpses out of the warehouse so they could retrieve the weapons, then returned to the elevator, piling up munitions at its entrance, holding on to a few grenades to start the charge.

They retreated.

"Ready?" Galen said.

"Ready."

They pulled the pins with their teeth and lobbed the four grenades at the elevator, then sprinted out the exit. Their escape was followed a few seconds later by the grenades exploding and setting off others in turn. Rubble and shrapnel spattered the walls and smoke rose out of the building's roof and broken windows. It would slow anyone down who thought to come after them. The front entrance was a concern, but they now had enough weapons to guard their flank.

They stripped the bodies of as many guns and ammunition as they could carry, working silently but diligently, side by side. They finished quickly and started to walk back to the exiles.

"By the way, how did you get down from the skyscraper so fast? Did you jump?" Emrys asked.

"What skyscraper?"

"That one. I saw you in the moonlight."

"I've been down on the ground the whole time."

Emrys stopped a split second after his heart. "But I saw you up there."

"And I'm telling you it wasn't me."

Laughter followed. High laughter. The laughter of a young girl with a woman's mind. It tickled the shadows and brought a chill to Emrys's heart.

"Nimue?" he said to the shadows.

The child Darisami, frozen in time with her small stature, dark chestnut hair, and too wise dark eyes stepped out from an alley up ahead, the moonlight hitting her body. "I'm a little hurt you didn't come to investigate."

"What are you doing here?"

She approached, ignoring his question. "I'm glad you're alive, Emrys. I was worried when the bond broke and you went silent. I thought the gold poisoning had done you in." She peered up at Galen, bathing in his light. A great smile appeared on her face. "Excellent! Well done. I was wondering how long it would be before you turned him."

"It wasn't planned."

"No, of course not. But I bet you're glad of it, aren't you? Both of you?" She winked.

"No!" they said it in unison, but Emrys only said it for Galen's sake.

She rolled her eyes. "Whatever, guys." She took up Emrys's hand and pulled them in the opposite direction. "There's something you need to see. I promise, you will like it."

"We have to leave, Nimue. There's a group of survivors we need to take to safety."

"Emrys, this is far more important."

"Nimue, there's no time."

"There is for this." She yanked hard on his arm.

They dumped the weapons, and he allowed her to drag them back into the city. She drew them to the high school where Emrys had killed Ragnar and Wyatt, down the dark path between buildings and onto the cracked basketball court where he'd slain the two Darisami.

"Why have you brought us here?" Emrys asked.

"Galen, give me your torch."

He passed it over, and the combined light from the torch and from her shone onto the patch of green grass growing through the—

Emrys stilled.

Grass? *Actual* grass? *Actual* green, growing, glorious grass?

"What is this?" Galen asked.

Nimue tutted. "It's grass. Did they never teach you about grass in Providence?"

"I know what grass is. What's it doing here?"

Nimue smiled. She grabbed Emrys and pulled him to the other side of the court to another patch of green. The sight was magnificent, like a breath of clean crisp air cutting through him. Its significance dawned.

"It's surely not."

"It surely is."

"But how?"

"Can someone explain what's going on, please?" Galen said.

Emrys crouched to the ground. "This is where I slayed Ragnar. And Wyatt died over there." He brushed his fingers through the tufts, their blades supple yet sturdy, that feeling of nature and life and possibility.

Nimue took over. "When a Darisami is killed, all the souls they've ever harvested in their lives escape. We always thought it didn't have any real effect except on us. We feel all those souls leaving, but apart from an occasional flickering of the lights, we didn't notice much else. But this…"

"This is caused by a Darisami dying?" Galen asked.

"Yes."

Emrys blew an ironic breath through his nose. "We really can turn the grass green and the soil fertile."

"That's what it looks like," Nimue said.

"But not without dying."

All those Darisami he'd slain in his life… He could have put them to much better use.

"But the effect is limited." Emrys stood up, the sensation of grass sticking to his fingertips.

"And yet it holds promise, doesn't it? Imagine if we could find a way to release the Darisami's power without it meaning death. Imagine what we could do." Nimue's voice bordered on child-like wonderment.

"We'd still have to feed. It still needs souls to work. And

no offence, but these two patches of grass aren't enough to help the planet."

"You're wrong. They give us hope." The shine in her eyes was almost as bright as the shine from her body. Her smile then took on a teasing turn. "And there's more."

"What is it?" he asked, wary.

"I've found us the perfect home to test it out."

"Where?" Warier still.

"Prosperity."

"Prosperity? That went dark ten years ago," Galen said.

"With very good reason. While Providence kept itself underground, Prosperity has expanded onto the surface. I've scoped them out in secret, and they're living up to their name."

"But what good will that do us?" Galen said. "It'll just mean more souls for you to eat and an ark for you to destroy."

Nimue raised *both* eyebrows. "More souls for *us* to eat and more souls for *us* to destroy. You're one of us now, Galen."

Emrys hurried on. "He has a point, Nimue. Why would we test this new theory at Prosperity? Should we even bother?"

"Yes, we should. Because there's already a Darisami living among them, and they know all about him."

"They know he's a Darisami?"

"Yep, and we know him too." That teasing smile went full taunt.

"Who is it?"

Nimue laughed. "Remember Ash?"

Emrys's heart sank so low that nothing could lift it. Not the sight of verdant grass. Not the hope of a new place to call home. Not having Nimue and Galen by his side. "Then it's hopeless."

"Why?" Galen's smile flickered to life. "If they know what he is, then there's a chance for us, too. Why is this not a reason to celebrate?"

But Emrys couldn't answer so Nimue did it for him.

"Because Emrys killed Ash's lover."

ABOUT THE AUTHOR

Daniel de Lorne writes about men, monsters and magic.

In love with writing since he wrote a story about a talking tree at age six, his first novel, the romantic horror *Beckoning Blood*, was published in 2014. At the heart of every book is a romance between two men, whether they're irresistible vampires, historical hotties, or professional paramours.

In his other life, Daniel is a professional writer and researcher in Perth, Australia, with a love of history and nature. All of which makes for great story fodder.

And when he's not working, he and his husband explore as much of this amazing world as they can, from the ruins of Welsh abbeys to trekking famous routes and swimming with whales.

Connect with Daniel and get a FREE short story. Be the first to know about new releases, cover reveals, giveaways and more.
www.danieldelorne.com